Double-Edged Reckoning

Double-Edged Reckoning

A Western Edge Mystery

Nicole Helm

TULE
PUBLISHING

Double-Edged Reckoning
Copyright© 2025 Nicole Helm
Tule Publishing First Printing, May 2025

The Tule Publishing, Inc.

ALL RIGHTS RESERVED

First Publication by Tule Publishing 2025

Cover design by eBook launch

No part of this book may be used or reproduced in any manner whatsoever without written permission except in the case of brief quotations embodied in critical articles and reviews.

This is a work of fiction. Names, characters, places, and incidents are products of the author's imagination or are used fictitiously. Any resemblance to actual events, locales, organizations, or persons, living or dead, is entirely coincidental.

AI was not used to create any part of this book and no part of this book may be used for generative training.

ISBN: 978-1-966593-05-8

Chapter One

Marietta, Montana

SAMANTHA PRICE KNEW what it felt like when something *bad* was on the horizon. It had been a skill honed as a child, brought into a home where her mother's constant health battles had been a roller coaster of *maybe she'll make it*, until she hadn't.

Sam had been ten.

At fifteen, her world had been rocked again, when her father had been arrested and then convicted of murder.

She preferred to think of it in those simple terms, instead of all the complications that year had started. Domino effects that still knocked over her life to this day.

Because she'd spent the fifteen years since trying to get him out of jail, trying to clear his name.

She knew her father didn't kill Marie Bennet. She also knew who absolutely *had*.

Evidence, though, was a hell of a thing. That was why she'd made it her life. Honor's Edge Investigations, headquartered in the pretty, picturesque Montana town of Marietta, was her entire focus. Not *much* went on in Marietta, but she didn't mind tracking down a cheating spouse, a deadbeat dad, or a kid who'd taken off with the family heirlooms.

Her latest case had taken her to Bozeman, gathering proof on a cheating bastard of a husband. She drove back into Marietta with plenty of evidence to offer the woman who'd hired her. There was nothing to celebrate there, but at least her client had the facts, with the evidence to back it up however she needed, and that was Sam's job.

Her next case wouldn't be quite as satisfactory. She'd somehow gotten roped into investigating a neighborly spat over some damaged petunias.

Still, Sam would take any case, and anyone's payment, if it helped her with her end goal. Prove to the police and whatever legal entities necessary that Benjamin Bennet had killed his wife. And her father was *innocent*.

Even with his release from prison last month, Sam was determined. She would clear his name. And Benjamin Bennet, great paragon of ranching goodness in these parts of Montana, would finally pay for what he'd done.

Fifteen years and her father making it out of jail on parole hadn't dulled her determination on that front.

That was what she should be feeling right now. Determination. Some relief her father was home. But that old familiar dread danced along her nerve endings today no matter how she tried to focus on other things.

Like getting home. Her childhood house had been sold a long time ago, and Dad had declined her offer to let him stay with her in the apartment above her office building upon his release. It was a relief that he'd declined. She might not have a social life—what with a fifteen-year penchant for truth and answers in a community that wanted to saint her sworn enemy—but what thirty-year-old wanted to bunk in a one-room apartment with their *dad*?

He'd moved into a rental cabin at his sister's ranch instead. Aunt Lisa had taken over custody of Sam when Dad had gone to jail. She was a tough widow of a ranch woman, who now left almost all the ranch work up to her hands while she managed a small number of rental cabins on her property and helped Sam out part-time with administrative duties at Honor's Edge Investigations. Dad helped out with the cabins and acted as a kind of custodian for Honor's Edge as well.

It was a family affair, all born out of the same belief that Gene Price hadn't killed a damn soul.

As it usually did, the sight of her little office with her apartment on the floor above soothed her. Maybe she hadn't righted the wrongs against her father yet, but this was a symbol that she would.

That she could.

Both Dad and Lisa would probably be inside. Lisa doing some paperwork, Dad keeping himself busy with some sort of renovation project since the building was old and historical.

Instead, when she walked into the office, she felt that same prickling dread she always felt when something bad was going to happen.

Lisa was in fact there, sitting behind the front desk, but she jumped to her feet the minute Sam opened the door.

"Sam. Thank God you're back. I didn't want to call while you were driving." Aunt Lisa stood up and began to move for Sam. "The police were here."

That nagging *something bad is coming* feeling intensified. "For what?"

Lisa's expression was grim. She reached out, put her hand on Sam's shoulder, just as she'd done when Dad's first two parole hearings hadn't gone their way. "Sam, I know I should have told you…"

Shit.

"You know that young woman Benjamin Bennet's been seeing that everyone's been gossiping about?"

Anything that involved Bennet was bad news, that Sam did know. "I've heard bits and pieces."

"They found her dead. The day you left for Bozeman."

It was hard to hear Lisa over the buzzing in her head, but Sam reminded herself to breathe. To *deal*. This wasn't fifteen years ago. It was now. "Where?"

"Bennet property. Somewhere along the creek."

"Why would the police come here then?"

"To talk to your father."

"What does any of this have to do with Dad? It proves Benjamin Bennet is the problem."

Lisa sighed, shaking her head. She wasn't a woman who cried, but the worry etched into the lines on her face was close enough. "Maybe if it had happened when your dad was in jail."

"What are you saying?"

"Sam. Your father is a convicted murderer. Whether we believe that or not, the law sees it that way. Recently released, now there's another murder near where the first murder happened? He didn't do it, but we know what happens."

Sam did indeed know. Too well. It twisted her stomach into knots. This couldn't be happening again. She wouldn't *let* it happen again.

"Not this time."

"They took him down to the station, Sam."

"Then that's where I'll be."

It didn't go well. Maybe she'd known it wouldn't. Everything about the past fifteen years should have prepared herself for this.

And still, she couldn't believe it was happening again.

They were keeping Dad in a holding cell. They could, for a few more hours yet, while they tried to get a warrant.

Sam wanted to believe they wouldn't, but she'd been through this. She understood the sheriff's department and the law too well now.

Still, they let her see him. She didn't know if it was procedure or a professional courtesy. Some of the deputies didn't mind her work as a private investigator, they even worked *with* her on occasion. Some rolled their eyes at her and thought she was a joke.

But what really grated in this moment of being led to a room she could talk to Dad in was the fact she could tell *everyone* involved felt sorry for her. Not in an empathetic way, but in a *Sam is pathetic* kind of way.

Dad was handcuffed to a table in an interrogation room when the deputy brought her in. His hair was all gray now, cut short. He hadn't shaved in a few days, and he was still far too skinny from his fifteen years in prison. Her heart twisted, but she had to remain steadfast.

For him.

She knew the drill. She would sit opposite him. The deputy would watch, listen.

"Sammy," Dad said. He tried to smile but it faltered at the edges. "You shouldn't have come."

She didn't know how he could say that, but there was no point arguing with him about it. "Explain how they could possibly arrest you on this, Dad. You didn't even know her."

Dad shook his head. "Of her, though. And we'd had a few interactions, just in the way Marietta neighbors do."

"That's not knowing someone."

"No. But I know Ben, and that's what they're going after, all the stuff the last trial was about. Ben and I hate each other. They asked me some questions, didn't like the answers. I imagine they're filing charges right now." He sighed heavily, looking old and beat down, even if his next words were optimistic. "It's all right."

"It isn't," Sam insisted, ignoring the lump in her throat. "You didn't kill anyone. Then or now."

"They wanted an alibi. I live alone at Lisa's ranch. I don't have any alibi, and I've got a history. I'm the easy answer. They've got to do their due diligence."

"Why are you defending them?" Sam demanded, temper straining. It was hardly his fault fifteen years of being imprisoned despite his innocence had beat him down. Had made him this *resigned* to it all happening again.

But she couldn't be.

Dad sighed. "Let the police do their work, Sam. And you

can do yours."

She wouldn't cry. Not after all these years. Not under the weight of this. "My job hasn't cleared you yet."

Dad smiled. How he could, she didn't know.

"Yet being the operative word." He tried to move, reach out and touch her hand no doubt, but his hands were handcuffed to the table.

Dad looked down at his lap. "I spent fifteen years in prison. If I go back, I can handle it. I know you'll fight for me, and even if it never clears my name, it keeps me going." He looked up, that sad smile still in place. "You don't have to worry about me making it through, Sammy. I do, because I know you're fighting for me."

She swallowed at the expanding, bitter lump in her throat. Then she nodded. "Always," she managed to say around the pressure in her lungs.

Another deputy stuck their head in the door. "Sam? Sheriff wants to talk to you."

Sam swallowed again, managed a smile for her dad. "Have you called your lawyer?"

He nodded. "Bert will be on it. You don't worry about my end of things, all right? If I need anything, Bert will be in touch with you or Lisa."

"All right," she agreed, even though she didn't *really* agree, but she didn't want Dad to worry. She'd handle everything. "You take care of yourself."

"You too."

She desperately wanted to hug him, whisper words of love and assurance, but she was pretty sure it would break them both. So she got up and followed the deputy out into the hall and then over to the sheriff's office.

He waved her in, pointed to the seat opposite his desk. She sat.

She assumed it would be some kind of warning. The sheriff had always been kind to her, even when she'd been young and brash and blamed his shoddy police work for her father's conviction.

"Sam, I know this is upsetting. And I know you're going to want to raise a stink, but he doesn't have an alibi."

"And Benjamin Bennet does?"

"You know I can't tell you that," he replied calmly. "It'd be best for all involved if you stopped harassing my deputies. I know you're going to look into this on your own, and that's all well and good, but you cannot interfere with my investigation. You have laws to follow, just like we do."

Sam said nothing to that. Best not to say anything that might get her into trouble.

The sheriff sighed. "You've got to stay away from Bennet."

Sam remained resolutely silent. The sheriff started to show some of his frustration. He leaned over his desk.

"You want it said plain? Fine, I'll say it plain. Your father has a history of violent acts. Benjamin Bennet does not."

But that wasn't exactly true. She knew there was violence deep inside of Bennet. The kind that would make it obvious he could murder.

And had. Twice now.

She hadn't been able to track down the evidence in all these years, and she'd tried off and on, never quite sure how to approach it. But now she would.

She had to.

Chapter Two

North of the Smoky Mountains, Tennessee

SUMMER WAS LICKING its way up the mountain and Nate Bennet scowled at the encroaching heat. It reminded him too much of the Middle East, the ache in his leg, and a rare Montana heatwave fifteen years ago that had changed his life forever.

Since he didn't want to dwell on any of those memories, he focused on the gutter currently clogged by a starling nest. It was a minor problem compared to finding his target in the deserts and mountains of Iraq, or taking out said target, but at least there was a modicum of satisfaction in solving a problem, no matter how minor.

He frowned as the faint, stray sound of a motor puttered somewhere a few miles off. He had chosen this cabin to rent on this never-traversed tract of land north of the Smoky Mountains for the simple reason he would *never* hear a motor up here that wasn't of his own doing.

This wasn't.

Ladder forgotten, Nate moved inside of his cabin. He wasn't a sniper anymore, but he was still a man who wasn't about to be ambushed. His neck prickled, and he counted the heavy heartbeats against his chest, slowing them, calming himself, *focusing*.

It felt good.

He unlocked his gun cabinet and pulled out the small pistol he could conceal behind his back yet have at the ready.

Someone was coming for him. He could feel it in his bones, one of those gut reactions honed in the army. You knew when you were a target. You always knew.

Or you tended to end up dead.

He stepped back into the yard around his cabin and the motor was closer, though still far enough away to give him more time to find that center of calm. The power and control he'd wielded and nurtured to become a successful Army Ranger sniper.

An SUV rumbled up the curving, rocky path to his cabin's small clearing amidst the birch trees that surrounded his little cove. Nate watched the car's approach, clearly a rental by the plate and stickers in the window, then it slowed to a stop.

A woman stepped out of the driver's seat and into the warm, partly sunny afternoon.

Petite. Brunette. Assessing eyes behind the dark lenses of sunglasses. Concealed weapon, probably a baby Glock. Not nervous, but determined.

"Nate Bennet. Found at last." She surveyed him as if she didn't quite believe it, while the words *found at last* made his grip tighten on his gun behind his back.

"Who the hell are you?"

She cocked her head and pulled the sunglasses off her face. "I suppose it has been a long time," she said, brown eyes surveying him with the kind of calculation that might have made him nervous if she was anything other than five-foot-two of fluff and nothing.

But the word *time* in that voice rippled over him. The sharp edge of rancher woman she wore on her narrow frame like an invisible rod holding her shoulders back, and her hips cocked.

Samantha.

There was the flash of a night he wished he could forget even more than he wished that bomb hadn't gone off last year.

He pictured himself pushing the memory into a box, locking it, and then throwing it far, far away, and focused on the present.

"Samantha Price," he said grimly.

A blast from his past. Unwanted, like blasts usually were. Certainly the one that had blown him to hell over a year ago. And the one that had met him fifteen years ago.

She stood there, expression and posture never changing, even as his expression got grimmer with every passing second of breathing the same air as someone from Montana.

Home. Hell. The place he'd escaped and never—not once—allowed any last connections there to find him. Even his own damn family.

Now Samantha Price had. The daughter of the man who'd killed his mother, the one Marietta resident who'd seen him at his weakest.

"Go away."

She didn't react. Oh, he assumed there was a reaction going on under that placid expression and too-stiff posture, but she hid it well. Too well for his comfort.

"I'm afraid I can't do that, Nate. I wouldn't have tracked you down, which took too damn long by the way, if I could simply go away because you ordered me to."

"Fine. *I'll* go away." He turned to the cabin door, though he kept his peripheral vision on her. He knew better than to turn his back on the enemy. Anyone from home was the enemy, no matter what her message was, or how pretty the package it came delivered in.

"I have questions for you. Important questions, and I don't have time for childish storming away."

He raised a threatening eyebrow at her. "Childish?" he repeated, a warning for her to back down.

She didn't. "Do you sincerely believe, after what your father did to you that night, my father was the one who killed your mother?"

Nate almost, *almost* twitched, and it was unacceptable. Army Rangers didn't twitch.

Except you aren't an Army Ranger anymore.

Nor was he the scrawny kid from Montana whose dad had beat the shit out of him after his mother's funeral. He was someone else entirely. The only thing he shared with that kid was a name.

And the nightmares.

"Your father's current girlfriend was found murdered last month. Now, I'm looking for proof he was responsible."

"Don't know what that's got to do with me," Nate replied, because he hadn't anything to do with the Bennet Ranch, Montana, or his father since that night. And he damn well didn't care *who* murdered some woman.

"You are the only one who knows what your father is

capable of, and as long as everyone in that county thinks Benjamin Bennet is a god among men, my father is in danger."

"As far as I know, your father murdered my mother. I think you're barking up the wrong tree."

Temper flashed in her eyes, but she didn't let it loose. She held it all together, and when she spoke it was with a deceptive kind of calm he had to respect against his will.

"My father didn't murder anyone, and I'm going to prove it. You can speak to your father's volatile temper. You of all people can put some weight behind the fact he isn't the saint everyone seems to think he is. Don't you want to hurt him the way he hurt you?"

Nate had to fight the swirling emotions to keep them under the surface, down where he could control their outcome. She was asking him for revenge, and part of him wanted nothing to do with it. Part of him was that weak, scared little boy who just wanted it to be gone and over.

But he was a man now. A former sniper of an Army Ranger. His father couldn't hurt him like that anymore, and this? Help prove his father was the monster Nate had finally known him to be? Hell, it was tempting.

Still, he gave nothing away. Not his interest, not his confusion. He made an effort to sound bored and disinterested. "How?"

She lifted her chin as if it would give her some height, some leverage. "Come home," she said so matter-of-factly and succinctly, it pierced through so much of the armor he'd built for himself in fifteen years.

He'd left *home* behind, erased it from all the parts of his brain he could, and never, *ever* looked back. He'd promised himself he never would. Over and over again as he'd worked his way through the army, to the Rangers. He'd *vowed* to himself the Bennet Ranch was dead.

But apparently ghosts existed in flesh and blood, in Samantha Price, and in his heart that had always wondered if there wasn't more to Mom's death than everyone assumed.

But it was a lifetime ago, and he couldn't go back. He couldn't. "Sorry you came all this way for nothing," he said, jerking his cabin door open. He stepped inside and closed it behind him with a definitive *bang*, because that was that.

But he couldn't quite help a glance out the window. Samantha stood by her car, her posture rigid, her expression fierce. She stared at his cabin as if she could raze it with her mind.

That didn't scare him any more than she did, but there was a prickle of foreboding across his body. The kind he'd learned to listen to in the middle of night in the cold Middle Eastern desert.

Something was going to happen, and now he had to decide if he was going to let it happen *to* him, or if he was going to lead the charge.

When an hour later, Samantha's car was still in his yard, her in it, he decided to lead the charge.

He watched her out of his window in quick glances as he prepared the cabin.

She'd pulled a laptop out of her bag some time ago, typing diligently. Though what she could be working on out here where there was neither Wi-Fi nor any kind of cell signal was beyond him.

She drank something out of a thermos, occasionally popped something into her mouth and chewed angrily.

But she didn't leave.

He'd promised himself never to set foot in Montana again. His mother was dead. His father had beaten the piss out of him in a drunken rage, and maybe, every once in a while, Nate had a twinge of *something* over disappearing on his brothers, but what was the alternative?

And still Samantha Price was in his yard in Tennessee, half a country away from where she and all these memories belonged, like a grain of sand stuck in his eye that wouldn't flush out.

He'd prefer the sand, the Middle East, a sniper rifle and an army mission to this, but he was also too practical of a man to let this fester. With one last look around the cabin to make sure everything was where it should be for a who-knew-how-long trip away, Nate knew no matter what happened, this was the only choice.

Samantha Price had tracked him down when no one else had, and he'd been very careful to make sure no one could. There was a sign in that. A signal from the universe that this bomb she'd dropped at his feet couldn't be ignored.

He slung the duffel bag over his shoulder and allowed himself a moment or two to truly accept what he was going to do. Who he was going to face.

There would be surprises along the way, no doubt. Challenges he couldn't foresee. To face down the people he'd left fifteen years ago was somehow more daunting than hunting down insurgents.

He glanced out the window at a storm brewing in the

west, and that prickling sensation of dread that had been brewing inside of him since long before Samantha had showed up here seemed to thunder and lightning in anticipation of it.

Storms came, and storms went. They damaged, but they were a necessary part of the cycle. Maybe it was time to step into the storm.

No maybes, Bennet.

Samantha stepped out of her car, but she didn't make a move for his cabin. She looked at the storm clouds gathering, a mix of concern and anticipation in her expression.

A ray of sun pricked through the gathering clouds and landed in a glowing ray across her face. She lifted her head to it as if basking in that last moment of brightness before the storm descended.

Something in Nate's chest kicked, a feeling he wasn't sure he'd ever had, or would recognize even if someone named it for him, but he'd learned to believe in signs. The world was ugly and cruel and full of evil, but good existed in the signs. In birdsong and sunlight.

Sometimes you had to wade through a few storms first.

SAM DIDN'T HAVE much more time. She watched as the clouds billowed and rolled, morphing together into an impressive array of gray and black threat. She could only hope it didn't delay her flight, and she could only hope she could find *something* to lure Nate Bennet back to Montana.

She turned to glance at his door. She needed to push him

harder, but she'd been pushing at hard-headed men her whole life. She knew which ones couldn't be swayed with a hard shove. Sadly, the years had worn any finesse off her.

She wanted a hard shove. She wanted to knock a few hundred skulls together until everyone stopped looking at her like she was some pathetic creature who couldn't accept the truth.

But she knew, *knew* in her bones, her father was innocent.

Now, she was going to prove it to all the sad-eyed people who had pitied her attempts to clear her father's name over the years. And if she had to use Nate's personal tragedy to do it, she damn well would.

She just couldn't figure out *how*. She'd spent the past hour going over all the research she'd compiled in the past week since she'd found him—after three dedicated weeks of trying. She'd considered bribery, demands, blackmail.

She'd gotten to the point she'd decided just to find him, show up, and hope the right scenario would pop into her head. Instead, she'd shown up, found Nate Bennet to be someone completely different than she'd expected.

Because it was a strange thing to know someone and not. She'd grown up with Nate, been in most of the same classes at school. He'd *dated* one of her friends in that way middle schoolers dated. She'd known Nate Bennet the boy, and when she thought about him, she pictured him as the scrawny, scared, bruised and bloody boy she'd helped escape Marietta, because her conscience, even at sixteen, hadn't allowed any different.

Nate was no longer scrawny or bloody or weak. Nate was

crew-cut, blank-expressioned … muscle. Chiseled, honed muscle. Leashed power.

And she didn't magically know what to say or do to get him to come home.

Her investigation on him hadn't unearthed too much once she'd finally, *finally* found him. A stint in the military, then in a VA Hospital. Some not-quite-legal searching had led her to Tennessee and a nowhere cabin rented to N. Bennet.

She desperately wanted to know how he'd taken the hundred dollars she'd slipped him on his way out of town fifteen years ago, probably with a broken bone or two, and survived, gotten into the army, and flourished?

He was an unreadable mystery and she solved mysteries for a living. But the mystery of Nate Bennet somehow felt like the most daunting part of this whole thing.

She had to act. Her flight out of Knoxville was scheduled for eight, if this storm didn't mess things up, and she couldn't waste any more time trying to think of the perfect leverage.

When he stepped out of the little cabin as a roll of thunder shook the ground, she couldn't help but shiver. It felt like she was unleashing something dark and dangerous.

But he had a bag on his shoulder, and she allowed herself something like hope.

He walked over to her, and no matter that the first drops of rain began to fall, he took his sweet time. His dark gaze held hers the entire way across the yard, and Samantha refused to fidget or lower her gaze though she wanted to do both and badly.

"I'll come back to Montana with you," he said in a voice that sounded rough and underused.

"Good. Won't get in till late, but I've got a car at Missoula. I'll drive you to Marietta. If you don't want to go home, I can find you a place to stay."

"I don't know exactly what you want from me, Samantha Price, but know I'm coming home on my own terms. Not yours."

It was her turn to raise an eyebrow. "That a fact?"

"Yes, ma'am. I'll answer your questions, I might even help you out, but you're not the boss of me. I'll handle where I stay, and how long."

She shrugged. "No skin off my nose."

The rain turned from the occasional splatter of drops to a heavier sprinkle. Still they stood there, staring at each other in the impending storm. Samantha recognized it for what it was, some kind of weird power play.

Well, this was her case, her *life*, and she wasn't about to give up the power. "Any other proclamations before we get going?"

His jaw tightened for a second, and that dark, unreadable gaze swept over her. She didn't so much as blink.

"Where'd you get the money?" he asked. Nothing in his expression changed, his voice sounded exactly as calm and underused as it had every time he'd spoken.

But she could *feel* something in the air. Like there was this throbbing wound living deep down inside of this man in front of her.

She could have pretended she didn't know what he meant. It'd probably be the smart, distancing thing to do, but she'd never been able to erase that night from her memory.

"I'd been saving up for a cell phone," she offered flippantly, as if that were the real answer to the hundred she'd slipped him.

His expression flickered, something dark and brooding appearing for a second before he wiped it back to blankness. She wondered idly when the last time this man had smiled would have been. Was his life this dark and oppressive always? Had he escaped his father and Montana only to be shrouded in pain and sorrow and loneliness?

She didn't want to consider that.

"What on earth possessed a sixteen-year-old girl to give me the money you'd been saving?"

"Broken nose, blood-streaked face, the fact you'd just buried your mom. You want me to go on?" Because she didn't.

The night she'd found Nate Bennet barely conscious on the road next to her family's mailbox was one that had haunted her nearly as much as her father's prison sentence.

"Not because you felt guilty your father killed my mother?"

Samantha ignored the temper snapping to be set free. She wouldn't give in. She wouldn't be provoked. She'd learned anger never got her anywhere. She needed cold hard facts and evidence to get what she wanted.

"My father didn't kill your mother. My father hasn't killed anyone."

"But you expect me to believe mine did?"

"I don't care what you believe, Nate. I care about facts.

And the fact is your father beat you near to unconsciousness some fifteen years ago whereas my father never lifted a finger against me. *That* story gives me the kind of solid ground I need to prove my theory. No one's going to believe me if I say it. I need you."

"Do you now?" he murmured.

Samantha didn't flinch even though she realized belatedly in her vehemence she'd given him something of an upper hand. Hardly the first time she'd let her feelings get the better of her. She'd beat herself up later when she had time. Right now, the only thing she had time for was proving her father was innocent.

"So, your plan is to drag me back to Montana and what? Put me on a soapbox and bang the drum that Benjamin Bennet is an abusive asshole?"

"We don't need a soapbox or a drum," Sam replied. "You only have to say it to one person, and it'll spread. The doubts. People will start wondering. They'll start looking, and hopefully, anyone who has covered for him will start slipping. Then, I'll find the evidence I need to take to the judge or the police or whoever."

"You're awfully optimistic."

Sam shrugged. It wasn't optimism. That word had some kind of hope associated with it. Her hope, her belief, anything *positive* had leaked out of her over the past fifteen years. Her father had already paid for a crime he didn't commit, and nothing she did would bring those fifteen years back.

But she had determination. She had the dogged fucking grit to make certain another fifteen—or more—weren't taken away from her father.

"You ready or what?" she demanded, the rain coming down in earnest now, soaking them both.

He tilted his head up to the rain, tiny rivulets running down his sharp, chiseled face. He took a deep breath, then those penetrating brown eyes were back on her.

"Advance at will, ma'am." He gave a little nod then skirted the hood of her rental car and pulled the backdoor open and tossed in his bag.

Samantha got into the driver's seat doing everything in her power to keep calm, to not show how much of a win this was for her. For fifteen years she'd done everything she could to prove her father was innocent, but this was the first time in all that time she had something to prove someone *else* in Marietta was capable of horrible things.

She swallowed at the unexpected lump of emotion in her throat, ignoring Nate as he folded himself into the passenger seat.

She didn't look at him and she didn't say anything. She drove away from his pretty little cabin and, instead of dwelling on this success or all this *hope* bubbling inside of her, she planned her next move.

Chapter Three

On the Way to Marietta, Montana

IT WAS A long trip. Two layovers, and not enough preparation to deal with being in cramped spaces. Isolation for the past six months had made all the things Nate thought he was good at enduring feel damn near unendurable.

But he'd made it to Montana.

And for perhaps the millionth time, he wondered what the hell for. It was morning now and jagged mountain peaks greeted him outside the window of Sam's car as they drove out of Bozeman.

He preferred the Smokies, with their green and their fog. The subtle rolls, the smooth edges.

Montana was all sharp angles. Ones that had nearly cut him to ribbons.

Why had he come back?

But the answer was there, no matter how he tried to ignore it. It wasn't revenge so much as justice. He didn't give a shit about Sam's dad. He wasn't even sure he gave one about his own anymore.

But his mother hadn't deserved to die. Not like that. And the right man should pay.

Sometimes, he pretended he barely remembered his

mother. Sometimes, he pretended he hadn't known her at all.

But if he got too deep in that, his subconscious usually came for him in the shape of dreams that featured her. Whole and just as she had been, her voice haunting him long after he woke up.

So, he was here for her, if nothing else. It wasn't a good reason, but it was a reason.

He glanced at Sam as she drove, sunglasses shading her face, but exhaustion weighed on her shoulders though she tried to hide it. He'd known her growing up, but he also knew how much fifteen years could change a person.

She'd tried to talk the first few legs of their trip. Asked him incessant questions he'd refused to answer. Told him things he hadn't been ready to hear that he'd pretended to ignore. His oldest brother Cal was a lawyer living in Texas. Landon, the middle, was still manning the ranch with Dad here in Montana.

Neither piece of information surprised him. Cal had been born to be something flashy and important, far away from Marietta. Landon had the ranch in his bones, in his blood.

Nate had never quite fit. He existed somewhere in a middle. Or had, because he didn't exist in the family structure of the Bennets anymore.

He resented Sam for bringing up things that reminded him of that. Because he wasn't here about old family structures. He wasn't here to be a Bennet. He was here to find the truth.

And the truth was… As much as it was hard to believe

his father had killed his mother—even knowing the damage his father could inflict, Gene Price had never made much sense either.

He glanced at Sam. "Your dad did fifteen years?"

"He did. Jury thought he did it, but not premeditated or even on purpose, exactly. You keep track?"

He turned his attention to the road as it rolled out in front of them, considered what he should say. "Not exactly keeping track, but sometimes my curiosity got the better of me."

"Nothing wrong with a little healthy curiosity."

"On that we disagree." Curiosity got people killed in the wrong situation.

Silence descended again. Sam, to her credit, didn't seem to mind it. She drove, hummed along to the radio sometimes. But as they creeped ever closer to Marietta, they both got a little fidgety.

She tapped her fingers on the steering wheel, and he kept moving in his seat, trying to find a comfortable position for his injured leg.

"So, what's your plan?" Sam asked into the silence. "Since you made certain to tell me you're not following mine."

"Just take me to a hotel."

She slid him a look before turning her attention back to the road. "Look, it's none of my business, but maybe you don't remember how things around here go."

Nate paused, looked over at Sam. "And how's that?"

"You so much as whisper the name *Bennet* anywhere in the county limits, you're going to have at least five people charging their way up to your dad's place to tell him you're back."

"I guess it's good I've got some aliases under my belt and don't plan on whispering the name Bennet." *Ever again.* "I'll just get a room somewhere." He could use a nice bed after this painful trip. "You know the town. You pick."

"You don't think anyone would recognize you?"

"Why would they? I didn't recognize you." At least at first, and he prided himself on being pretty damn observant.

But Sam seemed undeterred. "Maybe they haven't seen *you*, but they've seen your brothers. They've seen your dad. You might be shocked to find you didn't grow out of that Bennet family resemblance. People are going to know. Your family is going to know."

Nate didn't outwardly react to that. It wasn't like he thought he could waltz into Marietta and hide in plain sight for a long time. It wasn't like he hadn't considered what it might be like to see his family again.

He just hadn't come to any forgone conclusions about how to handle it. He thought he'd have some days to lay low, to reacclimate to Montana, and maybe talk himself out of this fool's errand.

"You get to handle this however you want, Nate. I'm just warning you. There's a pretty big chance it gets back to your family. If that's how you want them to find out, that's your deal."

He supposed it was a kind gesture, all in all. Maybe she didn't know just how out of touch with reality he'd been for a while. Maybe she did. Either way, he could at least listen to what someone who'd stayed had to say.

"And what would you suggest?"

She blinked once, a barely there sign she was surprised he'd ask her. "I wouldn't wait. I'd jump right into the lion's den."

The answer amused him. Both because it felt apt, and because the Samantha Price he remembered was indeed a fan of jumping in. She'd been the first to take a dare from the boys, to be loud and mouthy in gym class, to wade into a fight to prove she was tough, no matter how tiny.

But if Sam hadn't changed, that meant there was a whole host of Bennets that likely hadn't either. Jumping into the lion's den without knowing the players, without knowing what he was jumping into felt like a mistake.

"I go to the ranch, say hi to dear old dad, he's going to know what you're up to."

Sam shrugged. "Believe me, he already knows what I think and what I'm trying to do. He has for fifteen years. But *you* might give him some pause. Some worry. I want him shaking in his boots. I want him worried enough to make a mistake."

She said it with a venom he wished he had left inside of him, but these days anger felt like too much energy.

They crossed the city limits, and Nate tried not to feel like there was a pair of hands around his throat, squeezing. Because he wasn't a black-and-blue teenager anymore. He was a man who'd survived war.

He could survive the Bennets. He could survive the curse of his own family.

"How about this?" Sam said. "I'll take you to my office. We'll eat some lunch and hash it all out. Figure out a plan of action. And I know, I know, you want to be your own boss, blah, blah, blah." She rolled her eyes like it was ludicrous. "But we're partners in this, Nate Bennet. Whether you like it or not."

"I definitely don't."

She laughed, which amused him in spite of himself. "Well, regardless, up to you. A hotel or Honor's Edge Investigations headquarters?"

Honor's Edge. That felt a little too apt, all in all. And maybe it was another sign. That no matter how messed up this felt, it was finally time. Time to face everything he'd had to run away from. Everything he'd tried to bury.

He was here. There was no going back. "We'll skip the hotel for now."

Sam grinned, but she didn't gloat. She just drove.

When she parked in her usual parking spot, the tiny lot behind her building was empty. Dad was in a jail cell, and Aunt Lisa was probably out at the ranch. Sam hadn't let her know she was coming back today, let alone with a Bennet in tow. She hadn't known how to break that news over the phone or text.

That was a problem for later. Right now, she had to figure out how best to use Nate Bennet.

For *years* she'd wanted to find him. For *years* she'd wanted him to tell his story. It wasn't an alibi for her father. It wasn't absolution. But it was *something*.

Sam was desperate enough to pin all her hopes on *some-*

thing these days. Besides, even if they didn't find evidence, even if Benjamin Bennet didn't mess up, Nate could be used in the defense for her father's trial as a sort of anti-character witness.

Since that *seemed* to be all the police had. She knew they were holding their cards close to the vest, and that right now they were holding Dad on a parole violation while they tried to build the murder case against him.

And sure, there'd been a gun in Dad's cabin, but Sandy wasn't *killed* with a gun, so it was all just a farce. The cops wanted something easy, and Dad was easy.

The highest hope Sam had was that Nate's reappearance, Nate being willing to speak on the abuse he faced, would rattle the sainted Benjamin Bennet. Who never had a bad word spoken against him.

Sam had investigated enough cases, watched enough criminals to know that when faced with their misdeeds, when they were afraid of what might happen to them, they made mistakes.

If Benjamin Bennet knew Nate was in town, working with her, talking to different people, he would make a mistake.

And if he didn't, she just had to keep Nate around long enough for the inevitable trial. Which meant she needed to convince him.

She was under no illusions she'd done that yet. He was here for his own reasons, and that was fine. As long as she made sure he stayed.

She led him into the back, through a little kitchenette, then into a hallway and her tiny office room. She tried to keep it orderly, but that had never been her strong suit. There were piles of folders, notebooks, and other variety of things that had to do with whatever she was working on.

Right now, her entire focus was the two murders on the Bennet Ranch, separated by fifteen years. One pile of folders nearly teetered. The other was smaller, but it was growing. She put her hand atop the taller one. "Fifteen years of work trying to clear my father's name in your mother's case." She moved her hand to the shorter one. "Sandy McCoy's murder a month ago."

Nate surveyed her desk with no hint to what he was thinking. "Do you not believe in computers in Montana?"

"I've got a lot of things computerized, but I think better when I write it all out. Plus, I don't waste time scanning things into digital when I can just keep them organized."

This time his expression was dubious. "This doesn't strike me as organized."

Sam shrugged. "It's *my* kind of organized."

He didn't say anything to that, but he crossed to the desk, lifted the top file off the Sandy pile. He flipped it open. She couldn't see over his shoulder, because he was a good foot taller than her, but she was pretty sure that folder held all the police reports she'd been able to get her hands on.

"And this new murder victim was my father's girlfriend?" Nate asked, his voice devoid of any emotion.

Sam nodded. "She was living at the ranch." It grated that even that—dating and living with a woman fifteen years his junior—hadn't rattled the way people spoke about Ben. It was like he was untouchable.

And he knew it.

But Nate could touch him. Stain that reputation. He had to.

"And your dad was released from prison a month before the murder? That's quite the coincidence."

"So's the fact both victims were killed on Bennet property *and* were romantically linked with your father."

Nate only made a considering sound. After he read through a few pages, he put the folder down, looked around the room.

"So, what exactly do you do when you're not trying to prove my father is a murderer?"

"Prove other things for other people."

"Like a cop?"

"Private investigator. Leaves the law a little more open to interpretation." And gave her the flexibility she needed to follow her own case. Cases now. She blew out a breath, gestured at the whole desk. "You can familiarize yourself with the case however you want. My goal is for them to know you're here. Then to watch what happens once they do."

"Who's they?"

"Your dad. Your brother. Aly. Anyone else who closed ranks around your dad the first go around."

"Aly Cartwright?"

"Still working on your father's ranch. All wrapped up in Ben or Landon's business most of the time."

"Weren't you guys friends?"

Sam nodded. Years ago, Aly had been one of her best friends. Then the murder had happened.

Because her entire life was before and after that moment.

Why wouldn't her friendships be too?

If she could solve this, if she could *end* this, then she wouldn't have to turn the calendar on this year and enter more years in the after, in the *lies*, than the before.

"You really think them knowing I'm in town is enough for him to make a mistake?" Nate asked, still frowning at her folders.

But when he looked up and over at her, Sam met Nate's dark gaze steadily. "I do."

Nate nodded slowly. "Then let's make sure they hear it from me."

Chapter Four

The Bennet Ranch

LANDON BENNET WAS tired. Hard enough to run a generational ranch when things were going well, but ever since Sandy McCoy had been found murdered, facedown, in their creek things hadn't been *good*.

Even now, police were still coming to the house at any and all hours with new search warrants. New this and that, poking around and asking questions.

Landon hated it for a lot of reasons. It reminded him too much of fifteen years ago. His mother. His missing brother. Dad's drinking—a bad habit Landon had started to believe was kicked for good, only to be sorely disappointed.

But what wouldn't send a man backsliding if not for the murder of his girlfriend? Maybe Sandy hadn't been Landon's favorite person, maybe he'd never quite understood what Dad had seen in the brash woman, but having two people you were involved with murdered was too much for any man.

Even Benjamin Bennet.

Landon shook his head as if it would stop the worrying. He finished off the sandwich he'd made haphazardly. His morning had been unproductive. He needed to turn the course with the afternoon.

But before he could even leave the kitchen, Aly was walking in. Aly Cartwright was one of the few people on this ranch who tended to ease a burden rather than add to it, but he could tell from the expression on her face this wasn't one of those times.

She had bad news. Luckily, she didn't beat around the bush.

"Sam Price went into her office this morning with a guy."

Nope, not here to ease any burdens. Samantha Price was one hell of a burden. "Am I supposed to care about that?"

"I think you are when the guy looks suspiciously like you."

Landon snorted. "I wasn't in Sam's office. I can't stand that woman."

Aly huffed out a breath. "Put the pieces together, Landon."

"I am *tired*, Aly."

"A man around your age, who looks a heck of a lot like you, shows up in Marietta with Sam, who has a vendetta against your father. Who do you think it might be?"

Landon felt those pieces click into place, and immediately rejected it.

He shook his head. "I don't know what trick Sam is playing, or you are, but…"

"Who else would it be?"

"You think my brother who ran away fifteen years ago is magically back in Marietta hanging out with Samantha fucking Price? Aly… Why would you even say that?"

"Because it's the rumor going around," she said, with that stubborn firmness that he usually appreciated. Except when it was directed at him.

If she was any other ranch hand, he could have ignored it and her, because they wouldn't have free rein of the house to start, but Aly was something like… Well, not exactly family. Not a sister or anything, but her dad had been the foreman when they'd all been growing up, and when he'd died and left her something of an orphan in their early teens, she'd stayed on as a ranch hand and the Bennets had something like adopted her.

Something like.

"I don't know when I ever gave you or anyone else the impression I give a shit about gossip, Aly."

She sighed heavily, forever despairing of him. "What if it is *true*?"

He moved past her, out of the kitchen, down the hall, and to the front door. He had work to do. He couldn't entertain whatever this was.

"It's not true. If Nate's really still out there I cannot imagine what circumstances would lead him to pop back into town with Samantha fucking Price."

"Landon."

But he pushed out the door. Maybe it was because there was something like hope trying to stitch itself together inside of him. Maybe he couldn't stand Samantha and everything she stood for, but if his brother was alive…

He stopped short on the big wraparound porch at the sound of a car moving up the drive. Gravel popped in the quiet spring afternoon, only the trilling sound of birds to go along with the sound of an engine rumbling.

He recognized the car that came up the hill and into view. Sam Price had come onto their property unwanted enough in the past for him to know it by sight.

Surely this didn't mean…

The car came to a stop. The driver got out. Samantha. But then so did the passenger.

"Told you so," Aly muttered, right behind him. But she reached out, put her hand on his back, a supportive gesture.

Landon barely heard her, barely felt her. He couldn't find his breath. It wasn't like looking in a mirror exactly. The man's hair was shorter. His nose was crooked. His muscle sat on him differently.

But Landon saw those same eyes in the mirror every morning. In his father over the dinner table—when Dad decided to make an appearance. He saw that same widow's peak on his older brother the rare times he saw Cal anymore.

He might have stepped forward. He might have gone on with this soaring feeling of *relief*. Nate was alive. Nate was here.

But he was with *her*.

So, he held his ground and his heart—he'd had to learn how these past fifteen years.

"I don't know why you're here, but if you're here with her, you can both turn right the hell around and get off my property."

"Is it yours these days?" The voice was all adult gravel, low and terse, and nothing like the voice Landon heard in his head when he couldn't seem to ignore the memories of a childhood that had seemed fine enough.

Before.

Landon didn't have anything to say. For a moment, he thought this was actually some warped dream. He'd open his eyes and wake up in his room, the weight of another day sitting on his chest like a ticking time bomb.

But this was real, and the strangest tableau. Nate, alive and well and an adult, with Samantha Price standing behind him like they were some kind of unit. Him, yards away, Aly's hand still on his back.

And no one said a word. Except a few robins making an unholy spring racket.

"I came to see Dad," Nate finally said.

Dad hadn't been in great shape this morning, and even if he had been, Nate being with Samantha meant that he was a threat.

Landon didn't let any threats through. "He's not here right now. Not sure he'd want to see you if he was."

Nate made a noise, something like a scoff or a bitter laugh. "Didn't say he'd want to."

"Maybe next time you call ahead. Warn someone you're back from the dead. Ditch the careless asshole pretending to be an investigator."

Nate didn't have a rejoinder for that. His dark, blank gaze seemed to survey the ranch. Not with any sense of emotion. It reminded Landon too much of the way the cops who came to investigate the murder scene surveyed things. Cold. Detached. Looking for clues.

Nate wouldn't find any clues here.

"You go on and tell Dad I'm back," Nate said finally. "See how he takes it. I'll be around." He turned and got into the car.

Samantha followed suit without having ever said a word.

Landon turned abruptly. He didn't want to see Nate drive away. It unsettled something inside of him that had to stay settled if he was going to keep what was left of this family and the Bennet name together. He strode for the house, not quite sure what his plan was.

Aly was at his heels. "You have to call Cal."

Christ, not that. "And tell him what?"

"That Nate's back! That he's … working with Sam, I guess? I don't know. But he should know Nate's alive, and he should know…"

Landon stopped, looked down at Aly. "Know what?"

"If Sam is with Nate, it means something. Something about Sandy's murder and Gene Price's case. Cal can help."

"Help with what?"

"Landon, don't be a jerk to me just because you're pissed. Cal can help with the legal part of all this. You know that."

"You think someone's suddenly going to blame Dad just because long-lost Nate is hanging around Samantha Price?"

"Cal could tell us—"

"Fuck Cal, Aly. This is our fight. We'll fight it." He knew he was being too harsh, but he figured he was due a little harsh.

Nate was back. Nate was *alive*. And he'd been poisoned by Samantha Price? Why would he drag Cal into what was already too big of a mess?

"If they poke into your dad…" Aly trailed off, and Landon knew what she wanted to say, but didn't want to verbalize. For him. For herself.

But in the end, in the silence, she did.

"He's drinking again," Aly said softly. And it was impossible to be harsh with softness from Aly. She was the only soft in his life. Ever.

But did she think he'd somehow missed Dad's drinking? Why did she think he was so damn tired? It was one thing trying to run this ranch on his own, it was a whole other to add babysitting Dad to those responsibilities.

His father could be a mean SOB when he wanted to be, especially if he was drinking, but so could anyone. Ben Bennet was a gruff, taciturn mountain of a guy, but so were most of the ranchers around here. Montana made you tough or it chewed you up and spit you out.

But if there were more questions, if the cops sniffed around even more than they already had the past month, Dad might do something stupid.

"Sam isn't going to give up," Aly said.

"She didn't give up *or* succeed the first time her father killed someone, and I still recall him doing time. Too little time, but time all the same."

Aly sighed heavily. "Landon, what reason does Gene Price have to kill Sandy? It doesn't add up."

He looked at Aly, shock mounting through him that almost matched the shock he was trying to absorb at his brother being back.

He'd known this woman most his life, but she was saying… "You think *Dad* did it?"

"No, of course not," she said. "But I'm worried a case that doesn't add up means a murderer is still running free."

"Gene Price is a murderer."

"Yeah, but that doesn't mean he murdered Sandy." She put her hand on his arm. Squeezed. "Call Cal, Landon. We need his expertise."

Landon had spent the past fifteen years learning how not to need his brothers. They'd deserted him. In different ways, sure, but they'd both done it. Why would he seek one out to help deal with the other?

But Aly had planted the seeds of doubt, the seeds of worry. Sam hadn't succeeded in getting her murdering father off the first time around, but she somehow had Nate now. Nate, who wanted Dad to know he was back?

It was all bad news, and maybe he didn't need Cal's help, but his advice as a criminal defense attorney wouldn't hurt.

"I'll think about it," he muttered. Then he strode away from her, to the stables, to the work that sustained him.

That threatened to drown him.

ALY GAVE LANDON some space that afternoon. She had things to do, and she knew better than to push that hardheaded man too much. He'd dig in and then where would they be?

She could call Cal herself. He'd no doubt listen to her. But there were certain lines she tried not to cross when it came to the Bennets. Maybe they'd taken care of her when she'd been orphaned, but she wasn't family.

She *was* a friend though. To Landon especially, but to Ben as well. And she owed them, so she couldn't butt out entirely. It was obvious they needed help, and considering Cal Bennet was a *criminal defense attorney*, Aly had never understood why Ben and Landon were so against asking him for help.

Aside from sheer stubbornness. And that dogged Montana pride that insisted anyone who left was less.

Aly couldn't imagine leaving her life at the Bennet Ranch, but she also didn't blame Cal for getting the hell out. It hadn't exactly been a hospitable environment after their mother had died, after Nate had disappeared. No, they'd been hard years.

But they needed Cal now to make sure that didn't happen all over again, and considering what she'd witnessed, and what she knew was happening with Ben—a backslide with alcohol—that was all a little too likely. Whether Gene Price was proven guilty or not.

Aly drove up the dirt road that followed Bennet Creek and the western tract of the Bennet Ranch toward the little cabin that was her destination on the other side of the property line. She'd picked up her friend Jill's groceries, would deliver them, have a little tea and gossip, and then head back to the ranch to work.

She needed to enjoy this while she could because once calving started, she'd be lucky to even have time to deliver groceries, let alone have a chat with her friend.

She pulled her truck to a stop in front of the cabin and hopped out. The Harrington cabin was in a pretty spot where you could take in the mountains, the Bennet Ranch below, and the creek just by making a circle in the yard. Montana's beauty stretched out all around them.

Years and years ago, this had been part of the Harrington Ranch. But long before Aly had been born, Glenda Harrington had split it up—selling some of it and all her cattle to the Bennets, donating the more mountain terrain to the state. She'd retained only her little cabin by the creek.

Aly could hear that creek gurgling nearby and tried not to think about Sandy facedown in it, or the fight she'd overheard between Ben and Sandy that day that she hadn't told anyone, including Landon, about. She focused on the mountains and the pretty blue sky and grabbing Jill's groceries out of the truck.

The door creaked open, and Jill stepped out all bundled up. "Afternoon," she greeted, hugging her arms around herself. "Jesus, you're not even wearing a winter coat."

"This is practically summer," Aly returned with a grin.

She handed Jill a few bags then took the rest and followed Jill inside. They unloaded the groceries in companionable silence and Jill filled the teapot and set it on the stove.

"I'm betting the wildflowers start blooming in a week or so," Aly offered trying to infuse some cheer in her words as she placed cans of soup and boxes of pasta in the cabinets.

"I'll believe it when I see it," Jill replied, still wearing a sweater and a jacket, even though there was a fire throwing off waves of heat in the old-fashioned stove. "What's up with you? You're acting more wound up than usual. Or at least the usual since the whole … Sandy thing."

Aly sighed. Telling Jill what was going on wasn't too risky. Jill lived in this cabin with her grandmother, Glenda. Since Glenda had health issues, Jill didn't like to leave her alone or drag her into town, so she didn't leave the cabin much. And since Jill wrote mysteries for a living, she didn't often have to leave.

So Jill was a safe place for Aly to lay a lot of her concerns. When she didn't want to worry Landon. When she needed to work through things without *that* complication. She'd even considered telling Jill about what she'd overheard the day of the murder.

But she hadn't.

She couldn't stop herself from spilling these beans though. "Nate's back."

"Who's Nate?"

Aly sometimes forgot Jill was a full-on outsider. She hadn't grown up in Montana but had moved here about three years ago to look after her grandmother, who was something of an urban legend.

Glenda Harrington hadn't spoken a word in twenty years or so and had become a hermit. There were a million stories as to why, gossip melded with straight-up fiction to scare kids on Halloween.

Jill thought her grandmother had just had a psychological break due to a tough life, and Aly was inclined to agree with her. Glenda had lost a lot in her life, and rural Montana wasn't the kind of place that offered softness or comfort.

Sometimes Aly thought it might be kind of nice to be a mute hermit.

She explained to Jill about the missing Bennet brother. The implications of Nate returning with Sam in tow. She even explained Cal and trying to get Landon to call him.

"Aren't defense attorneys the scum of the earth?" Jill

asked, settling the teakettle on the stove.

"Maybe. But we need one. Besides Cal… Well, he's a little slick, but he has a good heart."

"You think everyone has a good heart."

"Not everyone," Aly replied, because she hadn't particularly thought Sandy McCoy had one, which made her whole keeping everything a secret feel even worse. Was it *really* because what she'd heard was irrelevant, or was it because she'd hated Sandy?

She shook those horrible thoughts away. She was protecting innocent people. Ben. Landon.

Jill raised a perfectly arched eyebrow in disbelief. When Aly had first met her, she'd kind of wanted to hate Jill. She was so sophisticated. Effortlessly female. She didn't have to threaten to punch someone in the nose to get her point across. She just raised a disdainful, well-shaped eyebrow.

Aly tried to give the look right back to her, but she knew she failed. She was rough and tumble at best. The only female presence in her life had been Mrs. Bennet before she'd died, and Aly had been scrambling to take care of the Bennets left behind ever since.

Either way, Jill dropped the subject. She was good at that. They drank their tea and, thankfully, chatted about the weather and a potential shopping trip neither of them would actually be able to leave Marietta to do—not with Aly's job and Jill being the sole caretaker of her grandmother. Still, it was nice to dream.

When her phone beeped, the alarm she set for herself so she wasn't late for her ranching duties, she slid off the chair and placed her cup in the sink. "If the calves start going, I may not be around much the next few weeks."

Jill smiled kindly. "I know how it goes, and I hope you know how much I appreciate—"

Aly held up a hand. She had a hard time expressing to Jill how much these visits meant to *her*, and she wished she could get across to Jill it was no burden or hardship to have a little girl time under the guise of delivering groceries.

But words weren't much of her forte either. "See you around."

Jill nodded and Aly stepped outside. She startled a little when she realized Glenda was out there, sitting on a rickety-looking porch chair.

"Hi, Glenda," Aly offered, trying to hide the startle in her voice. She knew the woman wouldn't reply, but she also knew the woman wasn't stupid for all her lack of talking. Glenda watched and thought and paid attention to everything.

Today, Glenda stared, dark eyes steady on Aly. Aly knew it wasn't fair. It was just all those stories kids had made up about Glenda over the years, but it felt as if the woman could read her soul. And her secrets.

Aly swallowed down the frisson of fear and climbed into her truck. She had work to do.

Chapter Five

Honor's Edge Investigations Office

THEY HADN'T SPOKEN on the drive back into Marietta. In fact, Sam hadn't spoken pretty much at all since they'd crested the rise that had brought the Bennet Ranch house into view.

It wasn't a hardship. She was trying to parse a lot of what had happened, but more ... separate her emotional reaction from the whole thing.

It was easy to forget everyone involved was a person. Easy to forget about Nate's tragic past in ways that didn't suit what she needed to do. It had been easy to drag him back to Montana on determination and tunnel vision alone.

Save her father at all costs.

She still felt that, would continue to live by that tenet and that tenet alone.

But seeing Nate and Landon square off against each other, having to imagine what that would feel like, had messed with her a little bit.

She didn't have siblings, but she had family. She had gotten to visit her father for the fifteen years he'd been in prison. It had been hard to not have consistent access to him. It had certainly been traumatizing for a variety of reasons. She'd seen him though. Talked to and seen him as much as possible.

Today, she'd watched two brothers stare at each other, only yards apart, with the fifteen years of absence throbbing between them like an open wound.

And Sam had felt guilty. Which was *rare*, because her life was proving her dad was innocent and she didn't have time for guilt. Regrets could come if and when Dad was free.

But Nate's silence had guilt creeping up her spine. Like it was all her fault that two brothers didn't talk, when the only thing she'd had to do with Nate's fifteen-year absence was the money she'd given him to skip town.

Because Benjamin Bennet was an abusive asshole and potential murderer. Did he hit Landon and Cal too? She wanted to ask.

She didn't. She just drove back to her office, and when she got out of her car, so did Nate. He followed her back inside.

"They know I'm back. From my own mouth, more or less. I guess it's safe to stay at a hotel. What's still around?"

But he certainly didn't sound like that was what he wanted to do. Sam didn't know how to handle this strange partnership, even if it had been her idea. Even if it was something she'd wanted to do for years—bring Nate back to town and unravel secrets that she knew had to have *something* to do with an old murder.

Not a new one, though.

Regardless, she supposed the answer was in all that unknown. There was no map to this, no blueprint. She could only do what felt right in the moment.

"My aunt has some rental properties on her ranch. It'd be more private, if that's what you're looking for."

Nate was quiet for a few uncomfortable moments. "I don't know what the hell I'm looking for," he muttered.

Before she could think of what to say, especially over the annoying stab of guilt she felt for bringing him here, he kept talking.

"That'd probably be best. Something more separate. What are they, cabins or something?"

"Yeah. I can drive you over, though you're probably going to want a rental car or something. Eventually. But I can drive you around wherever you need until then."

"I'll get a car worked out by tomorrow, but before you drive me to your aunt's, I want to look at some of these." He gestured at her files.

"Sure. Anything in particular?"

"You got the police reports from my mother's murder?"

Sam paused. She did, but they were … graphic. Normally she wouldn't have thought twice about it, but this afternoon had reminded her of all the *people* behind the characters she'd made of them over the past fifteen years.

The first murder victim wasn't just pictures and some disturbing words in a police report. She had been a real live breathing human being. She had been Nate's mother.

"You sure you want to look at that?"

"I was in the army, Sam. I've seen people die."

"Sure, but they weren't your mom."

He didn't say anything to that right away. He was an interesting guy these days. There were silences in him—ones he wasn't afraid of. Most of the men she knew either wanted to hear themselves talk or used their silences like weapons.

Nate just seemed to be figuring himself out.

Which was starting to create a really annoying soft spot. She couldn't afford soft spots right now.

"Maybe that's a good point," he said eventually. "What about your dad's statements about the first murder?"

"That I can do." She moved to her desk, pulled out the correct file.

They spent the next few hours doing that. He'd ask for something, she'd find it. He'd read it in silence like he was filing it all away. She texted Aunt Lisa about Nate renting one of her cabins, caught up on a few emails while considering her plans for this evening.

Landon Bennet knew Nate was back, and that he was hanging around her. She was well versed in what Landon thought about her. Sam didn't even really blame him. What was there to like from his—wrong—perspective?

There was no doubt in her mind that by nightfall, every single resident of the Bennet Ranch would know Nate was back in town—on the wrong side of things, fraternizing with her. She *hoped* the cracks would start immediately. She'd have to watch to make sure they did.

Which meant camping was in her future. Which meant, she needed to hurry Nate along if she was going to get him out to Lisa's ranch, eat some dinner, and then get everything she needed together.

"We should probably get out to my aunt's before dark. She'll want to check you in, get you acquainted with everything."

Slowly, Nate looked up from the file he'd been reading.

Then he took his time before he nodded, closed it, and set it back on her desk.

"What are you going to do?" he asked.

"Paperwork. Maybe make some dinner, if you're fishing for an invite. I can cook, but not well."

His mouth quirked ever so slightly. "No, I mean with the case."

Sam didn't say anything at first. None of her plans would sound normal, she knew that. Maybe they weren't even normal, but she'd given up on caring about what her actions *meant* a long time ago.

The only thing that mattered to her was clearing her father's name.

She shrugged. "Maybe a bit of camping."

Nate studied her, suspicion in the dark brown of his eyes. "On Bennet land?"

"Of course not. That's trespassing, Nate." She offered a bland smile.

Because she knew a place. Just off the Bennet property. Owned by someone who almost never left their cabin, and who couldn't speak, so the likelihood of being stumbled upon was slim. And with the escape route of state conservation land not far away.

Because the plan she had in mind allowed her undetected access to Bennet property. To the murder scene. To anything—or *anyone else*—that might be lurking around that spot.

There had to be evidence somewhere. She didn't believe the creek was a coincidence. It was meant to wash away *something*.

But beyond that, when people started getting worried, they sometimes returned to the scene of the crime.

So, she'd be staking it out for a while.

Sam blurred some lines. She risked a lot. And it was easy to say it was worth it when none of it had come back to bite her yet.

But her dad sat in a cell. *Again.* After thinking he was free.

She'd risk and risk big.

She hoped Nate felt the same way.

He studied her. "Mind if I tag along?"

For a moment, she didn't breathe. For a lot of reasons. One, she'd never had help. Even Aunt Lisa had always kept her hands clean of this whole thing. She'd encouraged Sam to get on with her life in those first few years, before accepting Sam never would.

There were other reasons. Then there was the fact she really didn't know if she could trust Nate. If she *should* trust Nate. End of the day, he was still a Bennet.

But she'd found him. Dragged him here. Didn't she owe him some piece of this? She was in charge, in control. She didn't have to show him anything she didn't want to.

Besides, he'd grown up on the Bennet Ranch. Maybe he'd know some things she didn't.

She kept her response casual. A little shrug. "The more the merrier."

First Sam drove him out to her aunt's ranch, got him

settled in a rental cabin, then she casually asked her aunt if she could use a truck for a few days. It must have been a common exchange, because Lisa handed over keys and asked no questions.

By the time they drove back to Sam's office and packed up some camping gear, it was dark.

Nate appreciated this for a wide variety of reasons. One of the main ones being he couldn't recognize where they were or where they were going as Sam drove. Memories couldn't swamp him if it was all just dark.

He hoped.

When she pulled the truck to a stop, killed the headlights, in a little gravel lot, he figured maybe she *wasn't* lying about camping on public land. Because he didn't recognize any part of this.

But as he listened to the dark night around them, he heard the telltale sound of water running over rock.

So he supposed he had some idea where they were. His mother had been murdered—or left—in the barn on the west side of the property near the creek that marked the Bennet boundary between their ranch and what was left of Harrington land.

A creek Sandy McCoy had been found facedown in.

Both Sandy and Mom had died of blunt force trauma wounds to the head. No deadly weapons ever found. With both murders, there'd been some initial confusion at first. Had his mother burned to death in the barn? Had Sandy fallen and drowned in the creek?

No.

Someone had beaten them both to death first.

Sam opened the truck bed and began to pull gear out. He took the backpack from her before she could swing it onto her own back. He watched her pause, but in the end, she said nothing and offered no complaints. Even when it ended up that he was carrying most of the stuff.

He read her fairly easily, so far anyway. She was used to doing all this on her own, and she didn't know what to do with help. With his presence.

She could join the club, because he'd spent most of the past year completely and utterly alone. Part of him had felt like it was a necessary step in the process. If there was one thing Nate knew how to do in this life, it was start over. He'd learned ways to do it effectively. Isolation was one such way.

So, spending an entire day—into the night hours—with someone felt strange and vaguely uncomfortable even when Sam herself was surprisingly easy.

She didn't demand things of him. She didn't make things awkward. She sat in the silences he needed easily enough. Even when she was *clearly* uncomfortable, or not quite so sure what to do with someone helping, she just rolled with the punches.

He supposed, all in all, that was the Sam he'd known before murders and beatings. Hell, wasn't cleaning him up and giving him a hundred dollars all those years ago a roll-with-the-punches kind of situation?

But the fact she was here was just ... off. And even though this felt familiar—he was an adept outdoorsman, he'd hiked through every terrain possible with only his own wits, he'd camped with less and for longer—she was the discordant note of the unfamiliar that didn't allow him to relax or fully focus.

"This how you spend a lot of your evenings?" he asked, following her in the dark along a path only she knew.

She didn't respond right away. "Maybe not *a lot*," she said eventually.

Which wasn't all that convincing. But he supposed it didn't matter. What she did on her own time wasn't his concern. Not even if they'd somehow ended up on this strange same team.

But it spoke to a woman who had … not just drive, but maybe an unhealthy obsession with what she was doing.

He'd never been emotionally obsessed with anything—except maybe turning all his emotions off. So maybe it wasn't fair to think *unhealthy* about anyone but himself.

"Here," she said, coming to a stop. She turned on a flashlight, and he could see they were on a flat-ish area of land. From the position of the shadowy mountains, and the quietly moving creek he couldn't see but could faintly hear, he had a feeling they were on the west side of the Bennet property.

Pretty damn close to two different murder scenes.

"It doesn't concern you?" he asked, shrugging her pack off his shoulders.

"What?" she asked as they worked in tandem to get out the supplies they'd need to set up their camp.

"Traipsing around in the dark? Knowing two people have been murdered here? If you believe your dad isn't the culprit, doesn't that mean someone out there is?"

"Yeah, except I know who that someone is. Because

there's only one thing the victims had in common fifteen years apart. And it wasn't *my* father."

It was his. Maybe he wasn't fully convinced his father had killed his mother, but what he did know was that it was possible. That while Benjamin Bennet might put on the mask of a good man, an honorable man, ninety-nine percent of the time, Nate had witnessed that snap. And it had made him question all the ways he might have seen the *almost* snap in the years leading up to it.

There was no doubt in his mind—then or now—that his father would have killed him that sunny, hot afternoon if Nate hadn't managed to be faster.

So, yeah, he knew his father *could* have killed someone. Even two someones. He just wasn't sure *why* he would.

He'd read the police reports. They'd questioned Dad, of course. Everyone at the ranch. All the answers had been pretty straightforward. No one had seen Sandy leave the house that night. Everyone asserted that Ben and Sandy had been getting along. No issues that they knew of.

Sounded pretty above board.

Or was it closing ranks?

That was the thing about his father. He used loyalty like a weapon. You just didn't realize it until you questioned it. And if you questioned it too much, too hard, you saw the snap.

Sometimes Nate wondered if he—and maybe his mother, and now Sandy—were the only ones who ever had.

"Before we settle in, I want to do a pass at the creek."

"You know the exact spot?" Nate asked.

"Yeah," Sam said. She led him there. Using the flashlight

to guide their path along the creek's bank. The ground was soft under his boots. Anxiety started small, a little quickening of his heartbeat. An involuntary contraction of the muscles in his shoulders.

It was the smell. Warm pine and pure water, while the chill of night wound around them. It was his childhood in an inhale, and everything that had soured on every exhale.

"It was at this bend," Sam said, pointing to where the creek curved. Her voice carried over the heavy beat of his heart in his ears.

She pointed her flashlight at it. Water was a little low, he thought. But then again, water eroded. It cut through stone and earth and changed everything in its path. Everything might feel familiar, like some nightmare that had kept him company through every night since he'd run away, but it was different, too.

"I guess they searched more than just this area."

"Reports say they did a full sweep of the creek, but… Well, I think there's something they could have missed. I think there's a reason one body was destroyed in a fire, and one was left in water to be tampered with."

She wasn't wrong. And if the murder happened a month ago, if the main winter melt had already started, the current of the creek would have been a lot stronger, a lot faster. Nate thought back to when he'd been a little kid.

He, Cal, and Landon on hot summer days running to play in the creek. The parts Mom let them play in.

And the parts she warned them not to go in.

So of course, that was where they'd gone. Daring each other to go farther into the bends and dips than they were allowed to go. Always pushing the boundaries—always pushing each other to push them farther.

He thought of Landon's face this afternoon. A shocking copy and paste of Dad, with very few differences. And Nate knew it was easy to see Dad in his own face when he looked in the mirror, but he didn't do that much.

Maybe that was what had made it so easy to be dismissive of him. That he'd looked like Dad, sounded like Dad. Maybe it had been the shocking and clear dismissal—even if Nate understood that had more to do with Sam and shock than it had to do with Nate himself.

"Getting a bit far from camp," Sam noted conversationally.

He realized he'd been not just following the creek but moving fast. Her legs were much shorter, and she was a ways behind him now, even though she was keeping up okay.

"We can stop." He did so now. He'd come back alone some time. Maybe alone was better.

"No. Keep going," Sam said when she caught up. "You seem like you've got an end goal in mind."

There was a little bend in the creek a ways down. The way the water had eroded the bank had created a deep swimming hole. Against Mom's wishes, they'd tied a rope to a tree and jumped in one summer. Over and over again.

Often laughing at the trash and debris they found when they dove to the bottom.

Maybe this was something he should do alone. Maybe this was something he shouldn't do at all. What did he know of Samantha Price? Not a thing, really. A shared childhood, a brief saving, and a dogged determination to clear her father's name wasn't much.

But he kept walking. Until even in the dark he knew the spot. When Sam's flashlight beam caught up, it hit the deep pool of still water.

"Can I?" he asked, frustrated with how rough his voice sounded as he held out his hand.

She put the flashlight into his palm. He moved the beam from the water to the bank, then up the tall tree that reached out over the deep part.

A frayed rope still hung from the tree branch—though the branch was cracked, dangling there just barely hanging on.

It felt a bit on the nose, all in all.

He moved the beam of light back to the deep area, moving closer. This part of the bank was high, the water cutting into the earth making a wide gap. Sam stayed on lower ground where the soggy bank was more even with the water.

Nate used the beam of light to study the bank, the tree, the water below. On the other side of this little cliff of earth, some boulders created the boundary to make the water deep here.

Nate climbed down, knowing that even with his flashlight, climbing around on wet banks and slippery rocks was dangerous. There were a trio of boulders, and Nate picked his way across flat, wet, slippery rocks, then climbed up one of the boulders.

He crouched on the flat part. He shined the light in between the boulders. Where no doubt things caught by the current might be trapped. Stuck.

Something sparkled down there. It could be a rock. It

could be just the weird movement of water with the light refracting off it.

But Nate thought it was more. He watched it. Fixed, stuck. If he laid flat, he could maybe get his arm in there.

He glanced at Sam, coming up behind him, carefully stepping along the rocks. Nate considered his options. Tell her? Touch it? Leave it? Before he could decide, he heard the subtle *snap* of something in the distance.

Nate had worried that he'd lost some of his instincts. That his injury and lingering aftereffects might have dulled everything that had once made him sharp. But he clicked off the light almost simultaneously, then unerringly reached out and grabbed Sam with impressive speed, and with enough pressure that she didn't even make a sound in protest.

Maybe she'd heard it, too. Her free hand curled around his wrist, squeezed, like a nonverbal confirmation she had.

They moved together. Across the boulders and back to the bank which offered a sturdier foundation. Once their feet touched earth, they stood in utter stillness, perfect silence except the wild night around them.

When a light clicked, it illuminated another woman's face not too far away from them. A much older woman. With light green eyes that glowed eerily like a cat's in the dim light.

He swallowed against the way his throat wanted to close up. He'd faced down worse—here and in the army.

Glenda Harrington might play the role of bogeywoman around these parts, but she was just a little old lady who'd no doubt seen plenty of trauma.

No one said anything. There was just the night, the

whisper of the creek, and Glenda's camping lantern. Nate didn't know how long they all stood there, simply staring at each other, but after long ticking moments, Glenda turned away from them.

She started walking away, path guided by light this time. He and Sam stood perfectly still, watching her departure. Light getting smaller and smaller and smaller until they were left in complete darkness once again.

"We better book it," Sam said on a whisper. "Get the hell out of here."

"You think Glenda's going to call the police? Did she start talking sometime in the past fifteen years?"

Sam shook her head. "She's got a granddaughter living with her now. If Glenda communicates she saw something, I bet Jill will call the police. Or worse."

"What's worse?"

Sam looked up at him. "She calls Aly, because they're friends. Then Aly tells your brother."

"Well. Shit."

"Exactly."

So, they hurried. Back to the makeshift camp they made. Sam started packing it up quickly, which made Nate realize they were definitely not on public land. Or at least the lines were blurry.

Once they had everything, he followed Sam as she moved at a quick clip back to her truck. But before they made it, a light appeared in their path. A sturdy flashlight pointed in their direction.

"You shouldn't be here," a voice called out.

The woman was mostly just shadow. Her voice had a

trace of East Coast and something else. And while he couldn't make out her face, he didn't miss the glint of her gun in the flashlight's beam.

"It's public land," Sam responded, calm and certain, when Nate was definitely not certain. Though maybe they'd moved far enough to be on public land now.

The woman was quiet for a moment. The gun didn't move. "I guess I'll have to call the police to find that out."

He could tell from the potent silence that Sam was concerned. Nate considered what he'd seen. What might take at least some of the heat off of them, if it was distraction enough.

"Why don't you go on and do that?" he said into the charged silence.

Sam made a little noise of distress, but he knew what he was doing. Maybe his first instinct had been to be quiet, to wait, to figure it out himself.

But he wasn't doing this alone. Maybe the whole point of this was the secrets that had stayed buried long enough and needed to be brought to light.

"Because I think there's something pretty important in this creek that they missed."

Chapter Six

The Harrington Property

JILL STALKED BACK to her cabin. She was angry. She was scared. And she *hated* dealing with guns, but Grandma had insisted that Jill know how to handle one once she'd moved in.

Jill had been grateful for that insistence when Grandma had come into her room—waking Jill up out of a dead sleep. Grandma's boots had been muddy, and Jill couldn't think about what it meant that Grandma was traipsing about in the middle of the night outside.

Not yet anyway.

The piece of paper Grandma had handed Jill had one word written on it.

Trespassers.

Jill had gotten out of bed. She'd scolded Grandma for scaring years off her life but had also dutifully dressed. She'd put her own boots on, not at all sure what she was supposed to do with this.

But that was the thing about her life here. Three years in, Jill liked to think she'd handled the transition from upper-middle-class city life to ancient-rural Montana cabin with a mute grandmother fairly well, but that didn't mean it wasn't still without its challenges.

The first few months had been tough, and her understanding of Grandma's own version of sign language had been a little rusty since she only used it when she visited Grandma, and visits tended to use the same words. Living together had necessitated new words. Dealing with Grandma's recovery from the stroke had required even more.

But things had been going so well lately. Jill had thought they were in a good, steady place. But charging out into the night with only a gun and a flashlight had been scary. It had made her miss her place in Boston, takeout, museums, *culture*. She'd even had a second where she missed awkward first dates from terrible dating-app guys.

Because none of that felt dangerous and terrifying and like she was responsible for an elderly woman's life.

But because she *was*, because in fact she'd insisted on being just that responsible—because Dad had wanted Grandma in an assisted living facility in Boston and Jill had known if anything was going to kill Grandma, it wasn't a stroke, a fall, or being alone up here in the middle of nowhere.

It would be trapped in a building in a major city. Glenda Harrington was not meant for any place but this wild one she'd made her own. In a trauma none of them fully understood.

Jill had stumbled upon the two people with camping gear quite on accident. But she'd held her gun firm and stood up to them. For Grandma.

And then, once she'd recognized Sam Price, and a guy who looked *far* too much like Landon Bennet to be a coincidence, she'd stood up to them for Aly too.

Now, she needed to call the police. How was she even going to go about that? This wasn't a 911 emergency situation, but it *was* a situation.

She didn't bother to scrape the mud off her boots as she entered the cabin. She'd deal with the mess she made later. Maybe once there was daylight and an ounce of warmth from the sun.

Before she could even move for the phone, Grandma—who had been waiting in the entry-kitchen-living room—handed her another piece of paper. In her shaky handwriting the word POLICE was written, along with a phone number.

"Thanks," Jill muttered.

Usually using the old-fashioned landline phone made her smile, but not tonight. She picked up the receiver and dialed.

When a woman's voice answered, she asked for Jill's *nonemergency*.

"I have some trespassers on my property. I told them that I would call the police if they didn't leave, and they seemed to want me to. I don't suppose you could send an officer up here?"

She answered some annoying questions, repeated the information, then gave the location.

"We'll have someone out within the hour. We recommend you stay in your residence. The police will come debrief you once they've assessed the situation."

Hour. Great. "Thank you," Jill offered, before hanging up.

She kept her hand on the receiver, debating. Then without even looking back at Grandma, picked it up again and dialed Aly's cell number.

Aly's voice was sleepy but concerned. "What's wrong? Is it Glenda?"

"No. Nothing *bad* has happened. Just something I thought you should know. Or Landon should."

Chapter Seven

The Bennet Ranch

IT TOOK LANDON a while to realize he wasn't dreaming. That Aly's insistent repeating of his name wasn't something … else.

But this was his bedroom, he was in bed, and it was dark. Only the light from the hallway shone inside.

"What the fuck, Aly?"

"I need you to get up," she hissed.

He sat up in bed, tried to shake away the sleep from his brain. That odd dream at the edges. "What's wrong?"

"Jill called me. She caught some people poking around her property. Or Glenda did, I guess. They called the police."

"That sucks for them, but why are you waking me…" It started to dawn on him, why this would have anything to do with them.

"It was Sam. So I assume the guy was Nate. Jill doesn't know him, but she said he looked like you."

Landon swore. What the hell was his long-lost brother doing? Why the hell was he aligning himself with Samantha Price?

When would this fucking nightmare end? He threw the

covers off, ignored the way Aly immediately moved out of his room and into the lit-up hallway. He tossed on a sweatshirt that was on the chair by his bed, then moved to the closet to find some pants.

Dressed, he met Aly out in the hallway.

"Why didn't you just text me?" he asked.

Aly lived in the back of the main house, mostly separated like her own private apartment. She was the only female ranch hand, and since her dad had died when she'd been a teenager, Dad had moved her into the main house. As she'd gotten older, they'd made the renovations to give her more privacy.

The only thing she shared with the Bennets was the kitchen, but it gave her access to everything else.

Like apparently coming to his bedroom in the middle of the night.

"Jill said she threatened to call the police on them, and Nate's response was, and she said this is pretty much word for word—they found something *pretty important* in the creek the police should see."

"Fuck."

"Yeah, so I figured we should probably be awake. Should we go over there? Is your dad…" She trailed off.

Landon hated seeing that look of worry on Aly's face—worry she would hurt him, worry about what Dad was up to. Just *worry*. And none of it hers. But she was always here all the same.

"Locked himself in his bedroom with a bottle of whiskey about three hours ago."

Aly closed her eyes, made a sound of pain. "What are we

going to do?"

Landon didn't have the first clue. But he did know one thing. "You're going to go back to bed. I'll handle this."

She frowned at him. Then shook her head and moved past him toward the stairs. "I'll make the coffee."

He followed her. God knew he'd need coffee to get through whatever this was going to be, but he also needed Aly to get it through her head that she didn't have to be in the thick of all this garbage.

"It isn't your fight, Al. It's not your—"

She stopped abruptly at the bottom of the stairs and whirled to face him. Almost like she was daring him to finish the sentence.

He didn't.

"Were you going to say it's not my family, Landon?"

He sighed, finished the walk down the stairs. So that they were facing off against each other.

Except he didn't want to fight. Not with her.

"I don't mean it that way and you know it. I mean it in the way that you shouldn't feel beholden to a drunk mess of a man drowning his grief and … whatever the hell mess I am."

They stood there in a poignant kind of silence. Her blue eyes held his, a million of those soft emotions she kept so deeply locked up most of the time. But she was still the softest spot and heart he knew.

He hated these fleeting times when he wondered why he'd ever made promises about her.

But wasn't this reminder enough? His family was a disaster. He was holding on by a thread, pretty much always, and that thread was getting tattered. Aly'd had enough pain and struggling in her own life.

She deserved better.

"Whatever mess you are, you're my best friend, Landon," she said, very solemnly, twisting the knife that always seemed lodged in his heart. "So, family or not, I'm in this. And if you think I'd walk away because you told me to, maybe I need to reevaluate that friendship."

"Aly."

She held up a hand. "I'm going to make coffee. We're going to drink it and try to ... figure out what's happening." Then she walked away, and Landon took a minute, just a minute, to close his eyes and wish that literally *everything* was different.

Except the floor he stood on. The land that was his. A birthright, a legacy.

He'd fight for it, if nothing else.

He forced himself to walk into the kitchen where Aly already had the coffeepot going. Landon slid into a chair at the kitchen table, and Aly leaned back against the counter, arms crossed, expression thoughtful.

"If they found something, the police will want to talk to you and Ben. Don't you think? Even if it's something innocuous."

"I think it depends. What did he find? Maybe they'll just go have more questions for the *actual* murderer." Landon shook his head. "What could they find? This is horseshit. She's probably trying to frame us," Landon muttered.

"I mean, if she'd sink that low why hasn't she done it yet?"

"She'd sink that low," Landon replied. Maybe Aly hadn't been friends with Sam since high school, but he still didn't think anyone fully saw Samantha Price for the enemy she was.

The source of all the trouble. The Price family.

Aly poured the coffee. Gave him a mug. Poured some cream into hers before she took the seat across from him.

"I know what you're going to say if I bring this up…"

"Then don't," Landon replied.

He took a sip of scalding-hot coffee. It felt better than thinking about his brother. Either brother. Because apparently Nate was alive and well and in Samantha Price's pocket and Landon couldn't work through if he felt like that was any better.

"Cal would know what the police are doing, what they'll *do* with this, even if it is Sam framing your dad. Cal knows how murder investigations work."

"Dad hired his own lawyer."

"Landon."

A knock sounded on the door. Three harsh thumps. And Landon knew too much. From the fifteen years ago he tried to forget, and the current month that he couldn't block out. That was a cop knock.

They must have found something. Damn and hell. He looked at Aly. He didn't want her part of this, but he needed help. "Go upstairs. Make sure Dad stays put."

"What if they want to question him?"

"I'll hold them off, and we'll sober him up. We'll … do something. Just make sure he doesn't come downstairs, okay?"

She nodded, then hurried off. Landon took his time making his way to the front door. He gathered up all the things that kept him going year after year. Masks and walls and the fundamental truth that he would protect this ranch, his family.

No matter the cost.

He flipped on the porch light then opened the door to one of the many cops whose face he remembered but whose name he couldn't. Because they all turned into a blur of people who somehow wanted to compound tragedy with putting his family through the fucking ringer.

"Help you, Officer?"

The cop nodded at him, and that's when Landon realized he did *know* this one because they'd gone to high school together.

"Landon. Sorry to bother you in the middle of the night."

"Are you? Feels like you guys are happy to bother us whenever."

Brian's mouth firmed. "Just a few quick questions before we run some tests." He reached behind him, pulled a plastic bag out of his pocket. "Do you recognize this?"

Inside the bag was a pocketknife.

Inscribed with the name Bennet and the ranch's brand—a B with three lines coming off the top, like a sunrise. Landon didn't have to see the inscription to know it. Everyone in his family had one. Him. Cal. Nate. Dad. Mom had had one. Aly had one, too, because it was also a gift given to any ranch staff who stayed more than ten years.

It wasn't damning evidence. Except he knew it wasn't

Mom's or his. Cal or Nate could have lost theirs in the creek years ago. Hell, Dad could have given Sandy his. A handful of hands over the years could have lost theirs. It didn't *mean* anything, but it had a knot of anxiety settle deep in his gut.

"Yeah, I recognize it. Well, sort of. Anyone who's part of the family or has worked for us for a while has one. Not sure whose that is."

"Yours?"

Landon could say yes. He considered it. There was no way to prove or disprove it. Except his was on his key chain. Hanging on the hook by the door. Landon could *maybe* hide it and the police officer would never know, but … it felt too risky at the moment.

"No, not mine. But it could literally be anyone else's."

"Like your father's?"

"Or my brothers'. Or even some ranch hands. I don't know how many Dad has handed out over the years."

"So, your dad is the one handing them out?"

"Is there something you're getting at? Considering it's…" Landon consulted the clock on the wall. "Four in the morning."

"I'm going to need to speak with your father, Landon."

Landon tried to find some kind of diplomacy. But everyone had always said Cal had soaked up all the charm in the family, and that had only gotten truer the older Landon had gotten.

There was a reason he was a rancher. There was a reason he didn't go spend his time in town. There was a *reason* no one heard the name Landon Bennet and thought charming smiles and easy jokes.

He was a grumpy, closed-off asshole who didn't like playing games.

But, damn it, for Dad he'd try.

He smiled. "Surely this can wait until the morning. This has been an incredibly difficult month. He's having a hard time sleeping, and if he hasn't come down yet, he needs his sleep. You can understand that right, Brian?"

There was a flicker of something like empathy on the officer's face. "We're going to need a list. Of everyone who has ever had one of these. And everyone who currently has theirs and can prove it."

"Look, I can get that for you. Before the end of the day tomorrow. Or at least our best effort."

Brian sighed. "Don't make me hold you to it, Landon." But he turned and left without demanding to see Dad.

Landon closed the door, and then his eyes, leaning against it as he exhaled. Aly's words from yesterday haunted him. *What reason does Gene Price have to kill Ben's girlfriend?*

Not that he had doubts about his dad. Or Gene's guilt for that matter. Just that ... he wanted this over. He didn't want Dad getting questioned and the police getting a grasp of alcohol problems and leaping to conclusions that weren't there.

"You have to call Cal."

Landon opened his eyes. Aly stood at the top of the stairs. He let out a slow breath, wondering how many wounds he'd have to pick at before this was all over. "Yeah, I do."

Chapter Eight

Austin, Texas

CAL BENNET WAS sleepily blinking into his first cup of coffee of the morning when his cell phone rang. He glanced at the readout, expecting someone related to work. Who else would call him this early?

Instead, he saw his brother's name.

Cal considered not answering. Landon only ever called with bad news. *Real* bad news. Like, oh hey, Dad's girlfriend was murdered and found halfway on our property. Not like, oh no, the cattle are sick and we're going to have to sell the ranch.

There had been times when Cal had wished for the latter with all his heart. But that was back in the day when he'd been trapped there. A shiny sports car dying to speed away from the muck and relentless work of the Bennet Ranch and legacy.

These days, he didn't think about Montana much. Not his brother. Not his dad. Not cattle or a pretty town named Marietta.

He thought about his work. When he had time, he thought about dating casually. Sports, on occasion. He liked to hit the gym. And more than anything, he liked to pretend the first twenty-one years of his life didn't exist.

But Cal figured Landon felt much the same way, in the opposite. That nothing outside of the all-encompassing Bennet Ranch mattered, Cal included. Traitor that he was for leaving.

Which meant whatever this was to rate a call from his brother was important and avoiding it would only put it off temporarily.

Might as well cut it off at the pass.

"Bennet" he answered, knowing that it would annoy Landon to pretend like he hadn't looked at his caller ID on the phone.

Landon's sigh was his reward. "It's your brother."

"Which one?"

Usually that was enough of a joke to rile Landon up. Another sigh. Another reminder how not funny it was to make jokes about their missing brother who was probably long dead.

Cal had learned a long time ago that anything was funny if you let it be. And often, the hardest most horrible things were best suffered through with a bit of humor. Laughing about something didn't change it, but it felt a hell of a lot better than crying.

Landon, in the land of humorless Bennets, would never agree.

But this silence was ... potent.

"Nate's back."

For a moment, Cal couldn't comprehend those two words said together. Back? Nate? Who was Nate? How could he be *back*?

But he had the image of a gangly teenager, somehow a mix of Landon's seriousness with those somber dark eyes too much like Dad's, but at least *some* of Cal's restlessness to make his baby brother more entertaining than Landon's endless middle child trudge.

He could remember Nate as a baby if he tried. He could remember his mother if he tried.

He didn't try.

"I take it he's back because he's alive, somehow."

"Alive and well and *somehow* aligning himself with Samantha Price."

Cal talked to Landon maybe *once* a year, unless there was trouble like this year, and still he was well-versed in Landon's feelings on Samantha Price. Cal couldn't quite find the fervor to hate her. Sure, she was wrong. Misguided. But he dealt with enough criminals to know love blinded people to all sorts of things.

But Nate was back.

"So, how exactly did this come about? Nate just… showed up out of the blue?"

"Samantha brought him up to the ranch. He said he wanted to talk to Dad. I told him if he was going to align himself with a fucking Price, he could go back to where he came from."

Cal used his free hand to scrape over his face. "Jesus, Landon, you really never do change."

"You know what Sam's up to as much as I do."

"Yeah, I do, but it's…" It was a waste of breath to remind Landon that Nate was their *brother*. Who had disappeared as a teenager. Cal had spent some time trying to track him down, but he'd never been successful. The only conclusion he'd been able to draw after a couple years was that like too many teenage runaways, Nate had died. Nameless and alone.

But he was back.

Cal realized he was so lost in trying to work through that, he'd missed part of what Landon was saying. He keyed back into the conversation at hand.

"They've uncovered some evidence. I don't think it'll amount to much, but Aly'd like your ... professional opinion."

"Aly would, huh?"

"Yeah. Aly. I figure there's a reason we're paying Dad's lawyer. So why wouldn't we talk to him?"

"You're thirty-two, Landon. Maybe you should stop using Aly Cartwright as a shield."

"And maybe you should give two shits about your family. Oh wait, that's too much to ask. You've got a fancy life to take care of. I hope your financial portfolio keeps you warm at night."

"Sure buys the nice sheets."

"Fuck you, Cal. I knew this was pointless," he muttered.

And before Cal could say anything else, the line went dead.

Cal was still a little too tired to get his anger at a full boil. After all, this was so very *common*. It was why they talked as little as they did.

But something about that evidence, whatever it was, had to have rattled Landon. Landon could blame the call on Aly all he wanted, but Landon wouldn't have made that call if it wasn't the very last resort.

Cal could call his dad's lawyer—they'd talked more about Sandy's murder than Landon and Cal had. He was … competent, Cal supposed, if he was being generous.

Cal could call the police handling the case. He knew how to get the information he wanted from the cops. There was a lot he could do from Austin just from phone calls alone.

But Nate was back.

Cal couldn't quite work out why that rattled him more than evidence and murders. Why it had him thinking, for the first time in *years*, if he should make a trip back.

"Back to hell," he muttered.

Why would he go back there? If Nate had been alive these past fifteen years, and never reached out, why should Cal care he was back? Aligning himself with Samantha Price. Wanting to talk to Dad.

None of it mattered to Cal's life here in Texas. His good, happy life.

Still, he dialed his assistant's number. She usually got into the office an hour or so before he did.

"Morning, Mr. Bennet."

"Morning, Mackenzye. Can you clear my calendar of anything in person for the next two weeks?"

"I can try. Everything okay?"

Okay? No, he didn't suppose so. "I guess I'm going to Montana for a bit."

"What the hell would you want to go to Montana for?" she asked, a laugh in her voice.

What the hell indeed.

Chapter Nine

Crawford County Jail

SAM HADN'T SLEPT, and she knew that was a mistake, even as she went through the process of checking into the jail as a visitor.

She wasn't a big crier. She'd learned how to deal with—okay, *hide*—her emotions most of the time. But exhaustion made everything harder to keep in check.

She didn't want to upset her father. Not now. As much as he seemed to be holding up, he had to be hanging on by a thread. Doing this all over again.

But she wanted to be the one to tell him about what she'd found with Nate. She wanted his take on it. She wanted…

Some hope. For the both of them.

She smiled as Dad took his seat across from her. He smiled back. He really did look like he was handling this better than the last time. He seemed to be holding his weight. There wasn't that same sickly pallor that had terrified her the first few months he'd been in prison last time.

She supposed fifteen years did that to a person. Beat them down or broke them. But Dad wasn't broken, and neither was she.

"Hi, Dad. Sorry it's been a few days."

"You don't have to visit me all the time, Sam. You've got to have a life out there."

She tried to smile. *Life.* She wasn't sure what she had *out there* but it didn't feel like a *life* so much as a mission. But a mission was bigger than having a life. More important.

"We found some new evidence, Dad. I'm sure your lawyer will fill you in once he gets more information on how the police determine to use it, but they're investigating it. Maybe once they get all this parole stuff taken care of, we can get you out of here."

"Who's we?"

Sam wasn't sure why, but the question made her uncomfortable. She shifted in her seat. Shrugged. "You remember Nate ... Bennet?"

Dad's eyebrows drew together. "Sure. What's he got to do with anything?"

She had never told her father about that night. She'd never told anyone. In the grand scheme of all the things she'd done, laws she'd bent, friendships she'd risked and lost, Nate's secret had always been something she'd kept.

It wasn't something she'd *consciously* done, so being confronted with the realization now was ... something. Something she had to set aside.

"He's back in town, and he thinks his father is capable of murder. So, he's..." She had to pause, consider how to phrase it. "We're working together a bit on this."

Dad's expression was one of concern. "Sam. I never thought I'd have to tell you this, but you can't trust a Bennet."

Trust. She hadn't really thought about Nate in terms of trusting him or not. Just that he was ... a tool to be used. Which felt like an uncomfortable admission, but when did she ever get the luxury of comfort?

"It's not a trust situation," she said firmly. "He has a unique inside track, even with his absence the past fifteen years. And he thinks his father is capable of murder."

"He's a Bennet."

Sam blew out a breath. "I think he's had it rough, Dad."

"Haven't we all?" Dad asked, and it was the first hint of any bitterness.

Which honestly relieved Sam. That there was *some* fight in there, not all easy acceptance—even if it was because of a Bennet's involvement.

She couldn't argue with his words either. It felt like the last fifteen years had been nothing but rough on everyone involved. At least anyone not lofting about on the Bennet Ranch.

Dad had spent fifteen years in jail for something he didn't do. Nate had no doubt seen trauma—his father's violence against him, his stint in the army that had clearly made a mark on him. Not to mention whatever injury had landed him in the VA hospital last year. Even in the short time she'd been around him, she got the impression he wasn't fully healed. Though Nate never said anything.

And maybe Nate could go be a Bennet in every sense of the word if he wanted to, but he'd helped so far. Nothing he'd said or done made her think he was some sleeper spy.

Sam met her dad's frowning gaze. "If he helps me find evidence Benjamin Bennet is behind one or both murders, then I'm going to take that help. It's the sensible thing to do, and it doesn't have anything to do with trusting anyone."

Dad's frown showed off the deep grooves around his mouth. He suddenly looked gray. He shook his head, gesturing at the guard that he was ready to go.

He stood. "Don't say I didn't warn you."

And that was all he said, before the guard led him away. For a few moments, Sam could only sit there feeling far too much, the silence of her father's departure echoing through her.

No, *I love you, Sam*. No *thank you for all your hard work*.

She shook that away. She wasn't doing this for thanks. Dad got to have his own emotional responses to all of this.

She had work to do. She got up and signed out of the jail. Then she drove out to her aunt's ranch.

She was going to drive Nate to the rental car place so he could get a car of his own for however long he planned to do that. She knew that meant he'd do some work on his own, and maybe her father's warning was timely.

She didn't know Nate, but she did know he was a Bennet.

It was a pretty spring day when she stepped out of the truck outside Nate's rented cabin. Birds were chirping. Butterflies flitted in the field. Morning mist still hung in the tree line.

Hope. This—a beautiful morning and new evidence—was supposed to feel like hope, and it just *didn't*.

She trudged up the porch and knocked on the cabin door. Nate answered, ready to go as he always was. There was something eerily put together about him. Like every second of his life was lived in military precision.

When that couldn't possibly be true.

Still, he didn't immediately step out onto the porch.

Instead, he held out his hand. "They'll probably go through and figure out who all had one, and who can prove they still have theirs."

In his palm was a pocketknife. It was almost identical to the one the police had fished out of the water once Nate had shown them to the place between boulders.

Down to the inscribed *Bennet* and ranch brand. Seeing it written out made her uncomfortable. Made her dad's words feel like omens instead of concerns.

He's a Bennet.

Yeah, and he was showing this to her. She turned it over in her hands. Finding this in the creek last night had felt like something to *her*, but no doubt the Bennets would explain it away. No doubt it was just … a wild goose chase.

She pulled out the blade. Shiny and bright, like it had never been used. She glanced at Nate. He hadn't come to Marietta with a lot of stuff, but she also got the feeling he didn't *have* a lot of stuff.

"You kept it all this time?"

"Yeah," Nate returned.

She put the blade away, handed it back to him. She wanted to dig into that—why? Did he still have some loyalty to his family, so he was eventually going to fuck her over?

But she didn't touch that thought. "I'm afraid it's going to be easy to explain away. Someone lost theirs and it just washed away in the creek, that sort of thing."

"Yeah, it's possible. But it's got them looking at things.

And it's like you said. Me showing up, the cops asking them questions, maybe it leads to a mistake."

That was exactly what she believed. Maybe it was just the exhaustion, but him essentially saying what she thought settled all wrong today. She resented his existence, when she was the one who'd brought him here. When he was the reason that knife had been found in the first place.

"You ready to head out to the rental place?" she asked, needing movement. Needing … something other than her own thoughts. Maybe a separation instead of feeling like they were joined at the hip and that she might be spearheading her own failure.

Nate nodded. He stepped outside then, pulling the door closed behind him. He walked over to the truck with her.

"Once we know the cops have cleared out, I want to go back. I think we can find more. If they don't, anyway."

We.

Sam climbed into the driver's side trying not to let on how much that *we* rumbled through her foundations.

She'd been an *I* for so long. Fighting this fight, only her. Over and over again, no matter the cost.

And suddenly there was this *we*. She didn't know what to do with it, but no matter what doubts existed within her overthinking, it was going to be nearly impossible to walk away from a *we*.

"Well, Nate," she said, managing to clear her throat as she spoke. "It's like you read my mind."

Chapter Ten

Marietta, Montana

CAL TRIED NOT to grimace as he drove the rental BMW down the heart of Marietta, Montana. It was just a visit, but even visits made the space between his shoulder blades itch. This *place*. He'd never understood Montana. Ranching. Not the harsh winters, the grueling work, or the steadfast love these people had to a land more than each other.

He laughed along with his colleagues when they made jokes about what a hicksville junkyard he must have come from. He even threw in a few redneck digs himself. He made everyone, including his family, think that was exactly what he felt.

But it wasn't. Marietta wasn't beneath him, and its denizens weren't stupid, but it was better to act as though it was, and they were than try to figure out what that itch *really* meant.

Nothing changed here. Not really. The baseball field he'd found glory on in high school was in the same spot, if maybe a little updated. Copper Mountain loomed as it always had, like a disapproving god in the clouds.

Sure, some minor details had changed, old business gone,

new businesses in their place. But mostly, it was like he was sixteen again, driving down Front a little too fast, wondering when the hell he'd escape.

At least now it was a BMW instead of a borrowed clunker of a Ford. Unfortunately, now it involved *murder*, and his brother being alive. Which was fortunate all in all, that Nate was alive and accounted for, just not something Cal knew how to deal with.

Because it all meant facing Dad, and Landon, and Bennet Ranch, and all the things he'd gotten the hell away from before they could eat him alive as he'd always suspected they would.

Cal paused at the edge of town even though there was no stop sign or light.

A left would take him back around town and out to the highway, back to Bozeman, and a plane ticket to Austin. Going straight would take him toward the rolling tracts of green and brownish gray capped in white, to Bennet Ranch and the life he'd escaped before he could ever figure out why it weighed on him so much when Landon loved it like a wife or mother.

Nate had loved it too, all those years ago, before Mom had died and he'd disappeared in what Cal could only assume was some misguided attempt at teenage rebellion. The baby of the family, Nate had always been the spontaneous one. If there was any similarity between Landon and Cal it was a dogged mentality to plan it all out then see it through.

Just in opposite directions.

But one day, out of nowhere, Nate had been gone, so

much like Mom, and Cal had seen too much evil in the world since to believe Nate might have survived.

Cal sighed and hit the gas pedal. All of *this* was why he didn't come home. Introspection and circular thinking and a whole lot of sitting on his ass not *moving*.

He flew down the bumpy, curving road that led him to the Bennet Ranch. He didn't let up till he skidded to a halt outside the wood-planked home of his youth.

His heart was beating too hard against his ribs, and he did everything he could not to take in the all-too-familiar scenery or the way the world had changed and not changed. He was here to do one thing. Just one thing. Then he could go back to where his skin didn't feel too tight, and everything didn't feel vaguely wrong.

Like a nightmare he couldn't remember.

A cold prickle of dread slid down his spine, and Cal ignored it by stepping out of his car and walking toward the porch.

Before he could get even halfway across the yard, the door opened, and a woman stepped out.

There was only one woman who'd be so bold to enter and exit the Bennet house as if she belonged, but even if that hadn't tipped him off, the bright red hair pulled back into a braid would have.

He watched her as she came to a stop. Recognized him. She looked back at the house for a second, just a second, but Cal knew for who and why.

He'd grown up with Aly, always thought of her as a little sister, but he'd never gotten the vibe that whatever weird ass relationship she had with Landon was *sisterly*. Codependent and fucked up, definitely, but whether they ever dated or whatever or not, they didn't view each other as siblings.

So, she was looking back at the house, worried about Landon and how he would react to Cal's surprise arrival. Even if Landon had called him, even if Dad needed help. Even if he *should* be here.

And yeah, maybe he could have warned them. And yes, definitely, he should not be a purposeful asshole in this situation.

But this was Bennet land, and coulds and shoulds had never been his strong point here. "Honey, I'm home," he announced as big blue eyes moved back to stare at him.

"You came," Aly said as if she didn't quite believe it. "You actually … came home." She took a few halting steps toward him. "Right away."

"Is this any way to greet an old friend?"

She let out a shaky sigh as he met her on the porch.

Then she smiled, and it was genuine even if a little wobbly around the edges. "I'm glad you're here."

Cal found he believed her. There was too much relief in that sentence. Even as she went into typical Aly mode and tried to lock it all up behind a friendly, breezy mask.

"I hardly recognized you. My, you're too skinny by half." She surveyed him, trying to hide something like disapproval in her expression. "You're a little overdressed for the ranch."

"I don't plan on getting my hands dirty, per the norm."

This time she didn't try to hide her disapproval. Even if she always ended up siding with Landon, she didn't like watching the Bennets fight.

He'd never understood why she'd stayed then, since that

was all any of them were good for. But stayed she had, and he was likely to get a clearer idea of everything from her over anyone else's bluster.

"How are you, Aly? Really?"

Her smile was tight, and she clasped her hands together. She seemed guilty, which was odd.

"Sandy dying, however she died, it's been a whole ... thing." She shook her head as if irritated with herself. "But you'll take care of it. Won't you?" She looked up at him all hope and worry, and Cal couldn't remember the last time someone here had looked at him with the thought he'd accomplish something good and right.

His collar suddenly felt too tight just like his skin.

"Of course he'll fix everything," Landon's voice offered overloud as he stepped onto the porch. "That's our Cal. Got himself that law degree, what can't he fix?" Landon's voice dripped with bitterness.

Cal knew a good half of that bitterness was his own fault. Cal had been young and cocky and a dick to the people who mattered, so it wasn't any wonder they hated the sight of him.

Lots of people did. He was used to it, or so he told himself.

"Howdy, brother," Cal offered, all smiles he knew would piss his serious little brother off. Old habits died hard. Especially on Bennet land.

"I don't recall you telling us you'd be visiting."

"How odd. I sent a note via carrier pigeon. Shocked you didn't get it here in the eighteen-hundreds."

"If you're expecting to stay here, you're going to work."

"Landon," Aly chastised under her breath, but if Landon heard her, he didn't respond. Or stop.

"I thought the whole point of calling me *was* to work. On Dad's case."

Landon scowled. "He's got a lawyer. I only told you about the possible new evidence to…"

Cal waited, but no answer came.

"We'd very much appreciate your help," Aly said firmly. "Advice on how to proceed. That kind of thing. Ben's been taking Sandy's death understandably hard. We're worried any change in the case, any focus that takes away from proving Gene Price is responsible will really send him spiraling."

Cal noted the way Landon looked at Aly like he was surprised to hear her say that. Or didn't quite understand what she was saying. Something more to the situation.

But Cal acted like he didn't see it. Best to observe some things before he decided how to handle this.

"I'm sure you being home will really set him at ease," Aly said.

Causing both Landon and Cal to snort.

But Aly was clearly determined to make this true. "I'll make a room up for you," she said. "And I'll make dinner. For *everyone*," she said pointedly.

"I don't want to put you out, but I'd appreciate it. I'm going to set up a meeting with Dad's lawyer. Go over strategy and what he thinks about this new evidence. Then I can give you guys some ideas on how to move forward." He said all this to Aly, ignoring Landon's existence completely.

But he was very well aware that Landon was standing

there scowling at the both of them.

"Setting up meetings and talking to people. Yeah, you really needed to finally show your face around here for that," Landon said, moving past Cal and to the stairs. "Must be nice to get to pick and choose which emergencies you care to join us for."

Cal had no smart retort to that. He couldn't even keep the bland lawyer expression on his face. He watched as Landon stalked away—off to do all those important ranch chores no doubt. Boots muddy, cowboy hat low on his head. Quintessential cowboy.

And, as Aly had pointed out, Cal wasn't dressed like he belonged here.

Because I fucking don't.

He turned his attention back to Aly and what he hadn't been brave enough to broach with Landon. "Has he seen Nate since he came here with Samantha Price?"

Aly shook her head. "No, but Nate's the one who found the knife in the creek. He hasn't made any overtures. I think… He clearly didn't come back to have a family reunion."

Cal understood the sentiment. "You happen to know where he's staying?"

"Rumor is a cabin on Lisa Reynolds's ranch. She rents them out and—"

"She's Samantha's aunt. Yeah, I remember."

Aly studied him, and he didn't know what *she* saw. Because she didn't have any of the disgust for him that Landon did, but he also knew she didn't approve of just about any of his choices.

"You going to go see him?" she asked.

Cal figured he should probably be as honest as he could, when it came to Aly at least. "I don't know yet."

Aly nodded like she understood that. Another surprise, in what was likely to be more to come. "Come on inside," she said. "And … listen. Landon is… Well, obviously, this is hard on him."

Cal gave Aly a reassuring smile and patted her on the shoulder. "No worries, Aly. He'll warm up to me."

"I won't hold my breath," Aly returned before heading inside.

Which left Cal alone to face an open door that felt an awful lot like that nightmare he couldn't remember.

Chapter Eleven

Marietta, Montana

WHEN SAM HAD dropped Nate off at the rental car place, he had told her to go on. He'd meet her at Honor's Edge this afternoon. He had some personal things to attend to.

He'd known she was curious, but she hadn't asked what they were.

Just like he hadn't asked her what was wrong when she'd come and picked him up. Even though *wrong* had been written all over her face. With a hefty dose of exhaustion.

He sure hoped she'd get some sleep. She needed it.

Not that it was any of his business what she did or needed. He had his own shit to handle. And there were lots of things he should be doing. All of them dealing with the reality he might be spending more time in Montana than he'd planned.

He managed, for the latter part of the morning and the early part of the afternoon. He hadn't thought about anything except his to-do list. Compartmentalizing like a champ.

Then, like it was some kind of cosmic joke, he'd driven past the cemetery. Except, not past. He wasn't fully sure what possessed him to take that impulsive, last-minute turn.

Maybe some nostalgic seed had been planted last night, remembering a childhood with his brothers. The smells and sounds of the land his ancestors had tamed infiltrating his bloodstream until there was an itch to poke at every wound he'd left behind.

Broken. Bloody. Desperate.

Mom dying had been the crux of everything going to hell. And he doubted that was even that uncommon. What was a family once it lost its foundation?

But it was the whirling, sharpened daggers his family had turned into overnight that seemed to expose there had been something dark and wrong underneath his mother's sunlight that no one had acknowledged. Maybe no one had realized.

Nate had spent fifteen years running from that realization. From the fear it planted deep within him, some involuntary terror. He'd thrown himself into surviving—in so many different ways. A life on the streets. A life in the military.

Only the past year of forced physical recovery had turned any of that inward, into some kind of psychological recovery. In some ways, he was almost ... almost grateful for that. He was getting too old to keep running headfirst into danger without the first thought as to why.

But in most ways, it was frustrating. Because what the hell was he supposed to do with his life now? Throw himself into a past that probably didn't matter as much as he wanted it to?

But here he was, traipsing around the cemetery in the middle of a bright spring afternoon. It took a couple walks around the grounds to find his target, his memory of the funeral not quite matching up with the actual layout of the cemetery.

But eventually he came upon the shiny gray stone he remembered from that day. The little plot was well kept, and there were flowers—real ones, a little wilted around the edges—in the small ground vase. Nate had to wonder who brought them as he stared at the name carved in stone.

MARIE LANE BENNET. Dates that marked a too-short life ended in violence. WIFE. MOTHER.

Nate inhaled. If there was a memory that haunted him against his will, it wasn't his father beating him that day. It wasn't the news, delivered by police, that a body had been found in the burnt-out barn or even that Gene Price had been arrested that sunny, overly hot morning a few days before they'd finally held the funeral. There was something about all the tragedy that had fueled him through his adult life.

But the memories that came out of nowhere, that cut him down at the knees or knocked him sideways, were happy memories. Of his mother, with her sunshiny blond hair singing at the kitchen sink or laughing as she taught him to ride a horse.

She had all the patience in the world, where Dad had never had much.

Nate blew out a long, slow breath. The pain was a dull ache, but all over his body. Pressing into his skin, making every organ inside of him feel twice as heavy, making his bones feel like weights, so that it seemed a great physical feat to stand at all.

Sometimes he wondered why someone like her should have died so horribly, when he'd run straight into war and come out still breathing. Still wondering what the hell this was all for.

Sometimes he wondered if there were whys to anything.

But something had brought him here. *Something* caused this pain. And someone had killed his mother.

He knew Sam believed wholeheartedly it wasn't her father, even though he'd paid a price for it. Nate admired that determination, that surety. He hadn't been sure of anything in fifteen years. He wanted some of it.

Which was why he hesitated to believe, wholeheartedly, that Gene Price was innocent. Even if he suspected his father wasn't.

But he wanted an answer. Clear-cut. Sure. And so, he was here to find it.

He heard the shuffle of footsteps somewhere behind him, pulling him out of his thoughts. Out of old instinct, he reached for a weapon.

It wasn't there. Because he wasn't on a battlefield. He wasn't a soldier anymore.

Even if this all felt like its own kind of war.

So, he turned slowly, carefully, bracing himself for something.

For a moment, Nate was sure he had to be dreaming. Maybe he was back in Tennessee. Or that VA hospital. Because this couldn't be real.

The man moving toward him, head bowed, clutch of flowers in his hands was too familiar. Older, different, and still so damn familiar.

Dad looked up briefly, barely looked at him standing there. "You're supposed to be at the ranch," he said gruffly.

It took Nate a full minute of reeling through time to realize Dad thought he was Landon. Nate took a step away from his father's approaching form. He wasn't afraid. He *wasn't*. Yet it gripped him, just as it had the last time he'd seen his father.

But the step turned into a stumble, and Dad frowned over at him. Then squinted. Then…

The slow dawning horror of his expression was too fascinating to turn away from. Like a train wreck. A drone strike. Horror. Horror. Horror.

Dad's breathing became more and more labored. He actually raised his hand to his heart, and Nate flinched. Like he was a ghost of himself here in this field of bodies.

"What…" But Dad did not finish his sentence, and Nate could not find his voice as he came to the realization that no one had told Dad he was back in town.

Nate couldn't fathom what that would mean.

"You shouldn't be here," Dad finally rasped out.

Dark and dangerous, even though Nate could see that, these days, Benjamin Bennet was hardly a physical threat against the likes of him.

But for all the ways he'd stood here only moments ago and thought he wanted answers, when faced with his own personal living ghost, he found he didn't. There was a reason he'd spent the past fifteen years away. There was nothing *here* that would make that moment fifteen years ago all right.

So he turned and walked away. Back to his rental car. Far, far away from all *this*.

Chapter Twelve

Grey's Saloon, Marietta

Sam walked into Grey's Saloon later that afternoon, though not late enough to find herself wanting a drink. She was here because there was nothing quite like gossip in a small town.

People were starting to figure out Nate was back. People might not be sure as to why, or to what end, but they knew, *somehow,* he was linked up with Sam rather than the Bennets.

A clear line drawn that everyone in the entire county probably understood.

Which was why she'd received a few drop-ins at Honor's Edge just wanting to chat about the weather, whatever happened to so-and-so's cheating husband, and then subtly drop the hint they'd seen Nate marching himself into Grey's *far* earlier than was appropriate for that look in his eye.

Sam didn't know if it was her place to interfere. Nate was a grown man who'd said he had things to do. That he'd come by Honor's Edge when he was ready to deal with the case. If he was drinking in Grey's, that was his business, not hers.

But enough people seemed to think it was hers that she'd

just been driving herself crazy back at the office. Going over files and then realizing she wasn't retaining any information.

So here she was. And there was Nate. He sat at the bar, one empty glass in front of him and one half full. And she understood what everyone had been saying. He did not have the look of a man getting a casual drink. He didn't even have the look of a man who wanted to drown his sorrows.

He looked dangerous and edgy, and Sam figured it was her own messed-up nature that made her want to fix that rather than stay far, far away.

She walked over to him, leaned against the bar on his right. It took him a few seconds, but eventually he looked over at her elbows on the bar, then up at her.

He stared at her for a long time, in one of those patented silences of his. Taking in everything. She wondered what he saw when he looked at her. What it made him think about. She couldn't even begin to fathom what would rate such scrutiny.

"Have a drink with me, Sam," he said, gesturing toward the seat next to him.

She considered it, him. Nate was hardly the kind of person who was going to invite someone to a drink if he wanted to be alone. If he wanted to drink alone, he had a rental cabin, a rental car, and access to a liquor store.

So she took a seat. She considered ordering a pop. She wasn't much of a drinker even at the appropriate time, but there was something about this entire situation that had her ordering a beer.

While Nate ordered another whiskey. Straight up.

Sam kept her mouth shut even though she had *so* many

questions. The bartender delivered both of their drinks. Sam took a sip of her beer, watched the baseball highlights play out on the screen above the bar.

"I went to the cemetery," Nate said out of nowhere.

Making sure she was in full control of her expression—no shock, no pity—she slowly looked over at him. He was scowling at his drink. He had both hands curled around the glass, almost completely hiding it.

"To visit your mom?" she asked, making sure to keep her voice neutral.

"Visit? Is that what you call it?" he asked, sounding almost disgusted.

Sam shrugged. "We always did when we'd go."

"Your mom died," he said, as if it was a little trivia piece he'd just remembered.

It didn't matter how long it had been, how sometimes she went entire days without thinking about her mother, words like that still stabbed like a sharp wound.

She kept that pain out of her voice. "Yep."

"You were little," Nate said, as if he was slowly remembering the details he might have known fifteen years ago and not considered at all in the time since he'd left. Why would he?

"Ten," she confirmed.

He studied her then, so she turned her attention back to the television. She almost wished she'd ordered something stronger, because the beer tasted sharp and bitter in her mouth and so did this entire encounter.

"Sorry," Nate said. "That wasn't the point. I happened upon my dad there. He was bringing flowers."

Sam said nothing to that, because what she wanted to say was something nasty about how guilt did funny things to people, but this wasn't the time for that.

"He never brought her flowers when she was alive," Nate said, in that same tone of slowly remembering old, old information.

Sam slid him a look. He was making it very hard to keep her mouth shut. But then he kept talking. Perhaps saying more in a few minutes' span than he'd said their entire time together. He'd likely blame the whiskey.

"She told me that once. I'd accidentally, or maybe the right word is *recklessly*, drove one of the UTVs over her tulips. I knew she'd be upset, so I picked all the ones I hadn't crushed and gave them to her." He drained the rest of his drink. "She said no one had ever given her flowers before. And it just figured it would be because they'd ruined them." He shook his head. "That's sad, isn't it? She was in her forties, and no one had ever brought her flowers."

And then she was murdered hung in the air, a silent specter of all the ways life could be so damn unfair.

"I'm in my thirties and no one's ever brought *me* flowers." Which was hardly the point, but she honestly wanted to get away from the point. Because dead mothers and cemeteries was bumming her the hell out.

They needed to be talking about murder investigations. Not exactly lighthearted fair, but at least there was a *point*. An end goal other than feeling so damn fucking sad.

"No high school dance corsage?" Nate asked her.

A question that felt oddly like fishing. Not that she had any idea what he was fishing for. "I was a tomboy for half of high school and then busy trying to figure out how one got their innocent father out of prison for the rest."

"I was busy being an asshole until I was busy being a homeless runaway," he mused in return.

"Show-off."

He snorted out a laugh. Maybe a little drunk, but it was a laugh all the same.

He sobered, scowling at his drink. "I saw him there, and I walked away. And I almost left. Marietta. Montana. This whole *thing*. What the fuck am I doing here?"

Sam held herself very still. In so many ways, she felt Nate was the answer to everything. She *needed* him to stay if there was any hope of breaking up the great Bennet blockade of lies. She didn't want to venture a guess as to what had *really* brought him here. She knew that even if they were working toward the same answers, it was for far different reasons.

So instead of answering that rhetorical question of his, she asked one of her own. "But you're still here. So, what stopped you?"

Nate considered his drink for another second, then slowly raised his gaze to hers. "No one told him I was back."

Him being Ben.

Sam let that new information settle inside of her, but she couldn't reason it out. "That… doesn't make any sense. Why wouldn't Landon tell him?"

Nate shook his head. "I don't know. I can't figure it out. There's too many things I can't figure out. So, I didn't leave. Maybe the answers all suck. In fact, I'm sure they do. But I deserve some this time around. And I want to know why Landon is keeping me being back to himself."

Sam mulled it over, taking a pull from her beer. What would Landon gain from keeping it a secret? Especially considering Ben existed in the Marietta world around them where people talked. No matter the subject. And Nate being back was a hell of a subject.

Except, come to think of it, she hadn't really seen much of Ben lately, had she? Not that they often ran into each other. She was pretty sure Ben went out of his way to avoid her if he could.

"I don't think he knows what happened," Nate said.

It took Sam a minute to figure that sentence out, but Nate was clearly lost in a past. And in the past, his father had beaten him near to death. Did he think Landon didn't know? Did he *hope* Landon didn't know?

Because if Landon did know, he was siding with an abuser. Doubling down on what Benjamin Bennet had done as being okay.

So, Sam hoped, in spite of herself, that Landon didn't know either. "He never hit either of them?"

"Not to my knowledge." Nate gestured for another drink. "But maybe we were all keeping secrets. Maybe there's nothing but secrets there. Choking out everything like a weed."

Sam considered suggesting he stop drinking. He wasn't sounding himself—at least in their limited adult acquaintance. But alcohol and maudlin weren't good combinations for anyone.

She knew he was hurting. He had every right to be, but he was starting to worry her. Before she could figure out how best to say it, how best to handle it, she heard someone behind them.

"Nate."

They both turned at his name. And Sam supposed it was her turn to be surprised by the appearance of a Bennet.

Not Landon. The resemblance was clear, but he didn't look *quite* as much like his two younger brothers to have any identity be confusing.

This was Cal Bennet. So, Landon had told *someone*.

And Sam couldn't stop herself from smiling. Because there was only one reason the Bennets had somehow dragged Cal home from his cush life as a *criminal defense attorney* somewhere in Texas.

They were *worried*.

And that was very good news indeed.

CAL HAD LEFT Marietta long before he'd been old enough to drink. He'd taken that full-ride college scholarship and used it as the propellor out of this life, breaking the Bennet cycle of martyring themselves to something just because a bunch of foolhardy pioneers had once made their way out to this godforsaken place.

He'd succeeded, but there'd been a time where guilt—more to Mom's memory than anything else—had brought him back on more regular visits. Which had often required a break from the ranch and a heavy dose of alcohol.

So, though he'd preferred the edgier Wolf Den back then, Grey's was familiar-ish to him.

As was the man who'd turned at the mention of his

name. And the woman next to him. Both familiar-*ish*, because it had been so long. Because they'd changed. Because age had stamped a few lines on all their faces.

Cal wasn't sure he would have recognized Samantha Price if not for her proximity to Nate and what Landon had said about the two of them partnering up for whatever reason. She was something like six years younger than him, more Nate and Aly's age, so he'd never paid her much mind growing up. He wouldn't have now, either.

Except she was *smiling*, which Cal couldn't figure. But his real focus was Nate. Who was staring at him with an expression Cal couldn't read. There were too many pieces to it. Too many emotions flitting in and out of his dark eyes.

Jesus, he looked like Landon. And Dad. Not that Cal didn't, but it wasn't quite the same. People would call his a *resemblance*. People would say Dad, Landon, and Nate all came from the same damn mold, with only hints of Mom in the shape of Nate's chin and Landon's mouth to tell them apart.

Cal had known he'd find Nate here. That was why he was *here*. In the end, no matter how nice and welcoming Aly had been, he hadn't been able to be at the ranch another second longer. Not if he was going to spend the night there.

So, he'd come to town. To get to work. And that had led him to asking questions about Nate, and that had led him … here.

And still it took Cal a few minutes to find his armor, his polish, *himself* and smile at the pair. To do what he came to do. Because this wasn't just about seeing Nate. It was about understanding.

God, he needed to understand something in this whole mess.

"Funny running into you here," he offered, before striding forward and sliding into the stool next to Nate. "What's it been? Fifteen years?"

Nate turned his gaze to his glass. Downed it. "You know how many years it's been."

"I do. I do indeed. Because I spent most of it looking for you, before I finally concluded you must be dead."

"Not yet." He motioned for the bartender to give him another.

Cal didn't miss the concern on Sam's face. Interesting. Cal didn't know how these two had found each other, but he wondered if there was something more to it than old grudges and revenge.

"Landon seems to think you two teaming up is some kind of … glove thrown."

When Nate said nothing to that, Sam leaned forward so he could see her around Nate. "We're looking for the truth."

"The way I hear it told, you're an obsessed lunatic who can't accept that her father is a proven violent criminal."

"The way I hear it, you represent those kinds of people for a living." Her smile went sharp.

Cal had to give her points for that. And as someone who did in fact represent criminals for a living—because he didn't waste his breath trying to explain due process and innocent until proven guilty to people who wanted to purposefully misrepresent what he did—he didn't have the hard line against Samantha that Landon did.

He understood, from experience watching people, what

love and devotion could do, and maybe even *should* do, to any sense of reality. What mother should have to believe her child was a monster? What child should have to believe their parent one?

Cal ignored the cold chill that worked its way down his spine. It was just the usual physical reaction to a little too much *home.*

"What are you doing here, Cal?" Nate asked, sounding not just tired but bone-deep exhausted. Weary.

Cal had a million questions he wanted to ask his baby brother. Why had he run? What had he been doing all these years? Why hadn't he reached out to any of them?

But maybe the Bennet blood was just too strong, because he didn't. He buried those questions down deep, kept the easy expression on his face, and surveyed an increasingly drunk *man*, who might have been his brother, but was essentially a stranger.

"Well, I figured since Landon would rather stonewall a statue to death than ask something direct, I would. What are you two up to? And why?"

Nate finally looked at him—really studied him like he'd been studying his drink before. Cal watched as his brother's dark eyes did the same tour. The determination of what was the same—between then and now, between brother and brother—and what was different.

"Why would I tell you?" he asked after long seconds of studying.

"Why wouldn't you?" Cal returned. "I don't know what you ran away from all those years ago, Nate. But I'm not your enemy. And while I'm sure Landon does an impressive impersonation of an enemy, he isn't yours either."

"What about Dad?"

Cal didn't have a quick answer for that. "Why would Dad be your enemy?"

"Why indeed." Nate drained the last of his drink, then turned to Sam. "You ready to head out?"

She glanced at Cal, then back to Nate, gave him a nod and slid out of her stool.

They walked out together, and Cal watched them. They walked side by side, no touching. Nate opened the door for her, but she didn't give him any flirty looks.

Cal could have followed. Could have demanded answers. He considered it, but there was something … tenuous about all this.

Cal wanted to laugh. Wasn't there *always* here in the middle of his own personal hell. Always so afraid to make the wrong step when nowhere else in his life did he feel this dread, this anxious throbbing portent.

It was why he stayed away, and he still could. Going back to Texas was always an option. But as his brother disappeared, he could only wonder.

Why would Dad be Nate's enemy?

He ignored that too-tight-skin feeling that haunted him always here. *Always.* He offered to pay Nate's tab, but the bartender said Sam had taken care of it, so Cal just left a few bills as a tip.

As he walked back into a sunny spring afternoon, pretty and perfect if he was just about anyone else.

But he wasn't. He *was* a lawyer though, and it was time to answer some important questions. Not about old feelings.

But about what was going on in the here and now.

How had Sam found Nate when Cal had never had any luck? What were the two of them up to and why? There was something more to that little partnership. And while Cal didn't care about the goings on of Marietta or the gossip about any of his brothers, he knew it wasn't that simple.

This had something to do with his mother's murder—and how it might connect to Sandy's.

And Cal was going to figure out what.

Chapter Thirteen

The Bennet Ranch

ALY WAS SHAKING. But she knew what she had to do. She had debated it all day, ever since Landon had told her he couldn't find Ben's pocketknife.

Worry didn't begin to cover it, but in the end, there was only one thing to do.

Protect the people she loved.

Something about Cal showing up only cemented her determination. Maybe that and eating the dinner she'd made alone, because they'd all gone off into their corners to avoid each other.

Ben had left the ranch sometime this afternoon grumpy and hungover. Landon was off handling the last of the evening chores, and Cal had suddenly insisted he needed to go to town after only being at the ranch an hour or two.

So, this was her chance. It was now or never.

She crept into the Bennet side of the main house like a burglar, even though she wasn't setting out to steal anything.

Quite the opposite.

Landon hadn't finished the list he was going to give police regarding the pocketknife. Aly knew he was putting it off with Ben's missing, but that would only last so long. Landon would feel honor bound to have it sent to the police department before he went to bed.

Which meant her time was running out and she had to stop being a coward. She marched up the stairs. Maybe her hands were sweaty, but she was determined.

She was trying really hard to be determined. Everything she was doing went against her nature, went against how her father had raised her, but everything she was doing was in keeping with what the Bennets had taught her.

Protect your own. Maybe the Bennets weren't *her* own, but they had taken her in. They'd made her one.

At the end of the day, she wasn't convinced Gene Price had killed Sandy, but she knew Ben hadn't. For reasons that had been beyond Aly, and even with the way they fought sometimes, Aly knew Ben had loved Sandy.

In fact, the way he was drinking only proved that. He was inconsolable. It was a heck of a lot like when Mrs. Bennet had died. Aly had been terrified the Bennets and the ranch would fall apart, and she'd done her level best to keep everything running.

Along with Landon, who had put everything on his shoulders. When Nate and Cal had deserted him, when Ben had sunk into a depression and an alcohol problem, Landon had stepped up and handled it all.

She hadn't been able to do anything then, not really. Oh, she'd helped with meals and ranch administration when and where she could, but she hadn't been able to step in and *do anything*.

Now she could.

On a difficult swallow, she reached out, opened the door

to Ben's bedroom and slipped inside. It was stuffy. A mix of alcohol and cologne too potent so that she was tempted to go throw open all the windows.

But then Ben would know she'd been in here or someone had. Eventually everyone would have to know what she'd done, but she wanted it to be after. When nothing could be done about it.

She knew Landon hadn't told Ben about Nate or the pocketknife. For all she knew, Ben didn't even know Cal was back. He'd been isolating himself, and so it felt natural to isolate him from all these truths that might make him sink deeper into his depression.

Once Gene went on trial, once it was *proven*, Ben would pull himself out of it. He'd done it before. He'd do it again. She knew Landon believed that, and she tried to believe it too.

So here she was, doing her part.

She considered the room. The unmade bed. The empty liquor bottle half hidden under the dresser—that had two drawers pulled out, clothes spilling out of them.

This wasn't like Ben. He was neat and organized and *with it*. He was a hard man, but so had her father been. Her father had loved Ben like a brother, had been devoted to him, though Ben had essentially been his employer.

Aly couldn't imagine betraying her father's memory by thinking Ben was capable of *murder*. Of hurting people.

The drinking made that harder, but that was why she was doing this. Once the murder was officially solved, they could move Ben toward healing. Drinking was how he grieved. She knew he would pull himself out of it. He had before. Why wouldn't he this time?

They just had to make sure nothing went wrong in the meantime. She moved over to his nightstand. Since it was already half open, all she had to do was drop the knife in there. She hesitated for a moment.

This was a risk. But it was *her* risk, and if it came back to bite anyone, she'd make sure it was her. Repayment.

Landon would hate for her to think of it that way. He always got so squirrely when she said anything remotely close to her owing the Bennets.

But she did. They hadn't had to let her move into the main house. They hadn't had to treat her like family just because her dad had been Ben's foreman for so long. They could have left her to be a ward of the state and called it a day.

But they hadn't. Maybe that didn't come with any prices or strings, but Aly felt them anyway.

She dropped the knife into the drawer. Because it was the right thing to do. But before she could turn around, someone spoke.

"What the hell are you doing?"

She jumped a foot, a little shriek escaping her lips before she could control it. Because it was Landon's voice asking that question. No reason to startle and scream.

She closed her eyes and blew out a breath. She was going to have to explain it to him anyway, so this wasn't a worst-case scenario. But, damn, she'd wanted to do it on her own terms.

"What are you doing, Aly?" Landon demanded again.

She turned and met his gaze with a lifted chin and a

bunch of determination that was more mask than what she actually felt. "What needs to be done."

ALY LED HIM downstairs, refusing to answer any questions until they were in the kitchen. "You have to eat something," she said.

Landon just watched her move around the kitchen trying to understand what he'd just seen.

She pulled out a covered plate from the refrigerator. He could reheat his own leftovers, but she seemed to need to do something with her hands.

"Aly."

"Listen," she said, focusing on the task of putting the plate in the microwave, not on him. "You said your dad's knife was missing. We both know that whether that was his found in the creek or not, it doesn't have anything to do with Sandy's murder. So, instead of trying to deal with police bullshit, I took care of it."

She hit the buttons on the microwave, turned to face Landon. "You don't have to put me on the list. No one would question it. My name isn't Bennet."

"All the ranch hands who've worked here for more than ten years have one."

"And I inherited my dad's. I still have it. There was no reason for Ben to give me one when I had Dad's. There was no reason for me to have two."

Landon could only stare at her. She was suggesting they lie to police. Fake evidence, more or less. And Landon had bent some of his own strident morals over the years. He'd had to, but this felt … like a step beyond hiding things from Dad, hiding Dad's drinking from the police.

"Who is going to know besides me and you and Ben?" Aly demanded. "Ben gave mine to me for Christmas before my dad died, before your mom did. Why would anyone know I had one except us and people who are dead?"

He couldn't find fault with her plan. Except it felt wrong. It felt like dragging her into the mud, when she didn't deserve to be there. When she *could* cut all her strings to the Bennet Ranch and all these damn problems and have some semblance of a normal life.

And yet, he'd never been the one to do the cutting, had he? He'd always wanted her tied right here.

"What if Dad tells someone he lost his?"

"He doesn't even know he lost it. Besides, we only have to tell him what to say. Hell, we could probably convince him that one is his. It's a simple solution to a simple problem."

"It's lying."

"Since when do you have a problem with lying to protect him, Landon?"

"Me lying. Not you."

She shook her head, turned her attention back to the microwave. "He didn't kill anyone, Landon. I believe that and so do you. So, this is to protect him, and I don't see why I shouldn't be part of that. He protected me when I needed it."

"It wasn't so you'd owe him." Not that he thought Ben had ever done overmuch for Aly. Letting her move into the house, rehabbing the back section to give her a little apartment. The first had been Mom's idea. The second his.

But they'd all let Dad take the credit, he supposed, for allowing it.

"I don't *owe* him or you. I'm just part of this, Landon. So I'm going to do my part. Don't put my name on the list."

He inhaled, trying to find some of all that inner strength he was forever finding new sources of. Forever building it up stronger and stronger, because otherwise…

He handled everything. Always had. Always would. He'd promised himself, his mother, his father he *always* would. But he felt like he was crumbling.

It didn't help when Aly moved forward and put her arms around him. And he knew, immediately, it was just a friendly, supportive hug.

They were careful around each other. Not with words. They depended on each other too much for that, but there was a physical carefulness. Landon had never asked her where hers came from. Being the only woman in a ranch full of men? Something else?

It didn't matter, because he knew where his stemmed from and whatever kept them physically apart was for the best.

But right now, she was hugging him. Out of comfort.

She smelled like soap and spring. She always did. Even in winter. Her strong hand rubbing up and down his back like he deserved any of the sympathy in this whole travesty. And he could only blame exhaustion on the fact that he hugged her back, that he let himself be comforted when he knew better.

When she pulled back, he knew he should let her go. He tried, but she grasped his face in her hands, and it felt like the only thing to do was stop his pulling away by resting his palms on her hips.

"This is the right thing to do," she said firmly.

Her blue eyes were direct, and he could see that stubborn set of her chin. She didn't take over often. She didn't try to wrestle the control away from his over-tight grip hardly ever.

But she was doing it now, and it had been ... maybe a decade since anyone had ... *hugged* him, let alone swept in and just done something, taken care of something.

Oh, Aly tried. She always tried. She was the only one who did.

Her thumb moved, ever so slightly, across his cheekbone, and he was just a little too aware of the warmth of her hips under his hands. Of this spooling thing in his gut he knew better than to let linger here.

But before something ... shifted, something behind him caught her attention and she dropped her hands. "Cal. I'll heat up your plate now that you're back." She smiled at his brother over his shoulder.

Landon had to take a few seconds to breathe, to remind himself of who and where he was, before he turned to face Cal.

And he didn't like the expression on Cal's face. Something a little too *considering*. "I've got to send that list in, Al. I'll be back in a sec."

She nodded, her attention on getting out another plate of food. Landon walked out of the kitchen and into the living room where the ancient laptop he hated was sitting on the desk. He opened the screen and didn't bother to sit. He simply highlighted Aly's name and deleted it.

"I seem to recall Dad sitting us all down and giving us quite the talking-to about not looking in that direction," Cal said from behind him. "Ever."

Landon kept his attention on the computer. He copied and pasted the list he'd typed out into an email, typed in the officer's email address. "I'm not looking in any directions."

"Maybe you should."

Landon rolled his eyes. Cal was just trying to get a rise out of him. Landon didn't know why Cal couldn't grow up, but Landon wasn't going to bite.

"Seriously. You're a grown man, Landon. And still jumping at just the right height to keep Dad appeased? Doesn't it get old?"

Landon thought maybe if he'd slept at all, there might be rage. A great volcanic explosion of it. But he didn't have the energy. So there was only shock, and outrage, sure, but the tired kind. The quiet *fuck-you* kind.

He straightened, faced Cal. "Do you really think that's why I'm here? Because Dad told me to be? I'm too brainless and spineless to have my own reasons for holding every damn thing together?"

Cal didn't have any smart retorts for that. He stood there, hands in his pockets, studying Landon.

If Landon let the silence stretch out, he was afraid of what he might say, confess, ask for. When the only way he'd gotten through the past fifteen years—dragging Dad and the Bennet Ranch with him—was to fight.

"Some of us have work to do to make sure Sam Price

doesn't get what she wants," Landon said to Cal. "You know, I'm sure you meant well by coming here." He wasn't sure at all, but maybe he'd found some diplomacy in Aly's hands on his face. "But we don't need you."

"No, everyone has always made that very clear," Cal said.

And for a moment, just a moment of weakness, Landon wondered what everything looked like from Cal's perspective. Would he have helped more if the Bennet way wasn't to make it impossible to help?

But weakness had no place here. "I'm hungry." Email forgotten, he walked away from the laptop. But Cal strode toward it and that had Landon stopping in his tracks.

He watched, something like discomfort, maybe even something *like* guilt, crawling up his spine and stiffening it.

Cal looked over at him. "Aly had a pocketknife."

Landon's body went cold, but he didn't let his reaction show. "No, she didn't," he said, managing to sound flippant.

"She did," Cal insisted. "I remember Mom harassing Dad until he gave her one for Christmas one year."

Aly had been so sure no one would remember. Didn't it just figure it'd be fucking Cal?

"I don't remember that," Landon said, even managing a bit of a shrug. "Are you sure it was Aly? Her dad had one, of course. She has that one."

Cal's expression was grim. "You purposefully didn't put her name on the list. What are you hiding, Landon?"

Landon stared at Cal. Maybe he could find sympathy, softness, understanding for his brother. But where would it get them? Where did it ever get them?

Cal didn't belong here. He never had. A fact he'd made

clear to the entire family, time and time again.

"Did you just come to make trouble? To make everything harder?" Landon demanded. "Because if so, you can just go back to Texas. I've got enough fucking hard without you."

Then he left the room without addressing Aly, the pocketknife, or the list at all.

Chapter Fourteen

Rental Cabins at the Reynolds Ranch

SAM HAD DRIVEN Nate back to his cabin. He was in no shape to drive, and she didn't know what else to do with him. She hadn't expected to feel responsible for a grown adult man, but somehow every step of this made her feel more like she'd done something *to* him, rather than using him as a step in this case to exonerate her dad.

She pulled to a stop in front of his cabin. "Thanks for the ride," he said, then got out. He didn't *stumble* exactly, but there was definitely a moment of watching him catch his balance before he closed the car door and started walking.

Frustrated with herself, Sam turned off the car and got out herself. She followed him up to the porch. She'd just make sure he got inside okay, make sure it felt … right to leave him. Then she'd go.

"I don't need a babysitter," he said, taking the stairs up the porch. "Been taking care of myself for almost half my life. Even when half-drunk."

"Is it only half?" she returned mildly, still following him up the stairs.

He made a kind of grunting noise at that, jamming the key into the door with more force than necessary. Though she noted he didn't struggle to hit his mark, so maybe he was a bit more of an alcohol heavyweight than she'd given him credit for.

Still. It was a lot of alcohol, a lot of emotional upheaval, and it didn't feel right to just … ditch him.

He opened the door, stepped inside, but he didn't close it on her face or anything. So, she followed him in. Like most of the cabins Aunt Lisa'd had built, the front door opened into a living area and a small kitchen. There'd be a bathroom and two bedrooms off the back.

Small, but cozy.

Nate headed for the kitchen. He opened a cabinet, got out a glass. Then he stared at the empty glass and shook his head, moving back out of the kitchen. He looked at Sam, crossed his arms over his chest and scowled. She figured she was about to get kicked to the curb.

"What's Cal's story?" he asked instead.

Sam studied him. She realized he'd likely been wanting to ask that for a while but hadn't. Because Cal was *his* brother. But she obviously knew more, and that must feel weird.

Then again, what about Nate's entire life right now could possibly feel less than weird?

"I didn't have to ask Landon's, because it's clear he did what he always set out to do. Marry himself to that fucking place." Nate made a sweeping gesture with his arm, because yeah, he was a little more than half-drunk. "But Cal got out. Mr. Full-Ride Scholarship. He didn't stay after Mom died."

He said it like a statement, but Sam heard the question in it.

"No, he didn't. My understanding is that he got whatever degree, then went to law school. Back in those days he used to come visit a lot more, so people would talk about what he was up to. He was a lawyer somewhere before Texas. Not sure where. A few years back, he joined a firm there as a criminal defense attorney. I don't think he's been back in Marietta for years."

Nate nodded. "Years, huh?"

Sam shrugged. "I think I'd have heard about it. My impression has always been that he doesn't get along with the rest of them."

Nate was quiet for a few ticking minutes. "I don't think he knows about Dad. Or he wouldn't have asked about him being my enemy."

Sam considered. Not just what to say, but if she should say it. In the end ... it seemed like there were layers of Bennet secrets, and maybe that was none of her business. But maybe it led her to answers. Could she really just ignore that possibility?

"My interpretation of that was a little different."

Nate narrowed his eyes. "How so?"

"He asked, *why would Dad be your enemy?* In that ... slick lawyer way. He wanted an answer. Not that he already knew the answer. Or ... it was like fishing. He wanted something."

Nate frowned at that, but he didn't say anything, even to mount an argument.

"And the fact of the matter is, even before your mother died, Cal left. He always wanted to leave. Right? Maybe there was a reason, and he wants to know if yours was the same."

Nate nodded. "I guess he and Dad butted heads, but it was more about the ranch, the future. Cal never wanted any part of the ranch. Never seemed to anyway."

"Did you?" Sam didn't know what had possessed her to ask that.

It didn't pertain to anything important. None of the reasons she was here, or she'd brought Nate here. And still, she was curious.

Nate blew out a breath, his hands falling down at his sides before he scratched one through his hair. "I don't know. I don't know what I wanted. So much of the *before* feels like another person. Someone outside my own body."

Sam didn't say anything to that, even though she recognized the feeling. Sometimes it was how she felt about her childhood when her mom was still alive. She didn't remember it that clearly, but what she did was like… it had happened to someone else. Like some weird movie in her mind of a time that wasn't really hers.

Which wasn't the *point* of this conversation, and drunk or not, she should keep Nate on track. Keep them on track. Goals didn't get accomplished with distractions.

"I'm not saying you should trust Cal. I'm saying… We don't actually know whose side he's on yet. And if we could get him on ours… It might be helpful."

"Is that how you think of it? Sides?"

It felt like an accusation, so Sam had to work very hard not to bristle. "I didn't. Not at first. But everyone in those first few years of trials made it clear. If I thought my dad was innocent, I was on a side all by myself."

"What if your dad *isn't* innocent?"

"He *is*."

"What if, Sam?"

She could leave now. She did not need to fight with him over this. She knew what she knew and there were no what ifs, and it didn't matter what Nate Bennet thought. Maybe things were already moving forward because of him, but that didn't mean she had to sit here and justify herself to a veritable stranger.

But she did it anyway. "I have fought most of my life to prove that he's innocent because I *know* it. I have never found one thing that had me even *waver* in that conviction. I'm not fifteen anymore. This isn't a little girl's daydream. I've worked my ass off for fifteen years, and I have never once been confronted with actual evidence *he* did it. So there's no what if for me, Nate."

She got the feeling he wanted to argue on that some more, but whether he realized it would be pointless, or he was too drunk to have much of an argument in him, she didn't know.

He gripped the counter, his head dropping down as he let out a sigh. "I'm not on your dad's side. I'm not on anyone's side. I just want the truth."

"Are you sure about that?"

For a moment, he was immobile. Then he shook his head, ever so slightly. "No. I'm not sure about anything these days."

She hated that she felt for him. Just like all those years ago when she'd handed over her hidden savings. When she'd bandaged him up and sent him on his way. She hated that this wasn't as easy, as focused, as straightforward as she'd always meant it to be.

Nate was silent for a long time before finally lifting his head, looking at her. "So, what do you suggest we do about Cal then?"

"We don't alienate him. We see if we can get a glimpse into what he might know, what he might think. Maybe it's not about sides with him, but it could be a glimpse into how they're closing ranks over there."

Nate nodded slowly. "It's the Bennet way," he said bitterly.

NATE WOKE WITH a pounding headache, a roiling stomach, a pain in his leg that hadn't been there in a while, and no idea how he'd gotten to bed last night.

On a groan, he pushed himself into a sitting position. He rubbed his hand over the back of his neck, aching from the way he must have slept on it—half hanging off the mattress apparently.

He was wearing what he'd worn yesterday, and it felt heavy and itchy. He reached back to yesterday. He was pretty sure he remembered everything—cemetery, bar, Sam bringing him back to the cabin. Maybe bits and pieces were fuzzy, but he'd hardly been blackout drunk.

A strangely comforting thought. Coping without going overboard.

Yay, you, a bitter voice in his head.

Still, he felt terrible. He'd take a shower. Put something

in his stomach to stop this uneasiness. Then... Hell, he didn't know. Something. He'd figure out his next step *after*.

But when he walked out to the living and kitchen area, he stopped in his tracks. There was a lump on his couch. A Sam-shaped lump. She didn't move when he entered the room.

She was fast asleep.

Nate didn't know how to fully ... absorb this information. He moved into the kitchen to find something to take the edge off his hangover. He moved carefully, silently, so as not to wake her. Found some pain killers, a half-full glass of water.

He downed the ibuprofen, watched Sam. Her eyes were closed, her breathing even, but he didn't know how she was sleeping comfortably all curled up in a little ball like that. No real pillow. No blanket. Sure, he'd slept in worse, but she was...

He tended to think of everyone around him who hadn't been in the military, who hadn't been deployed as slightly ... less hardened than him, he supposed. She'd likely always had a bed to sleep in, a roof over her head. Her dad hadn't beaten her. She hadn't dealt with the aftereffects of shrapnel tearing her bones apart.

But she'd also dealt with some shit that had likely given her the ability to sleep where she needed to, when she needed to.

She hadn't needed to, though. Stay here. Watch after him. Just because he'd been weak and gotten a little drunk, she hadn't needed to ... supervise. He could take care of himself. Hell, he'd had to.

He'd been on his own since he was sixteen. And it was some kind of irony that she was the one who'd allowed him that escape. That one hundred dollars she'd given him was the starting point. And he'd had a hell of a struggle there for a few years, but it had been better than dealing with what his father had done. Dealing with his mother's death.

Now, he was back, and maybe not dealing with either of those things, not really. But here she was, being the person who somehow watched out for him again.

He didn't know what to do with that. Maybe there wasn't anything to *do*. Maybe it was just another thing to endure.

Even if this was a lot nicer to endure than all the military challenges he'd faced.

Her phone buzzed on the coffee table in front of her, the screen lighting up in the dim room. She made a kind of noise, shifted, her eyes blinking open. She reached for the phone, brought it up to her face.

Nate forced himself to look away. To search out something to eat that wouldn't make his entire stomach revolt. He didn't need to watch her wake up, or how she'd react to whatever was on her phone.

"You hungry?" he asked, pulling a box of cereal from the cabinet. At least he'd had the sense to go grocery shopping yesterday before he'd hit the bar.

"Yeah, sure. I want you to look at something, once you're feeling up to it."

"I can handle a hangover," he muttered, irritated that she could see it on him.

"Sure," she replied, making her tone somehow bland

enough not to sound like approval or censure. He heard or felt her come closer. "You got any coffee?"

The kitchen was small, but two people could have worked in tandem easily enough. He didn't feel like sharing any space right now though. Not with her.

"I'll handle it."

She didn't say anything to that, but once he'd gotten the coffee started and two bowls of cereal full, complete with milk, and because she was here and he felt like he owed her something a little extra somehow, a banana, he realized she was sitting at the stool opposite the kitchen counter.

He put the bowl in front of her. She was still looking at her phone. But when he turned and got the coffee, he could feel her gaze on him.

Pitying, no doubt. It put an itch between his shoulder blades. He didn't like it. It reminded him too much of those early years of running away, before he'd managed to make something of himself.

"Anything in your coffee?"

"Black's fine," she replied.

When he put the mug of coffee in front of her, she pushed her phone across the counter toward him. On the screen was some kind of list. "What is it?" he asked, picking the phone up.

"It's the list of people who own a pocketknife like the one we found."

He glanced at her. "How'd you get that?"

Her mouth quirked ever so slightly on one side. "I've got a few friends here and there."

He might have poked into that, but he read through the

list instead. His family were first on the list, as they should be. Then ranch hand names he recognized. He read through it twice, just to get a sense of everything, just to be certain he hadn't missed anything.

Because it dawned on him, if only because Aly had been at the house when he'd seen Landon, that she was missing. Nate handed Sam the phone. "Aly Cartwright isn't on this list."

"Should she be?"

"Yes. She got one. I know she did."

"When?"

"It was like a rite of passage. Turn thirteen, get the Bennet pocketknife. Now, Aly's no Bennet, but Mom treated her like one. I don't think her mom was ever around, that I recall. So Mom thought she should have one too. I *remember* Mom being mad at Dad because he hadn't done it for her thirteenth birthday. So, with enough prodding, he did it for that Christmas. So, whatever year that would have been."

"You're sure?"

"Positive. Her dad would have had one long before that. Her dad was working Bennet Ranch before she was born, so he would have gotten his before she turned thirteen."

"That's … interesting," Sam said. She looked at the list again. "And not an accident. Landon would know too, wouldn't he? That she had one."

"I'd assume so. They were always kind of close. Still are, if the other day was anything to go by."

"Yeah, they're close. And if there's anyone Landon's going to protect, it's Aly."

Nate shook his head. Not that he disagreed exactly. Landon and Aly had always been good friends, and Landon had *always* had some kind of warped Superman complex. But Nate also knew Aly wouldn't let that happen. If she wasn't on this list, she was aware.

"They're not protecting Aly," Nate said grimly.

Sam met his gaze. Blinked once. "If they're not protecting Aly, they're protecting someone who should have had their knife and doesn't."

Nate nodded.

"You think she replaced it with hers. So they didn't put her name on the list."

Sam didn't phrase it as a question, but he nodded. "Yeah, and I think it was Dad's knife that was missing. Your friend who shared this list with you, would they be able to tell you anything about the tests they're running on the knife?"

Sam considered her phone. "Only one way to find out."

Chapter Fifteen

The Bennet Ranch

CAL WAS UP stupid early, wondering why he was here at the ranch. He could have stayed in town. He could have handled a lot of things differently than he was. He didn't have to be *here*.

But he was staring at the ceiling of his childhood room—long ago cleared of any of Cal's stuff, now just decorated like a generic guest room.

He hadn't slept much at all. He didn't like to admit it, even to himself, but he'd been terrified of the nightmares that might plague him if he *did*, and it had been easy to avoid sleep anyway. Too many things circling his mind. Old memories he didn't want. Wondering what Landon and Aly thought they were doing *lying* to the cops.

Did they think Dad had done it and they were protecting him? Maybe he'd never understood his brother, but he just couldn't see that being the case. No, it had to be some warped sense of *saving* Dad. Probably from his own self.

But apparently they didn't understand how bad it would look if anyone figured it out. From what Cal had been able to find out yesterday, most of the evidence against Gene Price was circumstantial, and the prosecutors trying to build a case while Gene was held on a parole violation were relying heavily on repeat offender, not the actual evidence.

The case was held together by a tenuous thread, and Landon and Aly had no idea they were putting unnecessary weight on that thread.

It wasn't Cal's responsibility to fix that. To handle any of this. If he had any sense at all, he'd wash his hands of Bennets and Montana once and for all. He didn't owe Landon or Dad a damn thing.

In the past, it had always been Mom's memory that had brought him back. The guilt he could only stave off for so long that she would be disappointed in him if he cut ties completely. But this time…

It had been Nate. He still couldn't make heads nor tails of the conversation he'd had with him. Couldn't reconcile the fearless, volatile, and impulsive teenager with the stoic, quiet man of carefully hidden depths.

There was something underneath everything. His disappearance. His reappearance. Not just Sam Price, however that all worked, but something with Dad. Something that, even now lying in bed, had tension creeping into Cal's shoulders.

But no amount of *thinking* was going to get answers. He had to get up and act. If he went down to the kitchen now, got some breakfast and waited around, he'd likely *finally* catch Dad.

Because even though Cal had been back two days, he still hadn't seen his father. He'd *almost* believe Dad was hiding from him, but there was something about the way Landon and Aly were skittering around, lying to people, hiding things that had made Cal remember his visits in the year after Mom died.

Dad had started drinking heavily. Everyone chalked it up to grief. Even Cal had. Landon had insisted he was handling it, dealing with it, and that he didn't need Cal's help with anything.

So Cal had thrown himself into school. Into the LSAT and working his ass off to make sure he could afford whatever law school would have him—without having to ask a damn thing from any Bennet.

Was Dad drinking again, and that was what Landon and Aly were trying to protect Dad from?

Cal pushed himself out of bed, threw on some clothes, and decided to go find out for himself. No one was in the kitchen when he got there, but someone had started coffee. Maybe he'd already missed Dad, but Cal knew how the ranch life went still. Even if Dad and Landon were out doing early chores, fueled only by coffee, they'd be back for some breakfast soon enough.

So, Cal moved about the kitchen that had once been his mother's favorite room in the house. *The heart of any house is the kitchen*, she used to tell him when he'd do his homework at the same worn kitchen table. She had liked to tell him his father and grandfather had likely done their homework right there too.

She'd been proud of the Bennet family legacy, even though she'd married into it. She'd been proud of him. His brain. His drive. His charm.

Bitter now, without her. Without anyone who felt the same.

He shook his head. It was a stupid, childish thing to feel as if ghosts haunted the corners of this house. It was just a house. Mom was dead, not standing at the oven in some spirit form, while he ate his breakfast, disappointed in him and his inability to make some kind of connection with anyone here.

Just as it was a stupid, childish thing to want to hide when he heard the door open and boots stomp on the mat.

When Dad stepped into the kitchen, Cal had to resist the urge to leave. To change his mind about what he'd come here for, or about coming here at all.

Time had etched lines into Ben's face, given his rangy frame a little bit more heft than it'd once had. His hair was whiter, his eyes grimmer, and worst of it all were all the similarities he saw in Dad's face and the man he looked at in the mirror every morning.

Dad glanced at the table, but his expression didn't change. "We don't need your help," he said simply. Not even unkindly. Just in his straightforward, truthful way.

We don't need you.

Cal forced himself to smile. "Lucky for you, I'm giving it regardless of want or need. If I billed you, you'd cry."

Dad didn't crack a smile, of course Cal had known he wouldn't. In Austin, he could make just about anyone laugh—even the toughest judges who hated him on sight. But here in Montana his humor only ever failed.

Just like you.

"Go home, Cal," Dad said gruffly, before exiting the kitchen.

I am home, some small voice in his mind said. He ignored it. The Bennet Ranch might be his childhood home, but it wasn't *home* home. He'd made Austin his home, his life. He loved it there.

Not here.

He looked down at his half-eaten breakfast, knew he couldn't stomach any more. Knew he couldn't sit here and *linger.* If he lingered, memories he didn't particularly want to face would surface, so he moved.

Because surviving Montana was all about forward movement.

Besides, he'd come here for a reason. Not to see Dad. Not to argue with Landon. Not to remember Mom or feel like he was home or wanted.

Maybe he'd come to see what the deal with Nate was, but mostly he had come home to make sure his father didn't get wrongfully mixed up in this murder business, and so that was what he'd do.

He went to the front closet, grabbed a coat that would fit. He considered stealing someone's work boots but stuck with his own sneakers. They'd do for a hike.

It would have been quicker to drive, but the rental car wouldn't stand a chance and he wasn't about to have to ask Landon to borrow a vehicle.

So, he walked. And walked, and walked, and walked. Christ, he'd forgotten how cold Montana could be even in May. Forgotten how he'd liked that cold, the way it seemed to make the air crystal clear. The way it could knock all the shit right out of you and all you could focus on was surviving it.

Of course, he didn't have to survive much of anything in

Austin. He could live and breathe and move any which way he pleased. Life was life, not a battering ram.

For some reason when he finally reached the creek, frozen to the bone, something beat in his chest that didn't feel like pain or surviving. A faint ghost of something he'd once known.

He ignored it.

He surveyed the area, trying to determine where they would have found Sandy, where Nate had allegedly found that pocketknife. At this point the police would have gone through the area, over and over again, but that didn't mean there wasn't any more to glean.

The water in the creek moved at a lazy current. No roaring rapids or water up to the bank, but it was certainly high enough to drown an incapacitated person. Cal walked down a way, then back up, then around. Behind him was the expanse of the Bennet Ranch, outbuildings and fields, cattle, snow, mud.

The place his mother had been murdered, then burned. A bright blue sky above, the Rockies in the distance.

He'd left this place because of that house down there, and he'd never allowed himself to miss it. He *didn't* miss Montana, but sometimes the shadows of those mountains haunted him. In dreams, in crowded courtrooms, in swanky bars with a woman sidled up to him.

They existed somewhere inside of him no matter how hard he'd tried to run, and they pressed down upon him, like they could crush him from all the way over there.

He turned away, abruptly, and looked down at the creek. There were enough logs and rocks sticking up he might be able to make it across without getting too wet. With a panic he didn't understand beating in his chest, it seemed like a hell of an idea.

So, he did just that, and slid off a rock and into the creek twice, completely soaking through his sneaker, sock, and jeans about halfway up his calf. He made it to the other side, slipping as he scrambled up the muddy bank—adding a streak of wet mud down the front of one of his legs.

He swore a few times once he made it to the other side, wiping his muddy hands on his coat, imagining the razzing Landon would give him, then he swore some more. What the hell had come over him? Maybe he wasn't a Montanan any longer, but he'd spent enough time playing in this creek growing up to know you didn't just—

"Who are you?"

Cal jumped and whirled, then raised an eyebrow at the overly bundled-up form in front of him. He'd guess there was a woman under there based on the voice, but he couldn't be sure.

"Who are *you*?"

She—Cal was fairly sure she was a she—folded her arms across her lumpy chest. It looked like she was wearing not one but two bulky winter coats. She eyed him in a way a queen might eye a … wet, muddy person cursing in their court.

"You're trespassing."

Cal looked around and realized that yes, he was. It was Harrington land on this side of the creek. Glenda Harrington lived in a cabin… He glanced behind the lump of coats and scarves and a giant knit hat, and there was the postage stamp of a cabin Cal remembered being the source of ghost stories when he'd been a kid.

He couldn't imagine the woman before him was Glenda, if her height and clear voice were anything to go by.

She sighed heavily then. "Ah. You must be Cal Bennet."

He flashed her a grin. "My reputation precedes me."

He couldn't read any kind of response from beneath all those layers, or even her posture, and yet he had the sneaking suspicion that whatever preceded him was not exactly flattering.

"Why are you lurking around here?" the woman asked as if he'd never spoken at all.

He straightened, though in his wet, muddy state he doubted he looked very stately or professional. "I'm not lurking. I'm conducting an investigation."

"Perhaps you should investigate the cause of hypothermia, because I'm pretty sure you're going to give it to yourself walking around like that." She gestured at his feet where the darkness of the bottom of his jeans gave way to the fact he'd stomped through the creek like an amateur.

"I don't suppose you'd have an extra pair of shoes. Men's size twelve?"

"Stay put," she muttered, turning and heading for the cabin. A woman stepped out of it before the lumpy woman could enter, and they stood talking to each other for a moment.

When the lumpy woman gestured back at him, the woman who'd stepped out glanced at him. He'd known who she was straight off because she was hunched and coming out of the Harrington cabin, but when her gaze met his he *felt* who she was.

A deep, dark foreboding slithered through him. Some memory from long ago tried to surface. That panic returned, beating hard against his chest, so hard he forgot about the wet cold in the lower half of his body. He forgot everything except escape.

He turned away from green eyes, glittering in the dark, and walked straight back through the creek, not bothering to even try to step on stones this time. He had to get far, far away from all that black in the middle of a sunny afternoon.

Chapter Sixteen

The Harrington Property

JILL WATCHED THE man who was supposedly some big-shot attorney scurry away like he'd seen a ghost.

She glanced back at her grandmother and smiled mischievously. "I don't know what you did to scare him, but I hope you did it on purpose."

But Grandma didn't smile like Jill expected. Jill knew Grandma got some enjoyment out of being the town's ghost story, even though she was flesh and blood. Maybe she even enjoyed it enough to lean into it a little. Dressing heavily in black, staring creepily at anyone who dared show their face around here. Then laughing about it after.

But there was no laughter now.

Grandma sighed and shook her head. She didn't sign anything. Just walked away from the cabin and to the back, where her gardens were.

Jill frowned after her. This murder business had made everything so *fraught*. Aly was a nervous wreck. Grandma wasn't acting herself. And Jill herself was having trouble sleeping.

Maybe the guy who'd murdered Sandy was in jail, but she'd finally started to feel safe here in this middle-of-nowhere place, only to have all that taken from her.

Everyone in town was all abuzz with it, some jumpy—like Aly. Some like vultures on carrion—viciously delighted to have juicy gossip.

And she thought they all could have weathered that well enough, but the sudden appearance of *trespassers* poking around a murder scene—even if they were all Bennets in some respects—had Jill feeling very much like she wished she was back in Boston with a security system and video doorbell.

Jill glanced behind her where she could see, through the trees that lined the creek, the tiny form of Cal Bennet hurrying away. She frowned.

Investigating. Why were all these Bennet brothers *investigating* separately? None of them were cops.

She went inside, because three years in Montana hadn't eased her into living through the cold, relentless winter. She could *see* the signs of spring outside her window, but she'd yet to feel them. She'd downgrade to one coat in maybe a month or so. Maybe.

Should she call Aly and tell her about Cal? She made tea and mulled it over. Aly made it sound like Cal, slick but with a *good heart*, wasn't a threat like Samantha Price.

But in the end, as much as she was worried about Aly and how much she was putting on her shoulders, Jill knew she needed to know.

She picked up the phone and dialed Aly's number. Aly answered sounding … tired. At best.

"Hi, Al. You got a minute?"

"Sure. I'm just cleaning up the breakfast dishes before I

head out to the pasture. What's up?"

Jill sighed. "I just ran into Cal Bennet. Near the creek by our property."

"Oh. Well, that's surprising. What was he doing?"

"He claims he was investigating."

Aly was quiet for a few seconds. "Well, I guess that's what I was hoping he'd do," Aly said, though Jill could read a false thread of positivity in her tone. "Thanks for letting me know."

"He was acting … weird. Definitely not the slick lawyer you described. He all but ran away from Grandma, like he'd seen a ghost." But even before he'd stumbled into their yard, something had rattled him. What had made him fall into the creek and get all wet and muddy? What had made him run like that?

"I guess this is kind of a lot. And … Cal doesn't spend much time here. I imagine being near where his mom was found might have some emotional responses from him. But it's okay. It's all going to be okay."

Jill knew it wasn't any of her business, but Aly was her friend. And Aly hadn't been acting like herself since this whole thing happened. Maybe it wasn't fair to find fault with that. Murder was enough to change the way *everyone* was acting.

But this seemed deeper. Like denial and secrets and… Jill didn't know why Aly got so wrapped up in Bennet business when they weren't her family, but Jill also didn't know what it was like not to have parents to call, a sibling to rely on, a grandmother to take care of. Aly was all alone, family wise. Maybe it made sense she felt like the Bennets were her responsibility.

Still… "I'm worried about you, Aly."

"I appreciate that, I do. And I get it. But… It's okay. It really is. Gene Price is going to be tried and found guilty of murder and then this will all go away again."

Again. Jill didn't understand the whole lore around the first Bennet murder. But she didn't understand it because people were … weird about it. Mysterious. She tried not to ask questions, though, because it didn't seem right for something so personal to Aly to show up in one of Jill's books.

And it would if Jill started poking around, whether she meant for it to or not. Still… She could focus on *Aly*.

"I thought you weren't sure Gene did it."

"I changed my mind. Who else would have done it? He's the only murderer around here. We just have to get through this trial. Once they set a date, it'll all settle. We just have to… It's all going to be okay."

Jill didn't know what to say to that. She didn't want Aly worrying. But the positivity just hit … all wrong. Like desperation. Because trial or no trial, justice or no justice, a woman was still dead.

"Aly, I never ask, I try not to ask, but…" Jill closed her eyes, shook her head. She shouldn't do this, and yet she couldn't help herself. She *had* to understand what was going on if it was going to keep coming stumbling to her doorstep. "Look, you don't have to tell me, but all this talk about the first murder and not one person has explained the motive to me."

Aly was fully silent for a minute. Jill even opened her

mouth to say it didn't matter, there was no reason for her to know.

"The prevailing theory was that Gene was ... infatuated with Mrs. Bennet. They'd worked together on something for the Copper Mountain Rodeo a few years before and he'd been sort of ... hounding her ever since."

"Did you ever see him hounding her?"

"Hey, I'm sorry to cut you short because I really do appreciate the call, but I've got to go. We'll talk later, okay?"

"Yeah, sure. Of course. Take care of yourself, Aly," Jill said before the line went dead on Aly's mumbled goodbye.

When Jill hung up, she stood there staring at the phone for a good while. That had been ... weird. Or was the whole thing just weird and she was letting her imagination get the better of her?

It had been an insensitive question. All her questions had been. She should have kept her mouth shut. But everything about today was leaving her feeling terribly unsettled.

If Grandma was in the garden, Jill could grab her laptop and get some work done. Maybe a couple thousand words. Maybe... She turned around to see Grandma standing in the doorway. A frown sunk into her aged face.

"Everything all right?"

Grandma didn't respond right away. Then she gestured for Jill to follow her as she stepped back outside.

Jill sighed and grabbed her coat. She was just getting the feeling back in her toes. Still, as she went back outside, she could *feel* that the day had gotten a *little* warmer.

Grandma led her around back. Every spring, Grandma expanded her garden a little more, pushing the boundaries of what little land she had left. Like it was never quite enough. Jill tried to talk her out of doing such backbreaking work, but Grandma insisted, in her way, that working hard was good and healing recovery from the stroke. That she felt more like herself when she worked hard in the garden.

And Jill knew the stroke had stolen some of Grandma's sense of self. So, she didn't argue. Even when she felt she should.

Maybe Grandma was actually asking for her help with something. Maybe she *had* worked herself too hard. Maybe Jill had failed and…

But Grandma pointed to some upturned dirt where Grandma was expanding, close to the property line and the creek, where Grandma was excited to plant some flowers that liked a wet environment.

But there was something in there, like it had been buried.

Jill didn't quite understand what it was at first, but as she got closer and studied it, she thought maybe it was the blade of a shovel without its handle?

"Do you want me to … get rid of it or something?" Jill asked, not sure why this was significant. She moved forward to do just that, but Grandma grabbed her arm. The grip tight and strong.

When Jill looked back at her, she shook her head, then pointed again. But she didn't let Jill go, so Jill could only lean forward and try to see what it was her grandmother wanted her to see.

It took longer than maybe it should have to notice the etching in the steel. And that she recognized that design. It was the Bennet Ranch brand.

Grandma finally released her, then made a sign that Jill was starting to become all too familiar with.

Police.

Chapter Seventeen

The Bennet Ranch

LANDON HEADED TO the main house after a long day of work. Punishing his body so maybe his mind would shut the hell up. He hadn't stopped for lunch, hadn't had much in the way of water, coffee, or anything else.

His head pounded. His body ached. He was so uncomfortable that he could almost, *almost* forget everything that was going on.

He entered the house, bracing himself for the next shoe drop, but none came. Everything was still and quiet, like no one was home.

Please God.

The kitchen was blessedly empty, and when he opened the fridge, there was a plate made up. Just one, and he had to assume it was his. And that Dad and Cal had hopefully already eaten. Which meant Landon could eat in peace.

He threw the plate in the microwave, considered taking it all up to his room so that he could spend the rest of the evening in silent privacy. Tomorrow … tomorrow he would deal with Dad, with Cal. Today was his break.

His head pounded. He was so hungry he was actually veering toward nauseous. *Some break.*

When the microwave dinged, Landon pulled out the plate, and started to eat—standing there, not even caring that parts of the meal were still cold.

"What the hell is this?"

Landon nearly groaned. Why hadn't he gone to his room like he'd planned? He turned, plate still in hand, to his father standing in the entry to the kitchen, holding something up in one hand.

His eyes were bleary, his cheeks a little red. Maybe not *drunk*, but certainly not sober.

Landon looked from the pocketknife in Dad's hand to Dad's furious expression. "It's a pocketknife."

"Yeah, in *my* drawer. When I know this isn't mine. I know where mine is."

For a moment, Landon didn't breathe. Then he saw spots and realized he needed to suck in some oxygen. "You told me you didn't know where your knife was."

Dad dropped the pocketknife on the table. "I lied."

Something like a buzzing started in Landon's ears. The word *lied* echoed in his head, like the heavy pounding of his heart.

Lied. Lied. So casually. *I lied.* Without an ounce of shame or regret or explanation. And then Aly had taken it upon herself to… "Why would you lie? Do you have any idea what you've done?"

"Boy, I've warned you not to talk to me like that."

"Aly *lied* for you. She's covering for you."

"So?"

It splintered through him. This total disregard for… *everything*. "What the hell is wrong with you?"

But that didn't get through to Ben. He just got angrier and with more bluster. "I didn't tell that girl to lie for me. Maybe she should keep her nose out of things. Be easier for her to do if you weren't so damn tied to her pathetic apron strings."

Landon felt something inside of him just ... snap. Like a rubber band had been holding him together, but the pressure, the pull was finally too much.

It broke.

"You can't do this again." He let the plate slam onto the counter. It cracked in half, food splattering. Landon didn't give a shit. "You're not going to do this again."

"Don't take that tone—"

"The hell I won't," Landon replied taking a step toward his father. "I'll take whatever damn tone I want right now. You *lied* to me? Do you have any idea what the fuck is happening right now?"

Dad took his own step toward Landon with a furious sneer on his face. For a moment, Landon thought things were about to get violent. And he hated that he wasn't sure how he'd react if Dad reared back and tried to punch him.

Would he take it? Would he land a blow of his own? It left a pit of nausea expanding in his stomach.

But all that violence kind of ... crumpled into itself. Dad's shoulders sagged. His breathing got ragged in a different way. "Maybe loving me is a curse," Dad said, his eyes filling with tears.

And Landon knew he was supposed to have empathy, sympathy, *care*, and he had. For fifteen years he'd buried every last one of his own wants or needs to fulfill Dad's.

And now Dad was standing there, half drunk, saying he'd *lied*. And poor Aly was the one who'd stuck her neck on the line this time.

No. No, Landon wasn't having it.

"Maybe it fucking is a curse." Maybe they were all cursed. "But if you drown your sorrows in alcohol you are going to fuck something up. This isn't as cut and dried as last time."

Dad's head whipped up, back to angry. "I didn't kill Sandy."

"It doesn't matter," Landon shot back. "It matters if it *looks* like you did. And you've got too many damn people covering for you. We're going to make mistakes. And that's on *you*."

"I didn't ask anyone to help—"

"Bullshit. When tragedy strikes, you hit the bottle so everyone else has to do all the heavy lifting. You can cry grief and addiction all the fuck you want, but it isn't true. You're forcing us all to pick up the slack. To save you from yourself. I've carried your sorry ass for over a decade, but I'm not going to let Aly do it. I'm not going to let Aly pay for it."

Dad studied him with a look that might have had him withering once. *Once.*

"I set very clear rules—"

"Fuck your rules," Landon said, because Christ. Didn't anyone get it? Here he was running around extinguishing fires everyone else set. Over and over again without thought to anyone else.

Maybe it was his damn turn.

He laughed, a little bitterly. Both at himself, and the

purple mottled look of fury on his father's face. Because he wasn't going to set any fires. He wasn't going to break anything.

But maybe he'd stop trying so hard to fix everything for everyone else who wasn't going to help themselves.

"Fix this," he said, pointing at his father. Laying down an edict in a way he never had before. Not to Dad. "Fix it now."

And Landon left. The broken plate. His broken father. All the pieces of everything he'd tried to hold together. Desperately, until his fingers bled, cut down to the bone.

But he didn't leave the house. He went to the door that led over to Aly's section, and he didn't bother to knock.

He wasn't going to bleed all over her. He *wasn't*. But she was a part of this, so he could hardly keep her out.

ALY FELT LIKE she was moving through her days on fumes. Dizzy and awful feeling, but not enough to actually just lay down and sleep. It was too early to go to bed, but she considered it.

Then rejected it, because she was tired of her own thoughts. Her own anxieties. Her own damn self.

She thought about going up to have tea with Jill, or maybe make some brownies to take up and binge on. They could talk about their never-going-to-happen shopping trip or the book Jill was working on or … something.

But Jill's call earlier had ruined that. She was voicing concerns and asking questions now, and…

Aly didn't have any answers.

So, she'd thrown herself into deep cleaning her place. Turned her music loud. Drowned out her thoughts as best she could.

The problem was she was a neat, orderly person, so even deep cleaning didn't take long. And she was left with her thoughts, louder than the music, once again.

But she frowned when she thought she heard something under the music. She turned it off. She waited in the quiet. Was that the murmur of voices? Someone would have to be shouting for her to hear it through the walls, wouldn't they?

She moved for the door between her part of the house and the main part hesitatingly, but before she could decide how to proceed, the door flew open.

She wasn't sure who she'd expect to make such a dramatic entrance, but it certainly wasn't Landon. He very rarely came to this part of the house, and if he did, he always knocked. And it was usually an emergency.

Then he just stood there, and she crossed to him in spite of herself. In spite of all those little lines they drew around each other. Because he looked … wrecked. Pained, like a throbbing, open wound. And she knew his usual control and stoicism hid all *this*. It wasn't a surprise there would be all that pain inside of him. He had to put it *somewhere*.

But she'd never seen it so clear all over his face. All over *him*. And it had worry overriding her usual careful steps.

"What's wrong?" she asked, reaching out, wrapping her hand around his arm.

"I need you to come with me," he said darkly.

Which didn't answer her question. But she didn't press.

Not when he sounded like that. So final. "Where?"

"To see Nate."

For a minute, she couldn't find the words to say anything. He'd made it pretty clear he wasn't about to deal with Nate if he was connected with Sam. So something had happened to change his mind on that.

Something terrible.

But if he wanted to see Nate, if he wanted her to go with him, she would. She nodded. "Okay, just let me get my purse and shoes."

But he didn't let her move. When she moved to take her hand off his arm, he grabbed her arm so she couldn't. Then he stood there, staring at her with too many things she didn't recognize in his expression.

Worry and fear echoed through her, so she stepped even closer, needing to soothe whatever this was. Fix it. "Landon. Are you okay?"

He shook his head, which scared the hell out of her. Landon admitting something might be beyond his tightly held control? That was absolutely terrifying.

"Something is wrong, Al. Something is deeply, deeply wrong." He sucked in a breath, carefully let it out. "But we're going to get to the bottom of it."

"And you think Nate has the answers?"

He shook his head, almost imperceptibly, like he was afraid moving would make everything come shattering down around them. "No, but I think to find answers we have to go back. To what happened after Mom… Nate left for a reason. He had to have. I need to know it. If he's back *now*, I need to know it."

Something inside of her recoiled at that, resisted going back. They'd survived all this by going *forward*. If they went back…

But she saw the determination in Landon's face, and she couldn't be the one to stand up to that. Not about this. This thing that didn't *really* pertain to her, no matter how she was tangled in it. Maybe she'd spent a childhood wishing Marie was her mother. Maybe she'd grieved losing her too, but she wasn't a Bennet. Never had been.

Never would be.

So she could hardly tell Landon not to go back, not to poke into the past. If *he* of all people thought it was the way forward, no doubt it was for him. And she'd have to be there. Every step of the way, just like always.

Maybe that was codependent, but she didn't—*couldn't*—care right now. Landon needed someone, and she always wanted that someone to be her.

Aly rubbed her hand up and down his arm. "I'll drive."

Chapter Eighteen

Honor's Edge Investigations

"WAITING SUCKS."

Sam spared Nate a glance. He was sitting in one of the office chairs, ankles crossed on one of the tables. He was tossing a stress ball back and forth from palm to palm, and she'd been barely resisting telling him to stop it for the last fifteen minutes.

She was determined to be *chill* in direct response to his impatience. Mature in the face of what was essentially the behavior of a *small child*.

In part, because it was fascinating. Mr. Stoic Soldier was showing some cracks. A better woman probably would have attempted to smooth those over, but she'd never been a better woman.

"Waiting is part and parcel with investigating. There's more *waiting* than there is doing, and you might want to get used to it if you're going to see this through."

He let his feet fall to the ground, pushed himself out of the chair. "That's why I left the army," he muttered. "Too much fucking waiting."

"I thought you left the army because of injury," she returned, focusing more on the police report she was going over for the hundredth time rather than him. But she noticed he stopped his pacing.

He *slowly* turned to look at her. Eyes narrowed. "How did you know that?"

She didn't meet his suspicious gaze, just turned over the page she was now pretending to read. "How do you think I found you? I got your VA records, and from there tracked you to Tennessee."

"That can't be legal."

"Never said it was." She grinned up at him. "Going to sue me?"

He shook his head. "You're a piece of work, Sam," he muttered, but she watched as he couldn't quite stop himself from smiling back at her.

He was a handsome son of a gun. She'd give him that. All those Bennet good looks, and none of the charm or bluster. Thank God.

"Why, thank you," she said cheerfully. "You're not the first to tell me that."

They'd eaten dinner in her office, and she'd kept herself from telling Nate he could go sit at his cabin alone if he hated waiting so much. Because she remembered what he'd gotten up to the last time he'd been alone.

It just didn't feel like a great idea. She wasn't the *smoothing* type, but she had a bad case of *soft heart* when it came to lost causes.

Or maybe just when it comes to Nate Bennet's lost cause. Because even now, in the grown *soldier* man in front of her, she saw that boy he'd been sometimes. Bloody and lost.

Her phone buzzed, and boy, was she grateful for the distraction. Thinking too long and hard about Nate Bennet wasn't going to get her anywhere.

She looked at the screen. "Jackpot," she said, answering it quickly. "What do you have for me?"

"Look, Sam, you've got to stop harassing me." It was her contact at the sheriff's department. Brian never told her *everything*, no matter what case she was working on, but sometimes he gave important tips. Like that list of names he'd sent her.

"Yeah, yeah. What have you got?" She glanced at Nate, who was paying a little too much attention. She stood and moved into her office. Very performatively closing the door.

Maybe they were working together, but she had a right to her privacy, and she'd promised Brian that no one would ever know he was where she got her intel from. It wouldn't cost him his job if people found out, but it could get him written up. It could definitely have some negative repercussions. So she was serious about protecting his identity. Even from Nate.

"What can you tell me about the knife?"

"Nothing, Sam. Give me a break."

She rolled her eyes since Brian couldn't see her. He liked to fuss and argue, but in the end, he always ended up giving her the information. She'd spent *years* cultivating this relationship … and making sure Brian didn't expect any *payment* for said information.

"Look, there is something I can tell you. The Harringtons dug something up on their property this morning. Called a unit out. It's been brought into the station and we're going to run some tests on it."

"What was it?"

"Can't say. But it's caused a buzz. Tests means it might be evidence in something. I bet you'll hear about it by tomorrow. At the latest."

"Is it going to get my dad cleared?"

"I don't know, and you've got to stop leaving messages for me. People already talk about it anytime we spend time together."

Didn't he wish? Sam thought, but she didn't say it out loud. "You get me more info in the next twenty-four, I won't call for a week."

"My ass," he muttered. "Hey, I'm off tomorrow night, maybe we could—"

"Sorry, bud. Gotta go." She hung up before he could ask her out again.

She scowled. He hadn't done that in a while. She thought he'd gotten over it. He must have broken up with whatever her name was.

Annoying timing. Sam drummed her fingers on her desk for a moment. The information was nothing, and yet it was *something*.

Evidence at the Harrington place. Because *technically* Sandy had been found on the boundary between the two tracts of land. So, while she'd focused on the Bennet side, that didn't mean there couldn't be something on the Harrington side.

In fact, it made more sense, didn't it? If someone was looking to hide evidence, they wouldn't hide it at their own place, would they?

She shook her head. No use trying to jump to conclusions. In the next twenty-four hours Brian thought they'd hear about it. So it had to be big, important.

She could be patient. Hell, it'd been fifteen years already. She pushed off her desk and opened her door. She stepped back into the main office to find Nate scowling. She ignored any signs of male temper tantrum, and just jumped into it.

"That was my contact at the sheriff's department. He's still hedging about the tests run on the knife, but he did tell me something new. Something interesting. Someone from the Harrington property called the police this morning. They unearthed something, and the police are considering it evidence."

"What do we do?" Before she could open her mouth, he was shaking his head. "Don't say wait."

"We can't go charging into the police station *or* up to the Harrington place, Nate. There is a certain amount of waiting involved in all this. And if the police were up at the Harringtons again today, we can't head back to the creek tonight."

"That's bullshit."

"It is, but you're not the one locked up over it, so maybe take the ire down a notch."

Nate shook his head, clearly not appreciating that *patience* wasn't just for fun. That she'd love to demand answers and go charging headfirst into anything if it meant getting her dad out of another cell.

But back when she'd been young and dumb and done that, it hadn't gotten her anywhere. In fact, it had caused more problems than it ever solved. She tried not to have *regrets*. She learned from doing, but damn she wished she'd learned all this all those years ago and gotten him out.

"You're not the boss of me, Sam," Nate said, helpfully interrupting her little pity party. "You understand that, right?"

"Yeah, I do. But we're a team. We do this together."

He studied her, eyes dark and arms crossed over his chest. It was the first time since back at his cabin in Tennessee that he looked at her with pure distrust. "We don't have to be."

That cut surprisingly deep. A sharp lance of pain right in the chest. She wanted to rub at it, to see if it was really there, but that felt like giving Nate more ammunition to hurt.

Before she could think of what to say—something flippant, or maybe *go to hell*, the little bell on the front door rang as someone pulled it open from the outside. Hadn't she moved the sign over to closed?

"Sorry, we're—" But she didn't manage to say *closed*, because it was Landon Bennet and Aly Cartwright standing there.

Voluntarily coming into *her* place of business, which meant they'd done it on purpose.

Sam opened her mouth to say something, but in the end, she couldn't think of even one word to say.

NATE DIDN'T KNOW what to make of Landon standing there. Maybe he'd come to yell at Sam for something, but he doubted Landon needed Aly in tow to do that.

So, he was here for him. Probably. Though Landon said nothing. Just stood there. But that hard, stoic gaze was on

Nate, not Sam.

"I need to talk to you," he said, his voice sounding old and gravelly and uncomfortably like Dad.

"Thought you wanted nothing to do with me," Nate returned, because why should he make this easy on Landon?

Landon hadn't made shit easy on him.

"I think, actually, he wants nothing to do with *me*," Sam offered with a sunny smile that he didn't think anyone here mistook for being *friendly*.

Landon turned his attention to Sam. "I know this is your place, and I apologize for invading it. But could you give us a minute?"

Nate noted Sam's surprise as matching his own. There was almost a *politeness* in that apology. Geared toward *Sam*.

What was this?

Sam didn't say anything right away, but once again the bell on the door interrupted anything she might have said. And Nate couldn't hide his continued surprise when Cal stepped inside.

Cal surveyed the room with his own shock. "Well, who knew this was Grand Central Station?"

Nate glanced at Sam when she didn't say anything. He figured she'd be kicking them out. Being snarky in *some* way, but she looked from his brothers to him, like this was his call. And she was here to support whatever it was.

Which made him feel smaller than he already did about his *team* comment. Even though they didn't *have* to be a team. He'd never fully agreed to be Team Sam. He was Team Himself.

But now he just felt like Team Asshole.

Maybe that was all that having the last name Bennet ever meant.

"What am I missing here at the family reunion?" Cal asked casually.

His demeanor reminded Nate of something he'd forgotten in all the years away. The way Cal had always liked to wade into tension, stir it up a little.

Nate had *hated* it as a kid. It used to make his stomach hurt when Cal waltzed in and said something *designed* to piss off Dad, or sometimes Landon. But Nate had also been fascinated by it. Had to watch every last reverberation of the argument, no matter how it twisted him up in knots to watch Dad or Landon yell, Cal act unaffected, *pleased even*, and then Mom always swooping in to somehow smooth it over.

And now they were all here, fifteen years removed from having anything to do with one another, their peacekeeper dead and their dictator somehow still pulling the strings.

Teams. Always on separate teams. Landon on Team Dad, Cal on Team Cal, and Nate on Team *I don't know what the fuck I'm doing.*

Or maybe that had been a kid's interpretation of adult problems. Maybe they each had more going on internally than Nate had ever considered.

Standing here in Sam Price's office, all tightly wound adults, that same old tension Nate had never had the language to express in the air sure made that clear.

"What the hell are you doing here, Cal?" Landon asked, sounding somehow exhausted and disgusted at the same time. "You working with them now too?"

So much for any politeness when he said *them* like one might refer to dog shit caked on their boots.

"I'm not working with anyone," Cal returned. "Why are *you* here? In the devil's very abode."

Landon sneered. "I want to know why he left." He gestured in Nate's general direction. "I want an answer to something in this godforsaken mess."

Cal nodded thoughtfully, his gaze turning from Landon to Nate. "I could stand to hear that answer myself."

So that he had his brothers' dark gazes focused on *him* for the first time in fifteen years. And he didn't fully know what to do with it. This moment that felt like the past and a dream but nothing like his actual here and now.

Marietta.

His brothers.

Sam Price and Aly Cartwright like strange little sentries on either side. Murder and mysteries. Secrets. So many fucking secrets.

Nate considered being petulant. Refusing to answer. It would feel damn good in the moment. And what did they care *now*? They didn't. They were just looking for some way to get Dad off the hook, not make amends with *Nate*.

Neither of them had even directly *asked*. No, just like usual, they were talking to each other, and he was this weird entity tacked onto the end, to be fought over or around. A pawn.

Maybe that was why war had felt so damn comfortable. He'd been living in the middle of one his whole life. Whatever weird peace treaty Mom and Dad had in front of them, whatever power trip Cal and Landon had always been fighting. Nate had never fit in. He'd just been … a bomb to be thrown about by someone else when it suited.

So, maybe this time he'd detonate himself. "Dad beat the shit out of me," he said, plain as day.

Landon reared back like he'd been slapped himself. But Nate was fascinated by Cal's reaction. Because his face went … pale.

Nate cocked his head, studied his oldest brother. "You don't seem surprised, Cal."

"I … am," Cal choked out. "I had no idea."

But it didn't sound convincing, and that had Nate—and everyone else in the room—staring at Cal.

Who cleared his throat. "Dad never laid a finger on me," Cal said, but in a way that had Nate paying attention.

It was careful. *Lawyer-y*, if Nate had to categorize it. Every lawyer he'd ever known knew how to twist and turn language to suit a moment—not tell the straight truth.

"So, who *did* you see him lay a finger on?" Sam was the one to ask.

Cal shook his head. "No one. No… No one. I don't…" He took a step back toward the door, but Aly was kind of in his way so he just kind of bumped into her, then looked at her like she was some kind of ghost.

"What's going on, Cal?" Aly asked, sounding soft and sad. "Jill said you were being weird at her place too."

"Jill Harrington?" Sam demanded. Which earned her a sharp look from Aly that Sam clearly ignored. "What's anything got to do with the Harringtons?"

Something had been found up there, that was what Sam's informant had said. *Evidence* they were looking into.

And Cal had been up there. What did it mean? Before they could get to the bottom of *that*, Landon had to throw out his usual demands.

"I want to go back to the *point*," Landon said. His gaze had never left Nate. "What do you mean, Dad beat the shit out of you?"

"I mean, the afternoon after Mom's funeral, when Dad wanted me to go out and do my chores, I told him no. I told him there was no damn point to any of this. If Mom was dead, what the fuck was the point in fixing a damn fence?"

Nate wanted to fidget. Rub the pain in his chest. Scrape his fingers through his hair. Do anything to release some of this pent-up … emotion, but the soldier was still stitched into him, and he stood perfectly, dutifully still and tried to recount the information. All fact, no emotion.

"He started with a shake. Just picked me up by the shoulders and started shaking me until my teeth were rattling. Started yelling about legacies and all the usual bullshit. Except he just … snapped."

Nate hadn't had to tell anyone about this in approximately fifteen years, and even back then he hadn't told Sam the whole story. Just that his dad was the one who'd done it. Back then, he'd tried to downplay it. Confusion and embarrassment and a million other things making the real truth of it too hard to actually verbalize to the girl who'd found him. The girl whose dad had no doubt killed his mother.

So this was like reliving something he'd spent years trying to forget, and since he'd never said them aloud, the words just poured out. Like they'd been piling up for years, waiting for a dam to break.

"He threw me against the wall. I wasn't even fighting back at that point. I couldn't believe it was really happening." Nate glanced at Cal, wondering if that was the source of Cal's weird reaction. Had something happened? Had he felt like it hadn't been real?

"But he wouldn't stop. He started hitting me. Closed fist, just pounding on me. It didn't occur to me to fight back at that point. Just to get out. I got a decent kick in, ran. Just ran. Out the house. Off the ranch."

Nate didn't want to look at anyone. He already knew what he'd seen on Sam's face, because he'd seen it when she'd given him money all those years ago. He figured denial or something akin to it would be on his brothers'. So, if he had to look at anyone, he supposed Aly felt safe.

She wasn't. Her eyes were wide, shiny, and her hand gripped Landon's shirt sleeve like it was some kind of lifeline. Like this was some kind of horror movie she was living through.

He couldn't take it. So he looked at Sam. She'd been his savior too many times to count. What was one more?

"I saw him," Sam said and her voice was surprisingly rough. Like the story affected her too, when there was no reason for it to. They hadn't even been friends. Just acquaintances. "After. Bloody and bruised. He'd collapsed right on the road, next to our mailbox."

"You saw him? You've known this all along and just…" Aly said. Almost an accusation, like Sam had kept something from her, when it was clear their friendship had ended around this same point. Maybe that was why she trailed off and never finished.

"And then what?" Cal asked.

Nate noted a tremor went through his hand before he closed it into a fist.

So he supposed that's why he looked at Cal when he recounted the rest. "Sam bandaged me up, gave me some money, and I ran away. Well, walked away anyhow. Hitchhiked. Did the homeless thing for a while. Once I was old enough, I enlisted. Deployed a few times. Quit fairly recently. Been living in Tennessee. That answer enough of your questions?"

Cal laughed. Bitterly. "Not even close, Nate."

"You never thought to tell us?" Landon asked, his voice surprisingly soft. "That you were alive? That he... that he did that?"

Nate couldn't take on board that there wasn't denial happening. Maybe there was surprise, but no one, so far, was pretending like it hadn't happened. And he hadn't fully realized how much he expected everyone to immediately take up for Dad. To tell Nate he was wrong, a liar, or worst of all, deserving.

He had waited fifteen years for every single one of them to invalidate that turning point in his life.

Had he thought to tell them? Nate considered, but those years were fuzzy.

He shrugged. "I don't really know. At the time, it just felt better to ... get out. To pretend it didn't exist. I was just in survival mode."

"And then?"

"The army was structure. It became home. Mom was gone, so what was the point in looking back here? Dad would just be here, running his same little kingdom of bullshit. I didn't want any part in it."

A silence settled over the room. Black and heavy. Ominous, but no one seemed to know how to break it. How to bring it forward.

It didn't surprise Nate, even with fifteen years between the last time he'd really been around Landon in any capacity, that he'd be the one to break it. To get to the heart of it. He was a hardheaded son of a bitch, too determined, too controlling, too rigid…

But he was no fucking coward.

"What's changed? What brought you back then?"

Nate didn't glance at Sam, even though she was the crux of it. Maybe someday he would have made his way back here. Maybe *someday* he would have felt the need. But mostly, he figured he would have kept on living in isolated autopilot for a very long time.

"Sam found me. Said there'd been another murder. I figured … maybe it was time to find the truth."

"So you brought him back to what?" Landon asked Sam, but his voice was little more than a rasp. Like he'd been physically hurt.

"To prove that Dad is capable," Cal supplied. He still sounded … winded, rattled, but there was a firmness to his words. "A character witness of sorts."

"Dad's not on trial. He didn't kill Sandy. He's not a murderer," Landon said, as if he could say it and make it true.

But the fact he sounded a little *desperate* made Nate wonder if maybe, just maybe, his story cast some doubts in

Landon's unshakeable loyalty.

Nate wanted it to feel like vindication, but it all just made him sick to his stomach. Why had he thought dragging any of this up would actually *heal* anything? The only healing was solitude in a little cabin in the middle of nowhere Tennessee, far away from the ghosts that haunted him.

Except wasn't that the point? No amount of solitude and *away* had gotten rid of those ghosts.

Half of them were standing in this room right now.

"So, what prompted this great reckoning?" Nate asked, wondering if any answer would be anything but a wound, and because he did wonder, his questions were bitter. "It's been days. Days when Dad remains free and clear. Why did you suddenly need to know why I left?"

Landon didn't speak right away. His gaze was on Aly, and there was worry there. A worry he didn't extend to his brothers. But maybe that wasn't fair when neither Nate nor Cal had stayed. Aly had. She'd no doubt been right by his side all this time.

"Something isn't right," Landon said, shaking his head a little. "I want to figure out what."

"Maybe if we work together, we can make it right," Sam said.

They all turned to look at her, and Nate saw that she looked like she usually did. Tough. Certain. Like she didn't care what anyone else thought.

But there was something about the way she *held* herself that made him wonder how much she actually cared.

Landon glared at Sam. "You mean if we work together, you can find a way to get your dad off the hook at the cost of ours."

"I mean find the truth, Landon," Sam replied, with a calmness Nate wasn't sure he'd have been able to find, situations reversed. "Because I'm not afraid of it. Whatever it turns out to be."

Nate studied her. He could tell she meant it. Because she believed, wholeheartedly, her father was innocent. No doubts there, when maybe she should have *some*.

Nate glanced at Landon and saw a whole slew of doubts. Doubts Nate felt too, bone deep. He looked at Cal and saw the same.

"He's no saint," Nate said, because it seemed the thing everyone in this room—except Sam—was afraid to admit. "Why should we be afraid of whatever truths he might be hiding?"

Landon said nothing, but he turned on a heel and left. Pushing out of the door with such force the bell rang wildly.

Aly looked at Nate. "Because it changes everything. That's why," she said, then she turned to hurry after Landon, but Nate hoped his words followed her out the door.

"Change is life, Aly. Whether we like it or not. Hiding from it doesn't stop it."

Chapter Nineteen

Honor's Edge Investigations

CAL HELD HIMSELF very still. In not going after Landon and Aly, he figured he'd probably made his choice.

Or maybe Nate's story had shaken him just enough that he didn't want to go anywhere near the ranch they were no doubt headed back to. Maybe it wasn't so much a choice as a … a…

Okay, it was a choice. It was a choice to stand here, to believe Nate, to feel this old … horrible thing twisting inside of him. Making all the confidence and certainty and *strength* he'd built up from sheer grit feel like it was on an ever-shifting foundation of dust.

"I don't want to make it seem like alcohol is the answer here, but Christ I could use a drink," Sam said. "Anyone else?" she asked, moving into a small room off the main one.

Cal managed a glance at Nate, who was staring at him intently. "Sure. Why not?"

Sam returned with a bottle of whiskey and three coffee mugs that were a little worse for the wear—chipped and coffee stained. She set the mugs down on the big desk in the main room, poured a healthy dose of whiskey into each of the three coffee mugs.

She took one, took a big gulp. "Help yourselves," she said, waving at the other two mugs. Nate took one, so Cal followed suit. He stared at the amber liquid in the odd cup. Then figured what the hell. He didn't pound a gulp like Sam, but he sipped. Looked around.

The main room of the office was dim. Night was outside. But inside, three people sat around a big desk, drinking whiskey out of mugs, digging into old pasts that should probably stay buried.

"Murder makes strange bedfellows," he offered when the silence got to be too much.

"Cal." Nate said this with a kind of ragged exasperation.

He'd recounted Dad *beating the shit* out of him with such… A mix of stoicism and shock, something that resonated within Cal in ways he didn't fully understand. Didn't want to.

Why would anyone be shocked about something that happened fifteen years ago? But there were pieces of his childhood he still … didn't fully believe were real sometimes.

Except his reaction to Nate's story wasn't *real*. "He didn't hit me. Really," Cal felt the need to explain. "I just wasn't surprised he'd do that to you, Nate, because … it wasn't real. It wasn't."

"How could it not be real?"

It was Sam who asked this, with a surprising gentleness. And Cal figured she was well-versed in how to question people in her line of work. Because considering *Sam* over the information at hand made him feel less like he was being haunted by some parallel universe version of himself.

"I had this dream, years ago. And it was *only* a dream.

Your story made me … remember it for whatever reason." Cal shrugged jerkily, then went ahead and took a hell of a gulp of burning whiskey.

"Tell us about it then," Nate said. He didn't have Sam's gentleness, but in a way it was better. It was more like … doing what Cal was ordered to do. Not his strong suit, but it gave him a framework for how to proceed.

It was an odd memory. Cal couldn't even call it a memory. It was just that when Nate had told his story, Cal had felt this … vision almost. Like remembering a scene out of a movie. Except instead of actors, they were all people he knew.

And he was in it.

But maybe he should approach it like that. A movie. A story. Recounting the scenes in his head that were just dreams. One by one.

"It's like any dream, really. A mix of real and nonsense. The dream starts real enough. The bedroom I shared with Landon, when we first got our bunkbeds, and you were first born. You wouldn't remember, but when you were a baby, they put your crib in that room. Most of the time Mom would just have you sleep in a bassinet in their room at night. The crib was more for naps and stuff."

Cal remembered it too clearly. How hot it had been up in the top bunk, but that he'd been terrified of getting down the ladder in the middle of the night. But he couldn't tell anyone that, because he was the oldest. Landon was too little to climb up and down the ladder in the dark, but he was brave.

Dad had told him he should be brave.

But even when he had to go to the bathroom at night, he'd just hold it until daylight crept around the windows and he could see the ladder. Trust it was there.

"I heard—in my *dream*—I hear a thud. A scream. Crying. I was afraid of getting off the top bunk in the middle of the night, that was real enough, I guess. So, in the *dream*, I just laid there." Cal ran his tongue over his teeth, trying to keep that barrier of reality up so the fiction of the dream didn't take over. "Then Mom came in, put you in your crib. She … it was like she knew I was awake, because she climbed the little ladder, crawled into bed with me and told me it would be okay."

"What would be okay?" Sam asked when he didn't continue.

Cal shook his head. "I didn't know. Not at first. It was dark, but a little sliver of moonlight was coming through the curtains, and when it hit her face, it was all bloody."

He could still see it, like it was burned into his brain. He'd been so scared he hadn't even been able to scream. Everything inside of him had seized up in terror. And Mom had just held him and told him it would all be okay.

Cal cleared his throat, had to in order to get through the rest. "But in the morning, there was no blood. Mom was fine. Everyone was fine. It was a dream. Just a dream. It never happened again."

Cal watched as Nate and Sam shared a look, one Cal couldn't read.

Cal downed the rest of his drink. "How could it have been real? You're thinking it was. That he hit her. But there was no blood in the morning."

"That you remember," Sam said in that gentle way.

"It was a dream. Probably a dream from then, so I was like *five*. It's not about remembering. Whatever the dream was, it was about not understanding."

Sam nodded, clearly not going to argue with him any longer, but her gaze turned to Nate. Who looked ... angry. Just plain fucking angry.

"That house wasn't happy," he said, arms crossed over his chest, eyes blazing with unleashed fury. "It was a fucking tightrope walk. And I don't think any of us fully knew it. Except you. Because you're the only one who chose to leave, all on your own."

"Maybe happiness is a myth," Cal said, a thought that haunted him more than he liked to admit when he was in a courtroom, twisting mistakes to his own advantage. Watching criminals and victims alike behave honorably or horribly at any given moment.

"Maybe," Nate agreed. "But when you go out in the wild world, you learn people didn't grow up the way we did. And you start to see the fucked-up cracks."

Cal couldn't argue with that. It was a succinct way to put what college had been like, part of why he'd been so reluctant to return to Montana, to visit, to come back to all the glaring cracks that existed even before Mom had died.

"Landon can't see them. He never left. Same goes for Aly. I can't even blame them for it."

Sam made some kind of noise. Maybe it was a laugh. Because *she* could blame them. She blamed all of them.

Except Nate. Who she'd helped run away all those years ago. Because he'd been bloody and bruised.

Cal saw that flash, his mother's bloody face in the moonlight. A dream. A fucking dream. But had it been symbolic of … more? Of something underneath those cracks he hadn't understood … but had felt?

It made him nauseous. Or maybe that was the whiskey. Or maybe he just needed to get the hell out of Montana.

"Is it possible, just *possible*, Dad was the one who killed her?" Nate asked, low and serious.

Grim and determined and adult and alive. An ex-soldier. A man. With real life experiences outside their childhood. Which had felt normal in the moment but hadn't since Mom died.

Was it possible his father had killed his mother? It was a question no one had dared ever ask him, though he'd known back at the time some people *had* wondered. Before the trial had brought out the whole story of Gene Price hounding Mom. Before he had been found guilty.

It was a question he'd never allowed himself to wonder about, because he believed in the court of law. In Gene Price's guilt. Was his dad a lousy son of a bitch? Particularly when he was drinking? Yeah. He was.

But a murderer?

"And now maybe this Sandy lady?" Nate continued. "Because that is what he does? That is who he *is*?"

We don't need you here. Go home, Cal.

Words of a careless father, but not a *murderer*. But Cal knew, from years of experience at this point, that violent criminals didn't all look or sound or seem like one thing.

He knew a lot of people saw what he did as getting guilty people off, but he saw it as making sure every person got their inalienable right of due process of law. Not just to prove they were innocent, or not guilty though.

Sometimes, to prove they were. Sometimes, he lost a case, because there was nothing but pure, unadulterated guilt. And then making sure the punishment suited the crime.

Was it possible, just possible, that Dad was a murderer? In some way, shape, or form? Yeah, it was. "We'd need evidence. To … determine that. To prove it."

"So," Sam said evenly. "Help us find it."

He flicked her a glance. He didn't have the hatred for her that Landon did. He understood, too well, the way people supported their loved ones. Innocent or guilty. But he couldn't say he trusted her the way Nate seemed to.

"We'll see," he said. He set the mug, now empty, down on the desk. "I should get going." Of course *going* meant back to the ranch and that had him hesitating.

God, did he really want to go back to the site of all these questions? Fuzzy dreams and bad feelings and a truth he couldn't deny—no matter what he might have *dreamt* or not, Dad *had* hurt Nate. When he'd been a scrawny little teenager.

The thought of it, the way he could too easily *imagine* it, made him sick to his stomach. That and the dream and the cheap whiskey were a roiling problem, there in his gut, and what happened if he went back to the house and Dad was there? What happened if he…

"You don't have to go back there tonight if you don't want," Nate said, as if reading his mind.

"What am I supposed to do? Have a sleepover with you

two?" he replied, probably too acerbically considering that Nate was trying to be … kind, Cal supposed.

"There's the Graff," Sam replied dryly. "I bet you can probably afford it."

"Indeed I could." It wasn't a bad idea.

Maybe it made him a coward, but it wasn't a bad idea. Nor would getting in his rental car, driving to Bozeman, and flying back to Texas and staying there for the rest of his life.

But he knew he wouldn't do *that*, even if he didn't quite know what he was going to do. Staying *here* wasn't an option though. He needed to move. He needed to … think. To get a handle on something.

He glanced at Sam, then Nate. No, it couldn't be done *here*.

"I'll be in touch," he said, then shoved out of the building into a quiet, chilly Marietta night with no clue where he'd go from here.

SAM WANTED ANOTHER drink, but with Nate still hanging around, she decided against it. Besides, she had so much work to do. There was new evidence and … and…

She didn't know what to make of Cal's dream. Part of her wanted to believe it was just the truth, not a dream—a memory. Benjamin Bennet had beaten his wife, and that was proof enough he was a murderer, wasn't it?

But part of her, the rational part she seemed to access more and more these days, knew it could have easily been a dream. If there was no proof it had been real, why would it be?

But maybe, *maybe*, it had been born out of a seed of Cal knowing they weren't safe, even when he was a little kid.

"You could gloat if you wanted," Nate offered grimly.

He was still staring at the door Cal had walked out of. Landon and Aly had walked out of.

She shook her head, still not sure any of this had actually happened. Except, it had. Landon Bennet had walked through those doors and listened to Nate tell his story. Landon Bennet had looked shaken. Like he had *doubts*.

And Sam wanted to hate him. God, she did. But between Nate's recounting of what happened to him and Cal's recounting of his dream, Sam was having a hard time thinking of all of them as anything other than victims in one man's warped life.

"I don't want to gloat. Even if I thought this was somehow enough to get my dad off the hook, I wouldn't want to." She pushed off the table. "Some asshole—be it your dad or someone else—ruined so many people's lives that night. And then again, with Sandy and whoever else loved her. She has parents. Siblings. Nieces. And for what?"

"Yeah, death tends to be pretty fucking pointless. I think that's what makes life … well, the point of having one."

"He's a philosopher," she muttered, feeling irritable and riled up and a million other things.

Cal *maybe* was on their side, if there were even sides. He might work with them and Landon…

She didn't think there was a snowball's chance in hell Landon was on their side, but he hadn't tried to argue with Nate. He hadn't refused to believe that was what happened.

It felt like some kind of miracle that changed very little.

"You have a lot of time to philosophize in the army," Nate was saying. "All that *waiting*."

She wanted to feel amused. She knew he was trying to make some kind of joke, lighten the mood maybe. But she couldn't smile or laugh. She was still stuck on that moment when Nate had rotely explained what had happened to him, and his brothers had *reacted*.

She'd been half afraid they wouldn't believe him. Had he been afraid of that? Was that part of why he'd stayed away? It made her heart ache, and it made this whirling *mess* inside of her worse, so she did what she always did when she was more lost than she wanted to be.

Aimed for something that hurt. "You never saw Ben hit your mom?"

Nate shook his head. "No. Over the years, I've looked back. Sifted through memories, trying to find some … evidence, some *sign* that Dad was capable of that. I could tell you a million little things that *maybe*, as a whole, look like he was some kind of abusive asshole all the time. But I could also tell you a million things I remember that prove the opposite."

Sam sighed. No easy answers. No, there had never been any easy answers. Why should she expect any now?

"You didn't say anything to them about Aly not being on the list."

"Neither did you," she pointed out, because she didn't know what to say about it. About the ways all his family stuff twisted inside of her, somehow dividing what had once been nothing but laser focus.

Nate sighed. "One sucker punch felt like enough for one night."

"It wasn't a sucker punch, Nate. It's something that happened to you. If it's a punch to them, that's on your dad. Not you." She watched as he seemed to consider that, turn it over in his head. She was almost sure he rejected her point, even though she was *right*. But he didn't argue with her.

"I should head back to the cabin," Nate said, studying her with something she couldn't read in his expression. "You should get some sleep."

She knew that was probably true. On both counts, but she worried about him now. Going to that cabin alone. Bearing the weight of all *this*. And now his brothers had come and stirred up even more old weight.

She wanted to find a reason to keep him here. Keep an eye on him. Make sure *he* slept and ate. But she couldn't think of a single reason that made any sense, and Nate moved for the door.

She moved with him, scrambling for something to say. He glanced over his shoulder at her, something flitting through his expression.

"You don't have to worry about me, Sam."

She shrugged and turned away from him, embarrassment slithering through her. "Who said I did?"

He didn't say anything, so she thought he left. But when she finally turned, ready to lock the door and call it a night, he was standing there. Half in. Half out.

"I appreciate it though," he said.

Then he was gone. A shadow in the dark night outside. And she had the strangest feeling in her chest, a kind of cracking down the middle. Pain, but a warmth to it. Because if he appreciated it, it meant something, right? All of this *meant* something?

She looked around her dimly lit office, feeling for the first time in a long time that something was within her reach. The truth. Her father's innocence being proven.

She'd thought it would make her giddy. Happy. Determined. But there was a weight in her stomach. A mixture of fear and anxiety and worry.

For everyone involved.

Chapter Twenty

The Bennet Ranch

Aly drove back to the ranch. A few tears leaked over and onto her cheeks, but it was dark aside from her headlights outside. Landon shouldn't see them. God only knew what was going on inside his mind, his heart.

She still hadn't fully absorbed everything they'd learned. She still couldn't fathom… She had known Benjamin Bennet all her life. He'd been her father's best friend, her dad's *hero*, and after Dad had died, Ben had always been kind to her, included her, supported her, and protected her.

She didn't know that she'd call it a loving relationship. Ben wasn't a *loving* kind of guy. He was hard, rancher stock. Her father had been that way too. The only softness Aly had ever really encountered was Mrs. Bennet and a few teachers over the years.

But that was just … life on a ranch. Life when you were an orphan. Sure, it sucked not ever having a mom and losing her dad so young, but what if she'd had no one? She'd never once been left on her own. Maybe Mrs. Bennet had died. Maybe Ben wasn't exactly a warm, cuddly man. But … she'd had stability, and she knew a lot of people in her situation had never had that.

And then there was Landon. He'd always been there. He wasn't exactly *cuddly*, sure, but she knew he cared. He stood up for her. Protected her. He wasn't exactly good with tears, but the few times he'd come across them he'd sat with her just the same. And over the years, he'd come to treat her like a partner or an equal, and it was the only relationship she'd ever had that felt that way.

So, she needed to be there for *him*. Stop worrying about what *she* felt about this. It was his dad. His brother. *His* past.

She pulled the truck into a stop in front of the main house. Before she'd even put it in park, he was out of the truck. Stalking up to the house, with something like purpose in his gait.

It made Aly nervous, so she scrambled after him, hurriedly wiping the tears off her face in case she had to follow him inside. But he came to an abrupt stop, staring up at the house. It was dark except the porch light. Which cast an eerie glow on Landon. She stayed in the dark, as she watched his breathing go shallow and he started to shake his head.

He started hitting me. Closed fist, just pounding on me.

Nate had said all of that, looking somehow just like the teenager she remembered and like this stranger of a man, all rolled into one. Reciting the facts of being beaten by his own father.

Benjamin Bennet. A man she knew. A man she looked up to in honor of her father's devotion. Maybe she'd seen him lay into people over the years—Cal, Landon, ranch hands, Sandy. But she'd never seen him lay a *hand* on anyone.

This had to be some … mistake.

But Landon was standing here, and he hadn't said anything. He hadn't said *anything*. Like somehow this whole evening had flipped him upside down. And she didn't want that. She couldn't *stand* that. She wanted everything to stay exactly the same. Firmly on the foundation they'd been building together all these years.

"Maybe he's lying," she whispered, finally finding the bravery to say those words. Even if they were on a shaky whisper. "We don't know him, not after all this time. We don't know what Sam said to him. Maybe it's a lie."

Landon looked back at her. Heartbreak in his eyes.

"You believe him?" she asked, even though she saw the answer right there on his face.

"It didn't even occur to me not to," Landon said, his voice little more than a rasp. "What does that say about it, Aly? That it didn't even occur to me to think it was a lie? Some guy I haven't seen for fifteen years says Dad beat him bruised and bloody, and I *felt* the truth in it."

She wasn't sure what she'd felt. Shock and horror. No, she hadn't immediately rejected the scenario when Nate had been telling the story. But if she thought about it, she had to.

She had to.

Unless… A new, terrible thought gripped her. "Landon." She moved closer to him then, even if it put her in the beam of light. Even if it meant Landon saw the traces of tears on her face. She had to touch him. Reach out and put her hand on his arm. "Tell me he never hit you."

He made a sound—a sharp intake of breath that made her incapable of taking one of her own.

"He never *hit* me," he said, in that same quiet rasp.

But the *way* he said that made her want to throw up.

"Then what *did* he do?"

Landon was still shaking his head. "Not before. Not when I was a kid. It isn't… He didn't hit me."

The tears were threatening again, because he was saying what she wanted, *needed* him to say, but it wasn't enough. It wasn't enough. "Landon."

"Those years after … when he was drinking hard … he never hit me. Never beat me. But he'd get mad, and sometimes he'd lose his temper a bit. Throw something at me. Give me a shove. I was too big for it to matter. I wasn't a kid. He was just … grieving." He was breathing harder and harder. "I told myself he was just grieving."

It was too much. How was it all breaking apart? Cracking into a million pieces. Everything she knew. Everything she held onto.

Landon, mostly.

"We need to go inside," she managed to scratch out.

He was shaking his head before she even finished the sentence. "I can't go in there. I can't…"

She began to pull him with her. "We'll go to my side," she said, trying to be firm.

Trying to hold it all together as she pulled him across the yard and then into the entrance of her wing of the house. She led him all the way to the couch and then nudged him into a sitting position. His head fell into his hands.

"I'll make us some … coffee or … tea … or hot chocolate. Something warm. It's cold. Isn't it cold?" Lord, she was babbling. Panicking. If she was going to make any of those things, she'd have to go through the door that connected her wing to the main kitchen.

But she could get him a bottle of water. *What the hell is he going to do with a bottle of water?* She didn't know. She just had to get him something. She had to *do* something.

She sucked in a deep breath as she marched over to the little refrigerator where she kept a few things in case she didn't feel like making herself decent enough to go into the main house. She grabbed a bottle of water, then marched back to the couch. She held it out to him.

He looked at it, then her, but didn't take it. She had never once seen him look like this. Even at his mother's funeral. He'd been lost, hurt, grieving. But there'd been a sense of purpose underneath all that. That he had to keep everything together. He'd always put that on his shoulders.

Right now, Landon had no purpose, and nothing had ever chilled her more. She knelt next to him, putting her hand on his knee.

"We need to start at the beginning," she said, trying to be firm. Trying to find Landon, a Landon she recognized instead of this lost stranger. "What happened that made you want to talk to Nate?"

He looked down at her hand on his knee, his brows coming together. "Dad found the knife you put in his drawer. He was mad. He said he'd had his pocketknife all along."

"Why ... why would he have lied?"

"I don't know. I didn't get an answer out of him. I just lost it. All the years we've been pulling him along, trying to keep him afloat. All these years, we have carried the weight of everything, and he has only ever added new weights."

Landon pushed to his feet, her hand falling off his leg as he did. And at least it was *something*. Movement. Reaction.

"I was so furious he'd put us in a position where you might be caught in the crossfire, and something about that… I don't know. It made me think of Nate. And that felt like something I could do. I could know. I had to know why Nate would leave like that. Cal was one thing. He was always leaving. Always one foot out the fucking door."

Aly rubbed at the lance of pain in her chest because no doubt Landon was questioning everything now, just like she was.

Had Cal always wanted to leave, had that foot out the door because of him, like they'd always thought? Or had something spurred him, like it had spurred Nate?

But if there were things that spurred them, things that caused it, it meant everything she'd ever believed for fifteen years might be a lie, and that wasn't possible. It just wasn't possible. They had to be logical, not emotional here.

"Okay, so. Everything … every bad thing happened *after* your mom died." Aly got to her feet, leaving the water bottle forgotten on the ground. "After she was murdered. I'm not excusing it. He was so wrong to hurt any of you, but … if it was after, he didn't…"

Landon turned to face her. "Aly."

There was something so stark and awful in the way he said her name then. She found herself moving away from him. Away from *this*. But when his dark gaze met hers, she couldn't. She couldn't leave him with *this*. No matter how little she wanted to engage in it.

"When Nate was telling that story, true or not, it reminded me of something."

Aly took another step away. She knew, without hearing

it, that she didn't want to. She didn't want this. But he kept talking.

"It was junior year. I was supposed to have baseball practice after school, but it got canceled. Nate still had track, so he had to stay after. I was excited practice was canceled because it meant I could go riding with you, no Nate."

It felt like a million years ago. High school and the rides they used to take. The way the three of them had been a ranch unit. But Landon had always been eager to shake Nate off, and Aly... Well, she'd always been eager to have Landon to herself.

"I wasn't supposed to be home that early," Landon continued. "No one was. She was in the kitchen. She turned, surprised to see me. She tried to hide it, but I'd had enough to recognize it. She had a black eye, fairly fresh. It sure as hell hadn't been there in the morning."

Aly felt as though her heart stopped. She even shook her head, a kind of denial that she didn't even know why she needed so badly. It just couldn't be true.

"I asked her what happened. She told me she'd just had a bad run-in with a horse. Laughed it off. Maybe it was. Maybe I'm only remembering it in this light because of Nate."

Everything was being torn apart. The foundations of her entire life, hacked to pieces. Mrs. Bennet with a black eye. Junior year? That was only a year before she died. Before she'd been *murdered*.

"Maybe it was just a damn horse," Landon said. "It was just the one time. One time. Maybe it was exactly what she said."

But she heard it in his voice. He didn't believe it. Maybe he wanted to, but he didn't.

"But you're saying maybe it wasn't."

He inhaled a shaky breath. "I look back… I look back and I see cracks. I have since she died. And I didn't run away like Cal and Nate. I couldn't. So I tried to fix them." He looked at her then, that lost look on his face. "Did I just hide the important ones, thinking I'd fixed something?"

She shook her head, but she couldn't tell him no. She couldn't take this away from him. Hadn't she done the same? They'd done it together. Tried to smooth over anything that didn't fit the world they wanted to see.

"All these years, I have never once let myself wonder," Landon said, like every word was a great effort, raked over hot coals and sharp gravel. "Never once, not for a second, could I let myself think *what if he did it.*"

But he'd voiced it now. And his eyes were a little wild, so she crossed to him. She didn't want to believe it, but more, she didn't want *him* to believe it. She didn't want him to lose the foundation he'd built. *They'd* built. Together.

"Gene Price was tried and found guilty, Landon. Gene Price didn't just *happen* to get out of jail a few weeks before Sandy was murdered. Maybe your father isn't perfect, not a saint like Nate said, and maybe we've spent so much time defending and protecting him that we've forgotten that, but that doesn't make him a murderer."

"Are we so damn sure?"

He was hurting her, he could see it in her eyes, and Landon hated it. He wanted to put the words back in his mouth. Handle this himself. He'd been so pissed at Dad for putting Aly in the middle of this by lying about the knife, and now Landon was doing the same damn thing.

Maybe you're the same.

Because the last thing he wanted to do was make Aly cry. He knew she'd been crying in the truck, but she'd reeled it in. Tears were threatening again though, and it wasn't that he blamed her. No, he blamed himself.

He had to fix this. He had to fix all of this. But he didn't have a clue how to fix the careless upheaval Nate had just introduced into their lives. Fifteen years he'd white knuckled his way through life, sure he was right. Sure he was the only one who was right. To stay. To fight.

But when Nate had recounted that story, Landon could see it. So vividly. Didn't he see it all the time? Dad's temper. And sure, Landon always saw Dad reel it back in. Maybe he should believe that over Nate's fifteen-year-old recounting of a moment Dad had *snapped*. The day he'd laid his wife of twenty some years to rest.

But Landon had spent the past fifteen years working his ass off to keep that snap from happening. Because, without ever fully realizing it, he'd feared it.

He couldn't anymore. Not just because he was a grown man, but because Aly was at stake. She was too willing to put herself at stake.

"Here is what we're going to do." He took her by the shoulders, led her back to the couch. It was his turn to nudge her onto it.

Because she relied on him. He was in charge of this whole sinking ship, and maybe he couldn't stop it from sinking. But he could save her. He had to save her. And saving her felt like his own floatation device. If he had something to *do*, something to *accomplish*, they could survive this.

"In the morning, I'm going to go down to the police station with a new list. I'm going to say it was a mistake that you weren't on it. That Dad gave you a pocketknife a long time ago, and I just forgot."

She was shaking her head, but he didn't let her mount an argument. "You're not going to get in trouble over trying to help. I won't let you. We're done protecting him, Aly. If he's innocent, we don't need to protect him. And if he's not…"

He didn't know how it had all changed so quickly. Yesterday, he'd been so *sure* of his father's innocence. He had been so sure of everything.

It wasn't like he was so positive now that Dad had killed Mom. It seemed … so farfetched. Why wouldn't it have been Gene? There was evidence against Gene. An entire trial had found Gene *guilty*.

But where had those conclusions been affected by the reputation Ben had—that his entire family, and Aly, had supported? No matter the cracks. No matter the past.

Maybe if Nate had come to him with that story then, everything would have been different. But the combination of Aly lying for Dad, Dad lying about the pocketknife, then tracking Nate down and hearing … all of that.

Remembering things he didn't want to remember. Mom's black eye. The tension in that house. How easy it had been to forget when his brothers weren't around. How easy to blame it on them.

But the three of them in Samantha Price's office was like, ripping away all the excuses and falsehoods he'd depended on to keep himself going all these years. If he could blame *them*, he never had to look at the root.

His father was the root of all of this. And there *was* violence there. There always had been.

Had that leash on it *snapped* when it came to Mom? When it came to Sandy? Would Nate have been a victim to it if he hadn't run away?

Was it all just a strange set of circumstances that didn't mean anything at all? Because wasn't it just as likely Gene Price had in fact killed Mom all those years ago in some thwarted attempt at an affair, then for whatever reason zeroed in on Sandy too? Mom's trial had made it pretty clear Gene had no love lost for the Bennets, going back long before Landon himself was born.

So didn't that make more sense? Even with this new information? And Dad *had* his pocketknife, apparently. So, whose pocketknife was missing? Why was he jumping to so many damn conclusions? Why did this feel like a rug ripped out from under them when it could mean literally *anything*?

Including, Dad had been lost in grief and taken it out on his son. Beginning and end of sad story.

It wasn't his job to know. His job, always, was to keep this ranch going. This ranch was the only thing he could save.

The ranch and Aly.

So, he'd give the police the truth and let them do *their*

job. Let Samantha Price do hers. And he'd stop protecting a man who would lie, who would let Aly take the fall for anything. He'd hand every truth over to the police and let *them* deal with it.

That was the decision. That was the thing to hold onto. "We'll let the police handle this. If Samantha wants to poke into things… If Nate does, that's their thing and that's fine. Our focus is this place, like always."

She was chewing on her bottom lip. "I don't think it's that simple, Landon."

"It is. We're going to make it that simple. We—"

"There's something … I didn't tell anyone."

He stood there, staring at her across the room, dimly lit only by the overhead light. She was wringing her hands together in the way she only did when she was really worried about something.

"I told myself it didn't matter, because we know he didn't do it. I told myself it didn't matter because it was just going to hurt everyone, and I just wanted… I just want the hurt to stop."

How many bombs were going to be thrown tonight? How many were going to destroy everything? "What didn't matter, Aly?"

"I heard…" She swallowed, looking up at him, her eyes swimming with tears. "The night Sandy was murdered. I heard your dad and Sandy arguing. Outside. Late at night. Long after he told the police he went to bed."

He didn't reel like he had at Nate's story. This felt more like a brick being laid upon his chest, pressing down, then a blow.

What had they all done? What spell were they all under?

"We'll both go to the police tomorrow. I'll tell them—"

"You can't tell the police that, Aly."

"But—"

"Do you know what kind of trouble you could get into for lying? You can't… You're not getting in trouble for us. You're not part of this."

She reared back, a bit like she'd been hit herself. And he knew she was sensitive about that, about feeling like she didn't belong, so he should have phrased it better, but he didn't know how. "I mean you're not fucked up with all of this. You're not a Bennet. This isn't your fight. It isn't your burden."

"I'm plenty fucked up with all of this," she returned stubbornly. "We have been in this together since your mom died. Since Nate disappeared and Cal stopped coming back. It is you and it is me. It's us."

"Yeah. It is. And I'm sorry—"

"When will you get it through your thick skull that I'm *not*? That this is where I want to be. That you are…" She trailed off, turned away from him. "I know you don't get it. But if we're deciding to be honest, to let the police do their job, I have to tell them this."

If we're deciding to be honest.

Was that what they were doing? He supposed it was. He'd been honest with Dad—that the grief and the drinking was no excuse. He'd demanded honesty from Nate and gotten it. Now Aly was throwing in a comment like *I know you don't get it…*

But he did get it. He'd always *gotten it*. But he'd made a

promise. He'd made a vow to himself. To her, whether she knew it or not.

"I need you to understand something."

She got very still, then shook her head. "No, I don't think—"

Maybe he should have let her stop this. But ripping apart everything meant this too, didn't it? Just rip it down to the foundations, and by God, she was the best part of his foundation.

"When your dad died, my mom set the three of us down and gave us a long lecture, about how you should be treated with kindness and respect. Then Dad made sure we understood you were part of the ranch, something to be protected. That no matter what happened over the years, we weren't to so much as *think* about touching you."

She turned, very slowly, to look at him. Wide-eyed, she said nothing. So he felt like he had to.

"I keep my promises, so I kept that one. Mostly."

"Mostly," she echoed, still wide-eyed. Still just *standing* there.

Not that he knew what he expected her to do when he was ripping up a foundation he'd laid, brick by brick, himself. Even if it had been because of his dad, he'd still done it. Honored it.

Mostly. "I'm only human. I can't say I never thought about touching you."

She didn't say anything to that. She was standing there so still, just staring at him. And he could be a hardheaded idiot, no doubt. But he wasn't completely ignorant to the fact Aly looked at him a certain way.

But she held herself back too, for whatever reasons she had. So taking this any further than just a clearing of the air, in this moment, was wrong.

"I should go." He turned, moved for the door.

Tomorrow he'd go to the police station. He'd handle everything. And they would go back to the way they were. And they would deal with whatever happened with Dad. Because that is what they did.

"Don't go." She'd barely said it above a whisper. "I don't want you to go."

He stared hard at the door. Found some strength inside of him to … be the better man. The man he needed to be. The man his father had never been—even if he *hadn't* murdered anyone. The man his brothers hadn't been because they'd run away and left him here with all these cracks and ghosts. Someone had to stand up, and maybe there was a part of him that wanted to let himself not be that guy. For once. Just this once.

But he was who he was. "It'd be fucked up, Aly. To touch you now."

"I hate to break it to you, Landon, but we're pretty fucked up."

Chapter Twenty-One

The Bennet Ranch

CAL WALKED INTO the main house at the ranch the next morning with a little more clarity. He'd made a conscious effort last night at the Graff to take out all the jagged, emotional pieces and put this down like he would handle a case.

If there was any chance Dad had killed Mom, they needed to figure that out. And it meant all of them working together. Putting together all the pieces of a past they'd all dealt with alone, isolated.

He didn't want to. God, he didn't want to, and even if last night had felt like a strange little truce, he was under no illusion that working together, rehashing a past they'd all run away from one way or another, was going to be easy, companionable, or painless.

But he could remember the lullaby his mother used to sing them. The way she'd walk them down to the bus stop when they were little, listening intently to all their little boy posturing, or taking whatever rocks or lizard they might present her along the way and treat them like treasure.

They'd all been a family once. And it wasn't all ugly, way back then. Maybe that was what made it so hard. It was fucking complicated.

But if Gene Price hadn't killed his mother, whoever did needed to pay.

No matter the pain.

So, Cal needed to round up Landon. Track down Nate. Get them all together in one room and create a timeline. From the beginning of what each of them remembered to the end. He'd been over the trial a million times, never quite satisfied with how it had turned out—even if he'd never suspected his own father, or felt Gene was innocent. It had just never fully sat right.

He'd figured that was the emotional, personal component. Now he wondered.

So they'd go over it. Whether any of them wanted to or not.

The main house was eerily quiet when he stepped inside. None of the usual morning smells of breakfast or coffee came from the kitchen. It felt all … wrong.

Hesitantly, Cal moved through the living room and toward the back of the house and the kitchen. Everything was quiet. Empty. And no coffee had been brewed yet—recently or even especially early this morning.

Had everyone lost their collective minds and slept in? Forgetting chores? It was impossible. Surely, it was impossible.

Then the door between Aly's side and the kitchen opened.

It was Landon. Coming out of Aly's side of the house. In the clothes he'd been wearing last night. When Landon saw Cal, he came to an abrupt stop. So they stood there. Both silent and still. Both staring at each other. And since Landon didn't immediately launch into excuses about why he might have been over there so early without having changed out of his clothes, Cal could only assume … he'd spent the night in Aly's space.

It was there, on the tip of his tongue. To be a dick. To put that pissed-off look on Landon's face by pointing that out. Maybe ask if all the pined waiting had really been worth it?

For once in his life, he didn't take it. "Morning," he offered.

"Morning," Landon returned, somewhat stiffly, clearly still waiting for the jab. When it didn't come, he offered his own olive branch. "You want coffee?"

Cal nodded. If this was a truce, he supposed they'd both just taken the first steps.

Landon went through the process of getting the coffeemaker going, and Cal went ahead and took a seat at the table. They went on like that, in complete silence, all through the coffee brewing. Landon got out one regular mug, and one travel mug. He poured coffee into each, then brought Cal the regular mug.

He slid into the chair across from Cal, and they simple regarded each other in more silence for the first few sips.

"I'm going down to the police station this morning. I'm going to say the list of pocketknife owners was accidentally incorrect and give them one with Aly's name on it. Apparently Dad has his anyway."

"I'm not sure what some pocketknife in a creek is going to do for anyone's case," Cal replied.

Landon nodded. "Yeah, it feels pretty irrelevant, but starting now, we're going to be as up-front with the police as possible. Even if it looks bad for Dad."

Cal nodded thoughtfully. He knew the *we* meant Landon and Aly, not anyone else. But it was good. The police should have all the facts.

"I'm also going to tell the police something I hadn't told anyone but Aly," he continued. "About the night of Sandy's murder. I ... lied to them before. I told them I saw Dad go to bed that night at ten and didn't have any indication he'd left between then and the next morning. But I did. I heard him and Sandy arguing outside around midnight."

Cal didn't allow himself to react at first. Lying to the police wasn't necessarily a problem—until you had to admit you had. Which told Cal what he needed to do.

"You need to let me go with you." Cal waited for the immediate, knee-jerk *no*. *We don't need you, Cal.*

It didn't come. Landon studied him. "You can help? I mean, isn't there some conflict of interest thing?"

"Sure, if I was officially representing the family, but I'm not. I'm just going with you as a kind of ... consultant. So you don't say something you shouldn't, and the cops don't try to pull one over on you. We can go over what you should say, what you shouldn't, on the way."

Landon took a sip of coffee, clearly considering. Then he slowly nodded. "I'd appreciate it. You got time now?"

"I've got nothing but time."

Landon got up, but before Cal followed suit, the door flew open, and Aly stormed out. She was in pajamas. Her hair was a mess. And her temper was *blazing*.

"I know you don't actually think you're going down there without me," she said, pointing at Landon.

"Aly," Landon said in that calm, authoritarian way that reminded Cal of Dad. That had always pissed Cal the hell off.

Looked like Aly was pretty damn pissed off.

"If you think…" She glanced at Cal, then straightened her shoulders and narrowed her eyes in a way that even *Cal* knew was bad news. "If you think you can sleep with me, then disappear and do whatever the hell you want, you're solely mistaken."

"Christ, Aly," Landon said with a groan. "I told you what I was going to do."

"And I told you I'm going with. But here you are. Sneaking off."

"I hadn't snuck anywhere."

"Yet!" She waved her arm around the kitchen. "Yet, Landon."

And Landon didn't *snap* exactly. That wasn't how he worked. But Cal watched in fascination as all that grim determination that had always been the very *essence* of Landon, even when he'd been a kid, slowly take over.

He straightened, he got very still, and he pinned Aly with that fierce, solid gaze. "I'm going to give them the new list. I'm going to tell them what *I* overheard Dad and Sandy fighting about. *I'm* going to handle it."

So certain he had to. Cal had never really sat and observed his brother while trying for detachment and understanding instead of all his deeply ingrained knee-jerk reactions. This was Landon trying to control things. This was Landon trying to do the *right* thing. Cal had always found it infuriating Landon was so sure his way was the right way, but for perhaps the first time in his life he wondered if that was Landon's own defense mechanism.

Against all the cracks in their foundations. Against all the ways he'd been left.

Maybe it had never been Landon's intention to leave. Maybe this ranch was somehow a part of him, the way Dad and their late grandfather had always talked about that Cal had never understood.

But he'd still been left, whether he wanted to be here or not.

"You?" Aly was yelling. "You!" She made a noise—somewhere between a scream, a groan, and that special sound only women could make when a man is particularly dense.

Landon glanced at Cal, jaw clenched tight. "Can you give us a minute?"

Cal held up his mug, because like hell he was missing this, even if it did piss Landon off. It was like finally seeing under all that armor his brother had been putting on since he'd moved from crib to toddler bed. "Still drinking my coffee."

"*I* am going to go down to that police station, and *I* am going to explain that *I* lied. Because I'm the one who did it, and I don't need your fucking *protection* just because your dad made you promise that however million years ago. Promise broken last night. It's over."

"Oh, that's real mature."

Cal let out a low whistle, which earned him a glare from

both parties. But Aly's glare whipped right back to Landon.

"If you leave without me, you'll see mature," she said, and then she stormed back into her wing of the house.

Which once again left him and Landon in the kitchen in silence. Finally, Landon moved. He threw back a gulp of coffee. "If you've got something to say, go ahead and say it."

"What would I say? Congratulations? You finally slept with your best friend like you always wanted to?"

"I should split your lip."

"Why don't you? We've done it plenty to each other." He surveyed Landon's grim face. "Nate's story makes it feel pretty shitty. Doesn't it?"

"Yeah, it does."

"Saves me a split lip. I'll take it."

"Do you always have to be such an asshole?"

"I'm a lawyer, Landon."

He *almost* got a laugh out of Landon on that, and he'd consider that a rousing success.

Cal leaned back in his chair, surveyed the door Aly had slammed, then Landon. "She's right, you know."

"I don't know that. I don't see why I can't handle this *for* her. He's not *her* shitty dad. And he never deserved her protection or the way she stood up for him. Why should she pay the price?"

"First, with me along, hopefully no one has to pay any prices. Second, because she's the one who made the decision to do it—whether Dad deserved it or not. And if there's any lesson learned in this godforsaken place that even *I* haven't been able to shake, it's that you have to face the music of your own choices. No one else gets to do it for you."

Landon looked at his mug, then over at Cal. "You think Dad learned that lesson?"

It was Cal's turn to study his coffee. Because hell if he knew. But maybe that was the whole point. "I don't know what I think on that front. Except that the three of us need to sit down and hash it out. Beginning to end. What we remember. What happened in isolation, and as a whole. We need—"

A frantic knock echoed from the front of the house. Landon set his coffee down and swore. "Now what?" he muttered, striding out of the kitchen.

Cal followed.

When Landon answered the door, a woman was on the porch. Tall, slim, with midnight-black hair and the eyes to match it. She wasn't just pretty, there was an elegance in the way she moved. Even with all that *frantic* in the air around her.

"Landon, is Aly here? I knocked on her door, but no one answered. I need her help. Or yours. Hell, anyone's." She glanced briefly at Cal, and in that moment, he recognized her.

She was the woman in the layers up at the Harrington place. Glenda Harrington's granddaughter caretaker.

"I can get Aly," Landon said. "But what's wrong? What can we do to help?"

"I can't find my grandmother," she said, and there was a sheen of tears in her eyes, but they didn't fall over. "She wasn't in the cabin when I woke up, and I haven't been able to find her."

Cal watched as Landon frowned. "All right. Well,

we'll—"

Before he could finish, Aly was bustling into the room, but she stopped short at the sight of Jill. Before rushing over.

"Jill. What's the matter?" She reached out and the women gripped each other by the hands.

"Grandma. She's missing. I can't find her anywhere. She's been … she's been walking around at night. I guess. I don't know if that's what happened. I just woke up, and she's not there. Not the cabin. Not the garden. Her shoes aren't there and…"

"Slow down. It's okay. We'll all go look for her, okay?" Aly looked back at Landon. "I'll take Jill in her car. Maybe you can round up a few of the hands on horses?"

Landon nodded. "We'll do a full sweep of the properties."

"Cal, maybe you can call the nonemergency line at the police department," Aly continued, already moving outside with Jill's hands still in hers, taking charge. "Explain the situation. Maybe they can offer a deputy to help us."

Cal nodded. "Sure." But neither he nor Landon moved right away as Aly and Jill hurried for Jill's car, parked haphazardly on the gravel drive.

Cal wondered if Landon was thinking what he was. "Is Dad home?" he asked, a cold, awful chill settling in his gut.

Landon looked at him, then the staircase. "He should be, but I didn't check."

"Before we do anything else, let's check."

Landon nodded grimly.

⭐

Aly felt Jill's anxiety on top of her own. It would have been a nerve-wracking situation no matter what, but with a dead woman in the creek a little over a month ago… It was just downright terrifying.

"I'll drive," Aly said to Jill, holding her hands out for the keys.

Jill shook her head. "I left them in the ignition."

Aly moved for the driver's side, but the sound of tires on gravel stopped her. She turned, shaded her eyes against the quickly rising sun, then noted it was Ben's truck ambling up the drive.

Ben was in the driver's seat, which settled all wrong. Why was he up, and out in his truck, this early? But then she noted someone was in the passenger seat.

A small, white-haired someone.

It should be a relief to see Glenda safe and whole. It should be a relief. Ben had found her. Brought her back here. All was well.

Nothing felt well.

Still, Aly moved forward with Jill as the truck came to a stop.

Ben immediately got out. "I should have called," Ben said apologetically to Jill. "I didn't have your number, but I should have thought to call Aly. I bet you've been worried sick."

"What happened?" Aly demanded, wondering if her voice was as sharp as it felt.

"She must have gotten a little turned around," Ben said kindly. He moved over to the passenger side of the truck, moving in front of Jill to help Glenda down and out of the passenger seat. "I think she might have twisted her ankle a bit. She's limping."

Jill immediately took her grandmother's arm. "Grandma…" She shook her head, clearly overcome with relief, even if there was still worry there. "Can you walk?"

Glenda nodded firmly. She didn't look at any of them though. She just stared at the blue sky ahead.

They all turned as the front door opened and Landon and Cal came jogging out. But then they stopped short at the sight of Glenda.

Aly watched them both turn their gazes from Glenda, to Ben, then to her.

She could only manage a little *I don't know* shrug before she had to turn her attention back to Jill.

"Why don't I drive you guys down to the ER so you can get her ankle checked out?"

Jill managed a shaky inhale. "I appreciate the offer, but I can handle it from here. Thank you. Thank you for being ready to jump in and help."

"Of course. Call if you need anything, okay? I mean it. Anything."

Jill nodded. With Ben's help, Glenda got into the passenger seat. He even whispered something to her that had Glenda nodding. Jill climbed in the driver's seat, gave a little wave, and then they were off.

Aly watched Jill drive away. She didn't want to look back at Ben. She was afraid all her doubts and worries and suspicions would be written all over her face, and she wasn't sure she could handle whatever his reaction to that would be.

Would he be angry? Disappointed? Hurt? Would he be

right to be?

"They'll be okay," Landon said, putting his hand on her back and rubbing up and down. "I know you'll worry, so why don't you plan on taking dinner up to them tonight? I'll handle your evening chores."

Aly managed to nod and swallow so her voice didn't sound as rough as it felt. "That's a good idea. Thanks." She wasn't sure he should be touching her like that, here in front of Ben.

Maybe she'd been quite happy to drop the *hey, we slept together* bomb in front of Cal when she'd been pissed off and worked up, but everything about Ben being around made her feel like … already cracked glass.

But because she did, Landon's reassuring hand on her back was a comfort, and she couldn't quite step away from it.

"All right. Well, I've got chores I'm behind on," Landon said. He looked from Aly to Cal. "I'll meet you in town later for that lunch."

Cal nodded slowly. "Sure."

What they really meant was going to the police station, at a time when Ben wouldn't be suspicious. What Landon really meant was cutting her out of the problems *she* had caused, because they could hardly both go to town for lunch and miss chores, especially if he was going to take her evening ones.

And he knew that he saw it as protecting her, and it wasn't that she didn't feel some sense of … *something* that he wanted to. That all these years she'd been so sure her ridiculous feelings for him were a *her* problem, or he was just impossibly blind, but no, he'd made some promise to his dad a million years ago.

God, it was so fucking Landon it *hurt*, and that had been an easy enough line to cross last night, with his mouth on hers, but in daylight it was so much more complicated.

And still, the lies he was trying to save her from had been her mistake. Her desperation. Not his. So, she'd have to find a way to get her morning *and* lunch chores done early, so Landon couldn't give one excuse why she couldn't go with him.

She set out to do just that, head for the stables, when Ben's voice stopped her.

"Aly, can I talk to you for a minute?"

She nodded, glanced briefly at Landon. His mouth was in a firm line. She could practically see the wheels turning in his head. They didn't trust Ben anymore. Nothing felt *safe* anymore.

But that was ridiculous.

"Go on to your chores," she murmured to him. "I'll be all right." She fixed a smile on her face, moved to Ben.

But everything had changed. For all of them. Landon was walking *slowly* away, and Cal was still surveying them from the porch. If she gave that too much credence, Ben might notice and then…

She just didn't know how to handle this with them all having doubts. She didn't know how to walk through this new life where the foundations she had spent the past fifteen years *determining* were strong and steady were unstable.

But she had *doubts*, not certainties. Maybe this was all … mixed up. Maybe Ben was the same man he'd always been, and they were all jumping to terrible conclusions.

"Maybe you can talk to that friend of yours," Ben said, his voice low so it didn't carry to Cal on the porch, or Landon still stalling on fully leaving the yard.

"Jill?" Aly returned, confused.

"You don't need to tell her I'm the one who's asking," Ben continued. "I don't want her worried that I'm upset about the trespassing, causing damages. It isn't like that. I just want to be certain Glenda's okay. Maybe if we understand what she was up to, we can help."

Trespassing. Causing damages. Up to.

Aly wasn't sure any of those words would have struck her as *wrong* if not for last night. If not for Nate explaining why he'd run away. If not for Landon believing him, remembering Mrs. Bennet's black eye. If not for all the *cracks* they couldn't hide anymore.

What damages could Glenda have caused? Why was maybe crossing the property line on a walk *trespassing*? She was an elderly woman, not quite all there. What would she be *up to*?

"Aly?" Ben asked, looking concerned. Genuinely concerned.

But Aly couldn't seem to find words, or the ability to act, or anything. She just kept trying to picture Benjamin Bennet beating Nate. Hitting Mrs. Bennet. Had she ever seen him that angry?

For a moment, she remembered how angry he'd sounded that night when he'd been arguing with Sandy.

He moved closer, and Aly had to hold herself still and fight the urge to step away.

He lowered his voice as he spoke. "If you're upset with

me about my drinking, about what I said to Landon yesterday…" He took a breath, looked off into the distance, and sighed. "I'm going to stop. Landon was right yesterday. Harsh, but right. I've let too many things fall on his shoulders, even if … losing Sandy was a blow. I shouldn't let that mean I'm not carrying my weight."

But it wasn't about *weight*. It wasn't even about all the ways Landon had been holding everything together for so long. It was like he was missing the main point. That before yesterday, they'd only been worried about *him*, because they cared about *him*.

And he thought it was about the work. Like transactions.

That doesn't make him a murderer, Aly, she told herself fiercely, making her head move up, then down. It felt too slow, so she did it again, trying to feel normal. "The ranch needs you," she managed to say, feeling icy straight through.

Ben nodded. "I know it. I'm going to do better. I promise. And you'll get to the bottom of Glenda wandering around on our property. Won't you?"

Aly forced herself to smile. "Of course."

Chapter Twenty-Two

Crawford County Jail

SAM SUPPOSED SHE'D slept *enough*. Maybe not well, and maybe it *felt* like she was running on fumes, but that was part and parcel with making progress on a case. *Any* case. Not just her father's.

She didn't want to discuss the progress with her father though, and she knew that made her ... weak. But she'd made a promise a long time ago, she wouldn't let too many days go between visits. So, she headed down to the jail, with plans to meet Nate after lunch at the police station so they could dig more into the evidence, and everything else that might be going on with Landon and Cal suddenly listening to what Nate had to say.

She didn't know what caused this dragging, dreading feeling. Usually, she was excited about progress, even if it was complicated. Usually, she was eager to visit Dad, even if seeing him in jail *hurt*, at least it was connection. At least it was hope for him.

She just didn't feel very hopeful, and it made no earthly sense since she was closer to proving Benjamin Bennet was a murderer than she'd ever been. Even if Cal's dream was just that.

If there'd been any violence *in* the Bennet home, before Nate's experience, there would be reason to look back. There would be a pattern. There would be *something*.

And still, sitting down to talk to her father required supreme effort to manage a smile. "Hi, Dad."

"Sammy. You look beat, sweetheart."

"We're making progress. I feel very positive about the direction we're moving in. Nothing is … certain. But there's movement. You and I both know that's rare." She smiled at her father, wondering why she couldn't find any sense of vindication. Of excitement. Every step forward just felt bleak.

But Dad had been there. All those years ago. And he'd been interrogated on his relationship with Benjamin Bennet—known to have always been antagonistic. His relationship with Marie—which he had claimed was friendly and nothing more, while plenty of people involved in the rodeo had suggested there were whispers.

But no fact. No eyewitnesses.

But they *were* friends.

"Did… When you were friends with Marie Bennet, did she ever say anything about…" Sam didn't know why she was having such a hard time coming out and asking. Coming out and saying it. She was hardly spilling secrets. Nate had never asked her to keep what had happened to him to herself.

But it felt … wrong, anyhow.

And how are you going to find answers if you're too afraid to hurt feelings? That had never been her. She couldn't let it be her now.

She leaned forward, forced herself to look at her dad. Focus on any potential connections. "I know the original trial went over this, but I'm just trying to put two things together. Overlap Marie and Sandy's cases, see where they match up. Did Marie ever give any hint she was unhappy with Ben? Or maybe even afraid of him?"

"Just like I told the cops and lawyers back then. She didn't talk about Ben with me. She knew my feelings on Ben."

"Then why would she be friends with you?"

Dad shrugged. "She never said."

"She never … asked you for help with anything? Never … suggested she might be unhappy. In all these years, you've never thought of something in retrospect and wondered if you should have brought it up during the trial?"

"She never asked me for anything. We only ever talked about the rodeo and our kids. Just like I said then."

Sam knew she shouldn't keep belaboring the point. Dad's story had always stayed the same. Because he was honest. He was telling the truth. He was *innocent*.

"When she talked about the kids … do you remember anything she said? About any of them?"

"Why are you asking me this, Sammy? Shouldn't you be focusing on Sandy? You need to find some evidence that links Ben to that murder scene, not rehash what happened to Marie. They weren't even murdered in the same place."

"Can you just humor me for a second?"

Dad sighed, leaned back in his chair. He looked around the room, like he was trying to cast back. "If I remember correctly, she mostly bragged on her boys. The oldest was so smart, going places. Landon was a rancher, through and through. Nate … I suppose she had some worries about him. About how he fit in with the other two."

Sam's heart twisted at that. Poor Nate. Always the odd man out.

"She did … I think she did say something once about the boys and Benjamin not getting on too well." Dad frowned, clearly thinking back. "I guess I don't remember how she put it, but I remember laughing. I told her if they ever needed an ear to bitch about their SOB of a dad, I'd be happy to listen. I think I even offered them a job at the ranch. Joking around but…" Dad shook his head, and Sam found herself waiting on a held breath.

"She wasn't laughing. I think she said something along the lines of she might have to take me up on that someday. Then… I don't really remember. Maybe we got busy with rodeo stuff. Maybe it was time to leave. I'm not sure. I only remember because the idea of any of the Bennet boys working for me tickled me to no end at the time."

Sam nodded as she let her breath out. It wasn't groundbreaking. She wasn't sure it even meant anything—it wouldn't, without all the context she'd been gathering.

She didn't know a thing about raising kids, but even *she* knew teenage boys were rowdy and oftentimes rebellious. Probably against their dads most of all. Maybe it was just normal stuff.

Or was it another crack?

Dad cocked his head. "Is that why you've got yourself connected to Nate Bennet? He doesn't just suspect his father, he hates him?"

Sam considered the question. Nate didn't speak about Ben with any … emotion, really. Everything about what had happened was very matter-of-fact with him. But wouldn't you have to hate the man who'd beaten you bloody? Who you thought was capable of killing your own mother?

"I'm not sure," Sam answered honestly. And she didn't know what else to say, but Dad was quickly getting fidgety.

"I still don't understand why we're rehashing Marie. Haven't they found any evidence from Sandy's murder pointing to Ben? I was sure they would by now."

"They never found any last time."

"Sure, but this time… It's different, isn't it? No fire."

"But a creek, and wildlife, and time. All the test results suggest Sandy was left to the elements for almost forty-eight hours before anyone found her. Evidence gets harder to come by in those conditions."

He leaned back in his chair, clearly frustrated and antsy. She wished she knew some way to ease this for him.

"I'm going to go talk to the police this afternoon. I heard a rumor there might have been some evidence uncovered on the Harrington property."

Dad scowled. "What possible evidence could be found on the Harrington property if Sandy was killed and left on Bennet property?"

"Nearly on the property line. Still, I'm not sure what it is, or where it was found. I just know the Harringtons found it. I'm going to go see what I can find. It might be another few days if things heat up, but I'll keep your lawyer informed and come back when I've got some real news for you."

Dad didn't say anything at first. He just studied her.

Then he nodded slowly. "You know best, Sammy, but I hope you don't go wasting your time on Marie's murder. I already did that unearned time. I want to make sure I don't do any more."

"I know, Dad. I want to make sure of that too." And maybe that was the source of all this anxiety, this terrible, weighted feeling. She'd failed for *fifteen* years. She was terrified to fail for fifteen more. And no amount of forward movement felt like answers.

Not *yet*.

"I've got to get over to the police station," Sam said, forcing a bright smile at Dad. "Lots of threads to chase up on. I'll keep you up-to-date, and I'll be back in a few days."

Dad nodded. "You don't have to worry about me, Sammy. Everything's going to be okay this time. You'll find that evidence. It'll all be good."

She wanted to believe him. She wanted to agree. But something just felt *wrong*. Still, she maintained her smile, said her goodbyes, and went through the steps to leave the jail.

When she met Nate in front of the police station, she was still trying to maintain that positive façade.

But he immediately frowned at her. "Everything okay?"

She didn't meet his gaze. Just straightened her shoulders and lied through her teeth.

"Sure. Let's go see what we can find out about this evidence the Harringtons found, huh?"

NATE MOVED BEHIND Sam as they walked toward the front door of the sheriff's department. He kept his mouth shut.

He didn't point out that every time he saw her after she visited her dad, she seemed depressed as hell. What was she supposed to be? Happy her dad was behind bars again?

It made sense that she'd be a little bummed out after a visit. It just seemed … deeper.

And none of his business.

"Is that…" Sam trailed off before they reached the doors.

Nate didn't know if he was surprised to see his brothers making their way out of the police station. After all, whatever had happened last night had changed things. For good or for ill, new cracks had been exposed.

He *was* a little surprised to see Aly with them. She was the first to notice him and Sam standing there. He watched something in her expression shift closer to hurt than felt fair. Because he wasn't doing this to hurt *her*, or anyone. Not then. Not now.

Back then, they'd all run around together in that smalltown way, but he'd been raised to think of Aly kind of like a sister. And still, hadn't he known, when he'd been beaten and bloody, that she wouldn't be the one to go to? Because she would have turned to Landon and … he hadn't known how that would go.

Landon seeming to believe him last night, even if he'd left somewhat abruptly, somewhat angrily, brought up too many old feelings of guilt, of hurt, of anger, of doubt.

Nate had long ago stopped trying to determine what was right. What was fair. He'd been a teenager. He'd just lost his mom. Just been beaten up by his dad. Whatever he'd decided, it had been the best he'd been able to do in the moment.

It had taken a lot of years, hell an entire *war*, to come to that conclusion. That acceptance.

Only to have it feel shaken in the moment.

"Fancy meeting you guys here," Cal said, in his usual slick way. But there was a seriousness under that little greeting that Nate couldn't miss. "Come to report a crime?"

"We want to talk to someone about what they found up at the Harrington place yesterday," Nate replied, figuring there was no point lying. "What are you guys doing here?"

Cal, Landon, and Aly exchanged looks. Looks that spoke to knowing what was going on, while Sam and Nate were left in the dark.

Nate didn't care for it.

"We need to talk. All of us," Cal said, ignoring the question. And Nate assumed that was his lawyer voice. No lazy jokes meant to hurt or stir up reactions. All business. "The ranch probably isn't the best place to handle this. Neither is somewhere public."

"What about my office?" Sam asked.

"Your office is pretty public, right there in the middle of Marietta."

Sam nodded. "Got any better ideas?"

"Why don't we meet at the creek?" Nate suggested, earning surprised and suspicious looks from the whole lot of them.

Nate shrugged. "It's private."

"And the scene of a murder," Landon muttered.

"Sounds fitting to me," Cal replied.

Landon rolled his eyes and shook his head but didn't mount any more arguments. "Aly's got something to handle this evening. We can meet there later. Eight, maybe," Landon said, as if he spoke for her.

And since she didn't offer anything, Nate wondered if maybe he did.

"Eight it is," Sam agreed. Then she marched right by them and into the police station. Nate hesitated, his brothers' eyes on him. But he didn't know what to say, how to make this not weird, so in the end, he just followed Sam.

She was chatting with the front desk attendant when he stepped inside. She turned to him, then gestured Nate to follow her over to a bench. They sat down, hip to hip.

Sam said nothing. He said nothing.

After a few minutes, a cop appeared from the stairwell. He made a beeline for Sam, who stood, so Nate did too.

The deputy looked Nate up and down. There was something *unfriendly* about it. Nate noted his nametag said MATHEWS, and he tried to remember anyone he knew with that last name but came up blank.

Which seemed fine enough because the deputy turned his attention to Sam.

"I told you not to do this."

Nate didn't care for the tone. Kind of whiny, almost. "Then why'd you come down?" Nate asked when he likely should have kept his mouth shut.

The deputy sent him a nasty look, but Sam was ever focused on the task at hand.

"I want to know about what was found on the Harrington property, Brian. You tell me that, I can leave you alone."

This *Brian* scowled, looked back at the stairwell, then shook his head. "Glenda Harrington was gardening when she came upon the blade of a shovel, with the Bennet Ranch brand on it, buried in the ground. Much like that knife in the creek, it's been there too long to be any connection to Sandy's murder. So, you can stop pestering me."

The Bennet Ranch brand on it. Too long buried to connect to Sandy. "What about my mother's murder?" Nate demanded.

Brian didn't respond right away, and even when he did, he didn't look at Nate. "We're looking into it."

"How long is that going to take?" Sam demanded.

"As long as it takes. You know that."

"Did you tell the Bennet brothers that while they were in here?"

Brian looked from Sam to Nate, then back again. "No. They came in to clarify a few things from their questioning."

"Like what?"

"None of your business," Brian replied, a little petulantly to Nate's way of thinking.

Sam scowled, but she didn't argue with him. "Well, fine. Thanks." She moved to go, but Brian took her by the arm. Sam raised an eyebrow at him, that had him immediately dropping her arm.

But he still leaned a little close. "You got a second?" he asked her. "In private?"

Sam sighed heavily, but she nodded, and they moved off to a little corner.

Nate could have pretended he wasn't watching them. He could have been stealthy, but he couldn't figure any reason why he should be. Maybe Brian *should* know someone was watching.

But it wasn't that interesting. Brian said something. Sam shook her head. Brian said something else, and even though he wasn't close enough to hear, Nate could clearly see her mouth make out the word *no* before she turned away from him and walked toward Nate.

Nate said nothing, just followed her out of the police station and into the sunny afternoon. She marched toward her car. She didn't look mad, exactly. Not upset. Just her usual determined self.

Still, he couldn't help wondering what that whole thing was about. Lover's spat? Sam sure hadn't acted like she was involved with anyone, almost all her time spent on this case, but maybe that's just because it was her focus as long as her dad was in jail.

"Don't look at me like that."

"Like what?" Nate returned.

She came to a stop at her truck, looked up at him. "Like you're wondering if I whore myself out for information."

"Christ, Sam," Nate muttered, immediately uncomfortable at how easily she said the word *whore*. "Not what I was thinking."

"Wasn't it?"

"No," he said firmly. He'd assumed relationship, not … *that*.

She shrugged. "Well, I don't. Brian just gets the wrong idea sometimes. Not my fault."

"No, it wouldn't be."

She slid a suspicious glance at him, and he really didn't

understand her a good ninety percent of the time. Why she'd be suspicious. Why she'd think he'd jump to conclusions.

"I don't like that everything is old," Sam said, frowning as she drummed her fingers against the bed of her truck. "Why can't we find anything to do with Sandy's murder? *She* was the one in the creek not all that long ago."

Nate didn't respond right away. Because he, for one, was glad. And maybe that was wrong. But he didn't care much about Sandy, or even Sam's dad. He cared about justice for his own mother. One way or another. Even if it meant his father wasn't guilty of *that*.

Still, he couldn't pretend it didn't all connect, weave together, and when that was the case… "Maybe they're far apart, but I imagine they connect. Even if only by the murderer. So maybe this old evidence will connect to Sandy. With the right investigative skills."

Sam frowned over at the mountainous horizon. Snow peaked and picturesque against a warm spring sky. "We have the right investigative skills, I'd say."

Nate was surprised how much he liked being included in that *we*. For all the ghosts that seemed to hover about him here in Marietta, it didn't settle on him as uncomfortably as he'd assumed it would.

He didn't know what to do with that, then decided he didn't have to figure it out until the case was solved.

"Let's go back to the office. Go through your mom's file again, see if anything about a *shovel* blade fits. I'll pick up some lunch on the way. Burger, fries, Coke?"

Nate nodded. Not quite sure why it hit him that she knew what he wanted, that she was offering to feed him, that it felt like they were this team. A weird team, but a team nonetheless. Something he hadn't had in a while.

He thought about his brothers showing up here with Aly. Agreeing to meet with him and Sam later.

They were all agreeing to work together. To find an answer. Nate wasn't sure what he'd expected when it came to coming home.

But it sure as hell wasn't that.

Chapter Twenty-Three

The Harrington Property

JILL HELPED HER grandmother out of her car, and then toward the cabin. They'd spent the better part of the day in town. First at the ER, which had taken forever just for a physician's assistant to tell her that Grandma was fine, just had a minor sprain. Grandma should probably stay off her ankle for a day or two, but the swelling was minimal.

Then, since she *was* in town already, Jill had run into the store, while Grandma had stayed in the car. Jill had picked up some necessities. Something to wrap up Grandma's ankle—that she knew her grandmother would never consent to. Restock the aspirin—for the both of them. A few grocery items.

She'd grabbed some books and magazines and puzzles for Grandma, hoping to find *some* way to keep the woman from traipsing about in the middle of the night, twisting ankles. On someone else's property.

Jill surveyed her grandmother, who continued to not communicate, even by sign. "Do you want some tea?"

Grandma shrugged.

Jill struggled not to snap, but she helped Grandma inside and into one of the dining room chairs. Without a word, she went back to the car and began to unload, then put away everything she'd bought.

Grandma didn't try to help like she usually did. She didn't even watch Jill, to make sure she was putting things where they belonged. She was looking out the window.

Once Jill was done putting everything away, she started to put the tea together. The weight of the day finally started to crash. Now that they were back in their quiet little world, it just seemed to cave in on her. How *perilous* it all was.

She turned and scowled at her grandmother. "Grandma. You scared a hundred years off my life."

Slowly, Grandma tore her gaze away from the window, then cocked her head and studied Jill. *Sorry*, she signed.

It didn't feel particularly genuine. Which pissed Jill off enough to demand, "What were you doing out there?"

Glenda shrugged. Then she signed. *I knew where I was.*

"In the middle of the night?"

Couldn't sleep. Just turned my ankle. Sat down to rest it.

Jill stared at her grandmother. She couldn't sleep so she went traipsing about in the dark without any way to contact Jill. Luckily, Jill had been taking care of her grandmother for three years now, so she knew better than to scold Grandma for that.

That would lead to even more nighttime walks. And Jill shuddered to think about the far worse consequences.

But all there had been was terror and a sprained ankle. Thanks to Benjamin Bennet, Jill supposed. But with *murders* happening in that same area, and the early hour, Jill was having a hard time feeling particularly *happy* that the man whose girlfriend had been murdered was the one who'd brought Grandma back.

"And Benjamin Bennet just *happened* upon you while you were sitting by the creek?"

She nodded. *His property.*

"Why were *you* on *his* property?"

I like to walk.

Jill was not immune to being frustrated by the grandmother she loved so much, but this was taking it to a whole new level. Circuitous answers were fine when it didn't really matter, but Grandma's safety mattered.

"What did Benjamin Bennet say to you?"

Grandma didn't sign anything. Just shook her head.

"Why are you being like this?" Jill threw her hands in there, then forced herself to take a deep breath and chill. "Why are you walking around at night?"

Can't sleep. But I think I will now. She got up, and Jill hurried over to help her, but Grandma waved her off. Limping a little into her bedroom.

"Grandma…" But Glenda closed the bedroom door behind her, and Jill didn't know what to do. She didn't have much time to think about it either. Someone knocked on the door.

Jill moved to answer it. Aly was on the other side, a soft-sided cooler in her hands. It looked heavy, but she held it up a little.

"I thought you guys might want some dinner."

Jill managed an exhausted smile. "You didn't have to do that."

"I don't mind. I imagine you had a rough day."

Jill moved so Aly could come inside. Aly went straight to

the kitchen. "Are you hungry now?"

Jill took her grandmother's vacated seat at the table. "I don't know what I am."

"Then you need to eat," Aly said firmly, and Jill was grateful that someone would swoop in and tell her what to do. Swoop in and take control. Because she didn't know what the hell to do about any of this.

Aly moved in quiet, which wasn't totally unusual, but eventually Jill began to notice … there was something wrong here too. In Aly's movements, in the *tenseness* in her shoulders. An anxiety. A pressure building.

"Is everything okay?"

"Of course," Aly replied, like a knee-jerk reaction. She piled a plate high with food then set it in front of Jill, before taking her own seat at the table.

But she didn't eat any food or drink any tea. Eventually, she leaned forward, looking at Jill earnestly. "I've just been thinking. About Glenda wandering around. It's… I think … whatever you can do to keep her inside, I think that's best."

Inside. It had a cold chill running through Jill and made it hard to swallow the bite she'd just taken.

"What are you worried about, Aly?" When Aly didn't immediately explain, Jill put it together herself. "You're back to thinking that Gene Price guy didn't do it, aren't you?"

"I don't know. I really don't. I'm just worried." Aly looked out at the window, just like Grandma had. "Nothing seems to make sense anymore."

Jill could only look at her friend. Usually Aly was so … *strong.* Yeah, the murder last month had rattled her, but there was something different in her expression now. Something closer to fear.

"Did your grandma say anything about Ben?" Aly asked. "What he did when he found her? What they talked about?"

Jill shook her head. She knew she should eat, but she felt too tied up in knots to take another bite. "I asked. She didn't seem to want to talk about any of it. Why?"

"Ben wanted to... He asked me to ask... That is, he said he wanted to know what Glenda was up to—his words. It just ... felt weird."

"Up to? She was just walking." But Jill couldn't get over the fact that this was new. Grandma's midnight walks. And it was weird one of them had ended up finding Nate and Sam by that creek. By where Sandy was found.

And then one had ended up in the same-ish place, found by Benjamin Bennet.

Did Grandma ... know something? But then why wouldn't she say? Why wouldn't Ben say?

"But why the middle of the night?" Aly continued. "Why Bennet property?"

"It's like Ben said. She got turned around," Jill said firmly, even though Grandma had claimed she knew exactly where she was. Especially since she'd spent her whole life in these damn mountains *not* getting turned around.

And maybe Jill sometimes worried that Grandma's mental state might deteriorate, that this could be the first sign of that, but she just ... doubted it. There was something deeper here.

Or your overactive imagination is taking over again.

"You don't ... you've always been very adamant Ben couldn't have had anything to do with Sandy's murder," Jill said, almost like if she said it aloud now, it would make it true.

"I have. Yes," Aly agreed. She looked down at her hands. "I needed to believe that."

"*Needed?*"

Aly scrubbed her hands over her face. Then she just … unloaded. About going to talk to Nate Bennet last night. Landon's memory of his mother's black eye. All these little things that were stacking against the Ben Bennet Aly had thought she'd known.

Jill didn't know that she was surprised. She found Ben Bennet a neutral figure, but she rarely trusted a man whose wife had been murdered, particularly if it was followed by his girlfriend being murdered, even if it was fifteen years between the two.

Professional hazard, she supposed.

"You think he killed Sandy?" Jill asked Aly gently.

"No. Maybe? I don't know. I just know I suddenly have doubts about everything I thought I knew." She looked down at her hands. "Like, what was he doing out with his truck this morning, really early? If he was doing chores, he would have been on foot or in one of the UTVs. Did *he* even come home last night? I don't know. Landon and I were … busy."

Jill might not have thought much of that, except Aly's cheeks were turning red. It was a strange kind of whiplash— all this worry and fear and uncertainty, and then Aly *blushing* over whatever she and Landon had been doing.

Jill leaned forward, intrigued and amused in spite of all those other things. "Just what were you and Landon busy *doing?*"

Aly shook her head, but she resolutely did not meet Jill's gaze. "That's not important. That's not why I came over. I…"

"You've been pining over that guy since I met you. I suspect you've been pining over him your whole life."

"Half of it anyway," Aly muttered. "It's not the point."

"We can come back to the point," Jill insisted. "What were you and Landon doing?"

Aly chewed on her bottom lip. "Well, it's just… We were frustrated with Ben. I think both rocked by what Nate told us had happened. And it made us … look at some things we have been very wholeheartedly trying not to look at."

"Like each other?"

Aly blinked up at Jill. Like it was a *surprise* that she'd figured it out, when Jill had always figured it was clear to anyone within a fifty-foot-radius that there was an *undercurrent*—that went both ways—when it came to those two.

"Apparently after my father died, the Bennets sort of warned the boys off of me," Aly said, kind of shyly, quietly.

It made Jill feel for Aly. They were about the same age, and in some ways, Aly seemed vastly more mature. More *seasoned*. But in this, she seemed younger. It was sweet, and Jill wanted something to be sweet for Aly, who really had been chewed up a bit by life.

Not to mention this whole *everything*.

"So, you and Landon were *busy*. Message received. So, you're like … a couple now?"

"I… He didn't…" Aly shook her head. "We haven't had

a chance to discuss it."

Jill didn't like the sound of *that*, or the expression on Aly's face. All confused. "Well, just know, if he turns out to be an asshole, I've got your back."

"He won't. He's not. It's just complicated with everything that is going on. Which is why I came here. Which is the thing we should be focusing on. I'm worried." Aly's blue gaze met Jill's. It was shiny and she reached out to take Jill's hands in hers—a rare physical gesture. "I want you and your grandma to be careful. *Really* careful."

Jill wanted to go back to talking about Landon, because this... this was going to have her not sleeping tonight. "You're freaking me out."

"I know, and I'm sorry. But... Well, *I'm* freaked out, and I hate that you two are alone up here when there's so much uncertainty. I don't suppose…"

"She won't," Jill said. She didn't know if she would leave if she thought Grandma would. It felt cowardly—not her favorite thing to feel. But she also knew she was going to have a hell of a hard time sleeping until this whole murder business was a little more … certain on who did it. "*She's* not afraid."

Aly sighed. "Must be nice."

Chapter Twenty-Four

The Bennet Ranch

LANDON WAS BEHIND on just about everything, and while the hands had certainly pitched in and handled the absolute necessities, he hated feeling like he wasn't holding everything together.

Any other day, he would have worked well into the night, but they'd agreed to meet Nate and Sam down at the creek. So, he was walking from the stables up to the main house to meet Cal and Aly before they walked over to the creek.

What the hell were they thinking? This was all Cal's doing. He'd been talking about *timelines* and all sorts of what sounded like lawyer bullshit when they should be leaving this up to the *police*.

Except, he had to admit to himself, it was also laying out the truth, and Landon had realized in the short span of twenty-four hours they were all operating under their own truths, and somehow, that made it feel like they were all existing in a lie.

Landon knew that he was pretty good at burying his head in the sand, at living in denial of things that were complicated or complex. He preferred things to be black and white. Who wanted to exist in a gray?

But he'd never been any good at accepting a wrong when he knew something was right. And it was *wrong* to ignore that his father might be, at the very least, a lot more violent than most people had ever given him credit for.

He heard the sound of an engine, tires against gravel, and Aly's truck made an appearance on the rise. She parked, got out of the truck, setting sun glinting off the red of her hair. She looked sad, and he hated it. But she also walked right over to him, sad smile, sure, but pretty as always. Coming to him as always.

He'd gone through the day wondering if he'd fully imagined last night. Because they hadn't acknowledged it or discussed it—aside from her little outburst this morning in front of Cal.

And maybe he hadn't directly mentioned it because he'd been all the more determined to save her from going down to the police station when he'd woken up before her. To protect her, even if he'd crossed that line he wasn't supposed to cross.

But he didn't want to uncross it. He didn't want *that* always. God, he wanted something that felt steady and bright and *good*.

She'd managed to finagle going with them to the police station this afternoon in spite of him. She'd insisted on telling Brian that *she'd* been the one to keep things from everyone. Landon had assumed he'd have to stand up for her. Instead, there hadn't been much reaction. A lot of questions, but Landon didn't know what to make of the police's muted response.

He wasn't sure what to make of anything right now. Except her. She stopped in front of him, shading her eyes against the setting sun. She didn't offer a greeting, and he found he didn't really have one in him.

Except to embrace that little shot of good. So he just reached out, gently brought her into the circle of his arms, her temple on his cheek.

He didn't like anything right now. Not being behind. Not feeling suspicious of his own father. Not his relationship with his brothers or all these damn questions about their childhood.

But he liked this. Not holding himself just enough apart to avoid wanting too much.

This was just gentle and nice. This was just … home.

He heard the door squeak, then slam. On a sigh, he looked over his shoulder to see Cal coming out to meet them.

He released one arm, but not the other, keeping it around Aly's shoulders and her next to him. Cal's expression was grave as he approached.

"Dad's passed out in his bed," Cal said grimly. "Empty bottle on the floor."

"He told me he was stopping," Aly said, sounding hurt, leaning just a little into Landon's side. Like she was leaning *on* him, not just physically. "Just this morning."

Landon gave Aly's shoulder a squeeze. "It's never been quite that easy, Al. But if he told you he was, that means he's at least thinking about it, so we're past the denial stage."

Cal frowned a little at that. "You're familiar with all these stages?"

"Yeah. Not that he'd get help enough to know, but I suspect it's not just grief. More like fifteen years of alcoholism."

"Fifteen years. Or more?" Cal asked.

It was Landon's turn to frown. *Or more.* It had never occurred to him that Dad relying on alcohol might have preceded their mother's death, but … it seemed quite a few things he hadn't thought were true.

"Come on," Cal said. "I locked up the house. Let's go meet Nate."

They set off, but Landon didn't feel right walking next to Aly like things were as they had been yesterday.

Because they weren't. So he took her hand, linked his fingers with hers as they walked.

She looked down at their entwined hands, as if it was a problem she was working through. A familiar dent between her eyes when she was really puzzling something out.

He didn't know what conclusion she came to. Except she didn't pull her hand away. She gave his a squeeze.

They walked, hand in hand, over land that had been their playground, their foundation, their home for their entire lives. Every day the same, only punctuated by tragedies of loss.

But things weren't the same anymore, and Landon realized that by … building a shell around himself that he withdrew into to hide from dealing with the emotional onslaught of those tragedies, he'd become some version of a coward.

And that settled inside of him like another jagged edge, ready to cut through a lot of his foundations.

They reached the creek, followed it up its curve toward where it became the border of Bennet and Harrington land. In the distance, he could see Sam and Nate. They were talking, heads nodded toward each other a way off the bank on the Harrington side.

Landon couldn't say he liked Sam's involvement in this. But the whole story last night had eased some of the *hate* he'd held against her.

Blaming her for the upheavals of his life since his mother died hadn't been fair. He knew that, deep down, but it was a hard habit to break.

Even knowing she'd been just a kid herself and had helped Nate out of town. Away from Dad after a violent encounter. It was clear, even having not seen his brother in fifteen years, that Nate viewed Sam as a kind of savior.

He could wonder why Nate hadn't come to him, but Landon understood why. They weren't brothers who *went* to each other. And a few days ago, he would have said it was just … natural. Their personalities clashed. The three of them weren't ever going to be the kind of brothers who liked each other.

But last night had shifted a lens through which he'd once looked through everything. Because now he wondered.

If there was some … undercurrent to Dad—volatile, manipulative, *violent*—wouldn't it have behooved him to keep his sons from banding together? Against him?

Cal had always been the enemy. The *leaver*. Even before Mom had died, Dad had laid that mantle on Cal's shoulders, and Landon had believed, wholeheartedly, it made Cal less.

Had Mom viewed him that way? Looking back, Landon

couldn't think of a time when she'd said anything negative about Cal going off to college. Of course, Dad had enough negative for legions of college-bound kids.

With Nate. He'd been the baby of the family. Always coddled by Mom. Cal and Landon had been expected to toe the line, carry the load, but Nate had been given a lot of leeway.

Or was that just what Dad had put into his head? Did Landon have any concrete evidence in his memories of Nate being coddled? Of Mom treating him better? Or was that something he believed because Dad had said it so much it just felt like the truth?

They all exchanged muted greetings. Sam and Nate on one side of the creek. Aly, Cal, and Landon on the other. It felt a bit too much like a symbol. This divide between them, comprised of fifteen years, trauma, and something deeper.

Landon was beginning to realize it was much deeper.

Cal was the first to try to bridge that gap. "I'd come over there, but I don't want Glenda thinking I'm a trespasser again. Why don't you guys come over to this side?"

Landon watched as Sam and Nate exchanged looks. Like they were the best of friends. When, as far as he knew, they also had a fifteen-year gap in knowing each other, and maybe Sam and Nate had spent more time together in this week that he'd been back, but he didn't understand how they could fall into nonverbal communication so easily.

He glanced at Aly. She was also staring at them, with a thoughtful frown on her face like she was thinking the same thing Landon was.

But, in the end, their silent discussion must have been

agreement to listen to Cal, because they both used rocks to carefully make their way across the creek without getting too wet.

Cal gave them a little nod, as if welcoming them to their side. "I want a timeline. Of everything we remember. In regard to Dad. Mom. We all have different memories. Maybe if we put them together in a clear progression, we come to some sort of conclusion about fifteen years ago."

"What about one month ago?" Sam asked, referring to Sandy's murder.

"Should she really be here?" Landon asked of Nate.

Because maybe he could start finding it in himself to give Sam some leeway, but she wasn't part of this family. Part of this godforsaken mess.

"Yeah, she should," Nate replied firmly in a kind of commanding tone that brooked no argument.

A tone that had Landon actually considering what Nate had done out there in a world on his own. Become a soldier. Been deployed. No doubt seen terrible things. And grown up because of it.

"Sam has a point. That we have to look at it as one big picture. Two murders, fifteen years apart, both women involved with our dad," Nate said. "How can we ignore that coincidence?"

"Maybe the fact that the murders only seem to happen when Sam's dad isn't in jail," Landon said in spite of himself.

Maybe he was struggling to still defend his father, but that didn't mean he was ready to full on jump into the belief Dad had killed Mom and Sandy. Not when there was enough circumstantial evidence to have Gene Price convicted of one murder and investigated for the other.

"It's a point. *One* point," Sam said. "Another point is that the dead women have *one* thing in common. *Your* dad."

"It … it is just that one thing, though," Aly said. "I've been thinking about this. Mrs. Bennet. Sandy. What they had in common. Who they were. Why they both would have been targets. And I don't know, because… They were so different."

"How?" Cal said, clearly hoping to stop any more arguing and give Aly a platform.

"Mrs. Bennet was … permanent. She was his wife. The mother of his children. She was kind and … gentle. Not soft, but *gentle*. Sandy was … this isn't a dig, I don't want to speak ill of the dead, but she liked the drama. She liked to rile him up." She shook her head, glanced up at Landon. "Sandy had an edge about her."

Landon had to nod. He'd never understood his father's relationship with Sandy. Hated Sandy moving into the house. He'd tried to chalk a lot of it up to feeling like Dad was replacing Mom, but hell, it had been fifteen years. He didn't begrudge his dad a chance to move on.

He had begrudged *Sandy* though. She was loud, edgy, yes, just as Aly had said. She'd liked to needle people. In a way, she *had* felt like an opposite of Mom, and Landon had always figured that was the point. Any reminder of Mom would have been too … much.

"Aly's right. Sandy loved a scene. She found Grandpa's watch and started wearing it around the house. Dad would tell her to take it off every time. She would just smirk and they'd get into this big argument. They both knew what they were doing. It was nothing like Mom.

I don't remember Mom ever raising her voice. Except maybe to be heard over us. But not in anger. She was … she didn't get mad. She tried to make peace, and if she couldn't, she got sad."

"Yeah, that's what I remember," Nate agreed. "Disappointment over rage. She was quiet. Gentle."

When silence descended, Landon turned toward Cal, realized Nate had done the same.

But Cal wasn't meeting either of their gazes, like he couldn't agree.

IT WAS THAT old nightmare feeling gripping Cal. Just like when he'd seen Glenda Harrington the other afternoon. A panic beat inside of him, and something horrible was on the other side of it.

He tried to shake his head, to get rid of it. He had a plan, a goal, and he couldn't accomplish this next step in a case without obtaining information. Observing patterns.

"Cal?"

Something about Aly's concerned voice mixed with the panic made her sound too much like his mother. He had to squeeze his eyes shut, count his breaths.

"I'm fine," he finally managed to say. But he could *feel* all their eyes on him, even as his were squeezed tight, and he knew he wasn't fine. He could barely breathe. He couldn't *think*.

God, he hated it here.

"It's a panic attack," Nate said.

Cal shook his head. No, he wasn't panicking. He wasn't … but he couldn't think of any explanation for this physical response to this physical place. He didn't have any bad memories here. The only time he'd ever spent at the creek was messing around with his brothers when he was a kid.

Aly—he thought it was Aly though his vision didn't seem to be working quite right—put her hand on his shoulder. "Maybe you should sit down."

He shook his head again, but someone was nudging him, maneuvering him into a sitting position onto a large flat rock that was still warm from the day's sun. He tried to focus on that. Warm stone. Real life. Not this … feeling whirling inside of him.

Like that nightmare trying to root and take hold, change everything inside of him. He needed to fight it. He'd always needed to fight it, and he *had*. He had.

"Jill said you … you had the same reaction the other day," Aly said. He was sure it was her hand rubbing up and down his back. "Something … freaked you out."

Cal looked at Aly. Something about the way she was looking at him, sincere blue eyes, with just a hint of suspicion. Of fear.

He wanted to argue with her, and wasn't he good at just that? His whole life built on the foundation of *arguing*. Of twisting the facts *just so*.

But the words wouldn't come. Because what she said was true. The last time he'd been out here, he'd had the same reaction.

"You don't act like this anywhere else, Cal," Aly said, like she was accusing him of something.

"It's … nothing. Or, if not nothing, I don't know. I don't know. This … spot just makes me feel like…" If he hadn't been looking at Aly, maybe he would have had a better excuse, but the truth slipped out. "I'm in a nightmare."

"Like the one you had about Mom?" Nate asked, making Cal realize he hadn't shared that with Landon and Aly yet. Not in any purposeful way keeping it from them, just that … he hated going back over it. Hated…

He was going to put it on the timeline. Even if it was a dream, maybe it stemmed from something real. So it was going on the timeline, but he hadn't explained it to Landon or Aly.

"What nightmare?" Aly asked him gently.

Cal swallowed. There was something metallic in his throat. He looked around. Was that smoke he smelled? His chest got tight, his lungs cinching in on themselves. He struggled to suck in a breath. Couldn't.

Dimly, he could hear Sam recounting what he'd told her and Nate the other night. He tried to see through all the dark gray creeping around him. There was no nightmare. No smoke.

But the gurgle of the creek was trickling through his brain like a drumbeat threat. Like terror. Like fire and black shadows and things he needed to run away from.

Was that thunder rumbling the ground? Or his own heartbeat? Or pounding footsteps.

Get away. Get away. Everything will be all right. Mom al-

ways said everything will be all right.

"Maybe we should take Cal back to the house. This wasn't a good idea," Aly was saying. "We'll do this later. Somewhere more neutral."

But he was stronger than that. He wasn't a *child*. He'd withstood too much. He wasn't a coward, damn it. Whatever was happening to him was something ... something...

He felt something wet hit his head, then his nose. Rain. It was starting to rain. It was something to hold onto. To focus on.

"I'm okay," he managed to say. He was getting it together.

"Cal, you're *shaking*," Aly said, softly near his ear. "Besides, a storm is rolling in."

Cal shook his head. "We need to do this." So what if they got a little wet? It was warm. It was nearly summer.

"You know, I had a buddy in the army," Nate said, and when Cal managed to look up at him, his gaze was dark and steady. But something else, something too close to soft when you considered what their relationship had always been.

And there was a moment, just a moment, where he saw Mom in those eyes. Except they weren't seeing eyes. They were lifeless eyes.

"If we went on a dangerous mission, and it went a little sideways, if people got hurt, if it was ... traumatic in some way, he'd struggle to remember it," Nate continued. "Even the next day. Weeks, months later. His brain just blocked it out. Sometimes, he'd have a panic attack if someone talked about it around him."

Cal let out a huff of a breath, trying to laugh, blinking

away any fake images of lifeless eyes. "I remember things just fine." He gently moved Aly out of the way so he could stand.

A little silence fell. He managed to focus. To stand. To be himself. Because this place might have some weird effect on him, but he was Cal Bennet, and he knew how to research and put together a case.

A *case*.

He held onto that. The familiar rock that was his job. What he needed to do. "We need a timeline. We have Nate's last interaction with Dad. What day was that? The day of Mom's funeral or…"

"Cal."

It was Sam addressing him, which was weird enough he looked over at her. Her expression was grim, almost apologetic. Her hair was getting darker with the rain gently pattering down on all of them. One hit her cheek, traveled down the side of her face.

"What do you know about a shovel?"

Some kind of pain seemed to explode behind his eyes. A flash of something he withdrew from, even in his mind. Away from the pain. Away from the fear.

Away from the screams.

Cal had gone fully and utterly white, then taken maybe three halting steps away from them before throwing up, right there on the soggy ground. Aly rushed forward and Sam stepped back and away.

Nate stood exactly where he was, a cold, horrible dread

filling him, until it was all he felt. A numb cold.

Like the battle was just beginning, and no one would come out unscathed. Lightning cracked somewhere in the distance, followed by a roll of deep thunder.

"See? I'm just sick is all," Cal rasped as he stumbled away from where he'd been sick, but Nate recognized that glassy-eyed terror. Shock and trauma and the brain refusing to accept the truth. Because the truth was too God awful.

He didn't know what Cal's truth was, but he had a feeling it would change everything.

Maybe part of him wanted to run away from that, but Nate knew they couldn't. They couldn't keep running.

"Dad lost it the day of Mom's funeral, yes," Nate said evenly, watching Cal. "We could chalk that up to grief, maybe. But I've been going back, thinking of old things I excused or didn't think much of at the moment. There was that ranch hand. Didn't last long. When I was in middle school, I think. You remember that guy? Him and Dad got into it. A fist fight, and Dad fired him. Don't you remember? Mom holding the ice pack on Dad's mouth?"

The rain was picking up the tempo, but no one made a move to find shelter. Everyone was focused on Cal.

"Mom…" But Cal trailed off.

Nate thought he might be sick again, but instead he kind of fell forward. Onto his knees.

"It wasn't her," Cal started saying, not making any sense. "It was a dream."

Aly had rushed for Cal, but Landon stepped forward, gently moved her aside before he knelt down next to Cal, and Nate didn't know what possessed him. Landon and

Aly—the people Cal actually knew—had it handled.

But he went and knelt on his brother's other side.

"It was a dream. It has to be a dream. It was a dream," Cal was muttering, his palms planted into the ground.

Nate met Landon's gaze over the top of Cal's head, both of them completely soaked. Both in rain and grim acceptance.

His own heart was beating too hard. Not panic, or maybe it was. Just not the life-threatening kind.

"I didn't hear a scream. I didn't. It was dark. It was shadows. I misunderstood," Cal was saying. "Someone threw her in the barn. And it was already too late."

Jesus. Everything in Nate went taut. Horrified. *Too late.*

Had Cal seen Mom die?

He couldn't breathe through the thought at first. When he eventually could, he tried to think of it clinically, without any picture of the mother he'd known in his head.

Too late. An image of her, already dead, seemed to sear in his imagination. Her body moved into that barn, where she'd be burned. But already dead. Blunt force trauma.

A shovel.

But Landon was a step ahead of Nate trying to sort through that. Because he looked Cal right in the eye and asked.

"Cal. Was the someone Dad?"

Cal didn't say anything for the longest time. He was shaking. There were tears in his eyes. When he squeezed them shut, they mixed with the rain soaking all of them.

Then he nodded.

Chapter Twenty-Five

The Harrington Property

THE STORM SHOOK the cabin walls. The wind was howling now, rain pelting against the windows. Sometimes, Jill liked the wildness of these spring storms. Rain instead of snow was certainly a comfort.

But tonight, with everything going on, she just felt … edgy and anxious. She'd tried to curl up in bed and read a book, but she'd been so nervous Grandma would try to go out in this mess that she'd moved to the couch. The cabin was dark except for the little lamp she had on. Which flickered every time the thunder let out a great, shuddering roar. She considered getting candles lit, but that worried her too.

She got out her notebook and tried to write out some descriptions of the storm that maybe she could put in her next book … if her agent ever got back to her. It was a comfort, to think about work, to write out words that evoked the creepy feeling around her. For a little while, she could forget Grandma was traipsing the woods at night, and Aly was worried about a murderer on the loose and—

When a loud pounding started at the door, she jerked and screamed in surprise. She closed her eyes, blew out her breath. The storm—

Three loud thuds this time. Clearly made by human hands. Jill swallowed at the nerves in her throat and got to her feet. Grandma poked her head out of her bedroom door.

"It's all right. I'll just … see who it is."

Gun, Grandma signed.

Well, even though Jill didn't think the bad guys *knocked*, it might be nice to have something lethal in her hands. She moved toward the drawer where they kept the small handgun Grandma had taught her how to use, then she inched toward the door as another round of thudding started.

Jill eased the door open, the storm door remaining closed … until she recognized Aly on the other side. Jill quickly unlocked the storm door and held it open.

"We're sorry," Aly said, by way of greeting. "We didn't have anywhere else to go. Not right now."

Jill blinked, taking in the strange tableau in front of her. Five very wet, muddy people. Some she recognized, some she didn't. But she knew Aly wouldn't bring her threats.

"I don't think…" Samantha was trying to take a step back into the night, but the missing Bennet brother held her firm.

"Come on."

"He's right," Jill said firmly. Though her allegiance was to Aly, Aly was the one who'd brought Samantha here. "No use traipsing through this storm. Come in."

There was a sound from behind her and Jill looked out to see Grandma surveying the group of bedraggled visitors.

Have them take their boots off out on the mat. Collect wet coats. I'll get towels.

Jill wanted to scold Grandma for walking around on her ankle, but in the end, she couldn't keep the door open with the rain blowing in and all of them standing there dripping.

So, she took Grandma's orders and made them her own, telling everyone what to do and where to put their things. She surreptitiously put the gun back in the drawer, turned on more lights.

Grandma returned with towels, began to hand them out before Jill took them and nudged Grandma into a chair. "Take care of that ankle," she murmured, then handed out the rest of the towels.

Everyone offered thanks, except Cal Bennet, who took the towel wordlessly, looking down at the floor. He was white as a sheet, and not steady on his feet. It was the other Bennet brother holding him up.

"Is everything all right?" she asked, focusing on Aly, though she noted the entire group looked … shaken.

Jill hated to think about why that might be.

Aly ran the towel through her hair. She managed a wobbly smile. "In the grand scheme of things, yes."

"Can I use your phone?" Landon asked after he wiped his face with the towel. "I need to call the police."

This brought everyone's eyes on him, but he didn't falter. And when she handed him the phone, and there was no choice but to be quiet and listen because of the tiny room, Jill understood why the tension was tied so tight.

Benjamin Bennet was a murderer.

SAM STOOD AS much in the corner as she could. It was a tiny cabin, the common areas not really fit for five soaking-wet people and the two people trying to help.

Like anyone in the area, she knew who Glenda Harrington was, and since Glenda had gone mute some time probably before Sam had been born, they'd never spoken. But she'd heard the stories. That Glenda was really an evil spirit, witch, or whatever the prevailing story at the high school would be these days. Whatever might prompt teenagers to shriek and dare each other to head up the mountain in the dark.

Sam had never partaken. Much of her teenage days taken up by taking care of Dad one way or another. So, while she'd poked around up here for investigative reasons, she'd certainly never been in Glenda's cabin.

She knew *of* Jill Harrington. She'd seen her around. And news of Glenda's stroke and East-Coast granddaughter coming to tend to her had been the talk of Marietta a few years back. She knew Jill and Aly were friends, or at least friendly.

She also knew Jill wrote compelling mysteries that Sam herself devoured when she had time to read.

There wasn't a lot Sam *didn't* know about the players in this strange life she'd been bare-knuckle fighting through for fifteen years.

And still, it was weird in so many ways to be standing here. She had none of her usual determinations to wade in, forgo discomfort and embarrassment because meeting the goal was more important than being worried about how anyone might *see* her.

She was the oddest of odd men out right now. Not family. Not a friend to anyone except maybe Nate.

His focus was, rightfully, on his family. Because they'd just been rocked by the news their father was a murderer, their brother had witnessed it … in some way.

Sam, on the other hand, had just been vindicated.

So where was the joy in that? Where was the sweeping satisfaction of victory and righteousness? Why did she feel like crying? And not out of any kind of relief.

Landon hung up the phone, then stood there very still for a few moments before he seemed to draw himself together, wrap up any strength he had left and use it. He surveyed all of them, clearly knowing all eyes were on him and these next few steps were his.

These past two days had turned Sam's feelings about Landon upside down. It had forced her to see that while she still thought he was kind of an asshole, she understood his motivation, his dedication to his family, to Aly.

In this moment, he'd become the de facto leader, because Cal was falling apart. Aly was a wreck. And Nate was … this periphery thing to them still.

So Landon was taking it all on himself to handle it.

It felt familiar, and it caused an empathy she didn't want to settle itself on her heart.

"The police want to come talk to you, Cal," Landon said very gently. "Since we can't do it at the ranch with Dad there, I thought I could drive you down to the station. If that's all right."

Cal didn't say anything, but he nodded.

"Aly, maybe you could stay with—"

But Aly was shaking her head. "No, I'm going with you."

Everyone watched Landon for his reaction to that. Sam figured it would be all manly bluster, but he just inclined his head, a very quiet agreement. Then Landon and Aly turned their gazes to Sam and Nate, like they were the unit who would decide how to treat the outsiders.

But Nate stepped in.

"I drove Sam. We're parked on the public land. We can drive you back to the ranch to pick up a truck," Nate said. His voice was rough.

There was a moment when Nate and Landon regarded each other. Like neither were quite sure whether Nate should go to the police station or not. Sam wanted to insist that Nate go with them. That she could handle herself. She wasn't *part* of this.

"It'll be quicker for us to just cut through the property and walk to my truck," Landon finally said. "We shouldn't run into Dad, so it should be fine."

There was another fraught silence, but no one mounted an argument to the plan.

Jill tried to offer warm drinks, a change of clothes for anyone that might fit into her things, but everyone refused. Thanked her for the towels. Then traipsed out into the wet dark.

The storm had mostly passed. A little drizzle still fell, and occasionally thunder rumbled off in the distance.

They all walked in a group across the Harrington yard, but as they got to the creek, they had to take different paths. Cal, Landon, and Aly across the creek. Sam and Nate along it until they got to his car.

There was a pause—mostly just Landon and Nate pausing. Cal and Aly were moving across the creek, Sam was moving in the opposite direction.

But she heard what Nate and Landon said to each other. In unison.

"Let me know what happens."

"I'll let you know what happens."

Another pause and Sam watched over her shoulder as Landon and Nate stood there, regarding each other. It was Nate who moved away first, taking those sharp, military strides toward her and making up ground.

But Landon stood for a moment, watching Nate's retreat, before turning and crossing the creek himself.

Sam and Nate walked back to his car in full silence. He got in, started the engine. The headlights came on, and he drove them down the dirt road that would take them back to Marietta.

"You're quiet," he offered finally.

"What is there to say?"

"I don't know. Figured you'd want to gloat. Aren't you happy? You did it. This truth is out because you tracked me down, brought me here. You were right. You should be happy."

Sam watched out the window as the car moved through the dark, mountain night. Happy. Why didn't she feel happy?

"I thought I would be," she said, considering all the ways she thought this would go, and how none of the feelings she thought she'd have existed within her right now. "Or vindicated at least. But two women are still dead, and my dad still served fifteen years in prison. So, I guess it all just feels like a fucking waste."

"Yeah, I guess it does."

They were silent the rest of the way to Honor's Edge. Nate pulled his car to a stop in front of the building. Sam made a move to get out, but so did he. She stopped, looked over at him.

He shouldn't be here right now. She figured he knew that, deep down, but maybe… Maybe he'd been gone so long, alone so long, he needed someone to remind him.

"Maybe you should be with Cal," she suggested gently. "Brotherly solidarity."

"We've never had much of that."

"Maybe you could start."

His expression went … arrested almost. Like that had never occurred to him. Like now that it did, he didn't know what to do with that feeling.

So, she pressed on it. "Be with your family, Nate."

"I'm not sure I know how. It's been fifteen years since I've had a family."

"You'll figure it out. Together. I think … I think you all need each other now."

He looked at her then, that serious dark gaze of his intent. Like if he looked at her hard enough, he could find the truth in her words. Or maybe more accurately, the lie.

"I'll see you later," she said, and she forced herself out of the car. Away from … the whole Bennet situation. Maybe once she was on her own and didn't have to see the ragged effects of all of this on the three Bennet boys, she'd find some happiness. Some satisfaction.

She got out her keys as she walked toward the door.

"Sam?"

She stopped at her front door, turned to him. He strode over to her, a determined look on his face she wasn't sure she'd seen before.

"Maybe this all feels like shit, even though your dad was innocent and paid for it anyway. Maybe no one's really vindicated because we're all just damn victims in all this, but you found the truth."

She wanted to argue with him, even though she didn't know why. Fifteen years of hard work, and it had been in Cal's head the whole time.

But why had Cal remembered? Why had Cal come back here? Wasn't it because Nate had? That was on her. Her bringing him here, it was the domino. *She'd* done this.

She should feel victory. She just felt nauseous.

Nate reached out, gave her shoulder a squeeze. "So, thanks for that."

She managed a paltry smile. She couldn't find words.

He released her and walked to his car and got in this time, drove away. She stood there in her doorway, her heart feeling bruised.

It had felt like goodbye. And maybe it was. He'd done what he came to do. Benjamin Bennet would hopefully go to jail. With this new evidence, he'd have to be tried and convicted, no doubt. So maybe this was it. Nate was done and going back to Tennessee.

Benjamin Bennet would be found guilty of two murders.

Her father would be cleared, and hopefully this parole nonsense would be dropped.

Sam went up to her apartment, straight into her shower.

Where she cried until she was spent.

Chapter Twenty-Six

Marietta Police Station

LANDON SAT IN the police station next to Cal in a utilitarian room that was somehow both uncomfortable, intimidating, and bland. Brian had led them in here, and now they were waiting for a detective.

In the end, Landon had asked Aly to wait outside for them. It didn't feel right to bring her into this—and not because he wanted to protect her or save her from anything. It just felt like … Cal didn't need a bigger audience.

He supposed that was the only reason she'd agreed.

"The questions are going to be annoying," Landon said, trying to interrupt some of the anxiety that seemed to tie itself in knots all around them.

"Don't worry about that. I can out-annoying-question anybody," Cal said.

Landon thought he *almost* sounded like himself. The sarcasm. The sharp confidence. But there was something robotic underneath, and he was still pale. They'd dried off some, but their clothes were still damp and bedraggled.

The door opened, and Detective Hayes stepped in. But that wasn't what surprised Landon, it was the man behind him.

Nate.

"Since this seems to be a sibling affair, I thought you'd be okay with Nate being here, but we can do this one-on-one if you prefer, Cal."

Cal glanced at Detective Hayes, then Nate, then looked back at his hands. "It's fine."

The detective put a laptop on the table then took a seat across from Cal and Landon. Nate stood in a corner, leaning a shoulder against the wall. Landon didn't know what to make of him being here.

"So, why don't you explain to me what you told Brian when you called this in."

Landon opened his mouth to speak, but Cal was quicker. And he laid it all out, in firm, succinct statements. The nightmares that had dogged him. What going up to that creek, discovering that his brothers also had violent memories or interactions with Ben, had done to unlock something that had previously been out of reach.

"I've spent most of my life wanting to believe these things were just that... nightmares. Leaving, putting it all behind me. But a second murder... You can't discount who Benjamin Bennet really is."

Detective Hayes leaned back in his chair, took his time surveying all of them.

"That's quite a story," the detective said, not unkindly, though it had Landon bristling. Why would Cal make up a *story*? One like this?

"It paints a picture of what happened. What really happened," Landon said forcefully. "I have been a staunch supporter of my father, but... I can't be anymore. Because this is clearly the truth."

Detective Hayes looked at him, dispassionately. "It's not proof."

"I saw it," Cal said. "It's an eyewitness account."

"Cal, it's not that I don't believe you," the detective said, with a hint of empathy this time. "It's just that it's been fifteen years. We've got to convince a judge and the district attorney that this is … irrefutable proof. And it's not."

"Any lawyer will tell you they can consult a psychologist. At the trial. To discuss memory … issues like this. To prove it's a real condition that can affect people."

"Dissociative amnesia," Nate supplied, like he knew. Like he was an expert. "It's real. And Cal's right. A psychologist could testify in any case that it's viable. And if what Cal remembers lines up with what happened, why wouldn't people believe it?"

"Especially with our testimony," Landon added. He glanced from Cal to Nate. They were all, maybe for the first time in their lives, on the same page. "Now that we've all come together and put the pieces of our father's behavior on the same table, it paints a picture of violence."

Ironic that coming together would be over something this awful.

"It's still not proof."

"What about the shovel blade found at the Harrington property?" Nate asked. "The one that's having testing done on it? The one with the Bennet Ranch brand on it?"

Detective Hayes eyed Nate. "You've been palling around with Samantha Price, haven't you?"

Nate's expression didn't change. He leaned there against

the wall, arms crossed over his chest, as if nothing could ever bother him, when the Nate Landon remembered was bothered by *everything*.

Something his brothers had often taken advantage of.

"I've been consulting on an investigation," Nate said, equally as blandly as the detective.

"We're still running tests on the shovel blade."

"What kind of tests?" Landon asked.

"Some... potential DNA was found. It's being analyzed."

"It's the murder weapon. You never found it," Cal said, leaning forward. Insistent. "That's it. Of course it's it. He was carrying her *from* the Harrington property *to* the barn."

Detective Hayes inhaled, let it slowly out as he surveyed them all once more. "It's a stretch, but I'll take it to the DA. I can't promise it'll lead to an arrest, but we'll see where it goes."

"You'll let us know? Give us some warning?"

The detective shook his head. "I can't do that, Landon. Not with you living on the same property."

Landon supposed that was fair, though he hated it.

"While I've got you all here, would any of you be willing to submit DNA, should that be necessary?"

For a long moment, not a sound was made. Detective Hayes was making it pretty damn clear what that implied.

"You mean if it's our mother's DNA on the shovel," Cal said flatly. "You think it could be."

"Would any of you be willing to submit DNA?" the detective returned.

But he didn't have to confirm Cal's suspicions. Clearly

that was why.

"I will," Landon said firmly.

Cal and Nate agreed as well.

★

THE ONLY THING Cal really wanted to do was go back to Austin and dissociate all the fucking way out of this.

He felt that even *before* they made it to the lobby where Aly was pacing. She looked so worried. Pale and stressed. He felt like he'd done this *to* her. Which he knew wasn't sensible, but it felt that way all the same.

"How did it go?"

"They're going to look into everything," Landon told her, putting his arm around her shoulders. "Right now, we should all get some rest."

"I can't go back there," Cal said, stopping on a dime. Just the thought had his hands shaking again. He balled them into fists.

Landon and Nate surveyed him, then glanced at each other. Like somehow the three of them were family when all they'd been for a long damn time were strangers.

"I think I should go back," Landon said, sounding gentle and not at all like himself. "Do our best not to raise any suspicions. Cal, you can stay at the Graff. He won't think twice about that. Aly, maybe you could—"

"Go back home, just like you? Yes, precisely what I was thinking."

Cal wished he could find humor in the pinched look on Landon's face. In the way Aly wasn't going to let him play lone-ranger protector.

But he wanted to get in his rental car and drive as far away from Montana as he possibly could.

"I can drive you over to the Graff," Nate said gruffly.

Cal could have walked. Would have preferred it, except he didn't want to speak. Didn't want to … exist. So he let everyone usher him out of the police station.

The dark Montana night with its brisk cool, even here at the end of May, made him want to die.

"I'll text in the morning," Landon said when they reached his truck. "We'll figure out how to proceed."

Cal didn't even bother to nod. He just followed Nate down the sidewalk, toward his rental car.

Except. He didn't want to stay at the Graff, or anywhere in this godforsaken nightmare.

He wanted it to be a nightmare, but … it so clearly wasn't. The need to throw up was building again.

He stopped, bent over at the waist, resting his hands on his knees, trying to breathe.

Nate gave him a light pat on the shoulder. "My cabin's got two rooms. You could bunk with me."

Cal studied this brother of his that he really didn't know. They'd become men far apart from each other. Hell, Cal had thought Nate was dead.

"You shouldn't be alone," Nate continued. "You shouldn't be around Dad. Maybe it's not ideal, but it's better."

Cal straightened. Nothing was better. But he still didn't want to speak, so he got into Nate's car and remained silent as Nate drove out to the Reynolds ranch and its rental cabins.

He followed Nate from car to cabin, mentally calculating the time it would take to wrestle Nate's car keys away from him, drive to the airport, and fly anywhere. Maybe New Zealand. Antarctica. Siberia. Somewhere far, far away.

"When was the last time you ate something?" Nate asked, tossing the keys on a little table by the door. Cal wouldn't have to wrestle them away.

"I don't know," Cal replied.

"Sit," Nate ordered, pointing at the sturdy-looking table.

The sharp order seemed to grip him. He turned his attention from the keys to the chair. Eased himself into it. He put his palms on the scarred wood of the table, spread his fingers wide.

Dad's hands.

He balled them into fists, then shoved both hands under the table where he couldn't see them.

A few minutes later, Nate put a plate in front of him. A sandwich.

"Eat it," Nate ordered.

And again, being told what to do seemed to engage something in his brain. Nate took a seat across from Cal. He wasn't eating anything. He just watched Cal, for a long time before he finally spoke.

"I know people who've dealt with this. You should find a therapist to talk it out with."

"What's a therapist going to change about the fact the truth has been in my head for over fifteen years?" Cal returned, trying to sound flippant. Failing. "All this time it was just sitting there. All this time an innocent man was in jail, because of me."

"No," Nate replied evenly. "Because of a murderer, Cal."

"If I'd remembered…"

"But you didn't. Brains are funny things. Sometimes I wake up, and I can *feel* the desert all around me. I'm sure I've got a gun strapped to me, my boots on, missions to complete. I've been out for over a year."

Cal looked at his baby brother. He could remember him toddling around at Christmas wreaking havoc. He could remember trying to teach Nate how to drive but getting so frustrated because Nate never listened to any fucking instructions.

Now he was talking about guns and deserts and *mission*s, a grown-ass man Cal didn't know at all.

Taking care of him anyway.

"Why didn't you come to us?" Cal heard himself ask. Because it wasn't a conscious thing—asking him this. He didn't know where it came from. Just that it escaped. "That answer you gave when Landon asked was bullshit."

Nate was quiet for a while. When he spoke, it was with all the grave certainty mixed with wistful regret that spoke of being an adult.

"It wasn't, but I'm not sure I ever thought of it like that. Maybe if Mom hadn't just died, I would have. But there was nothing more I wanted in that moment than to get away from not just him, but all that grief, all that fear. The unknown felt more safer than … hurting like that."

Cal supposed he understood. Maybe everyone had known where he'd gone, but he'd escaped. Even before Mom had died. He'd always been running away from the painful memories it seemed his mind wanted to block out.

Or turn into dreams. Nightmares.

All this time…

"The thing is, Cal. You're the oldest. It makes sense you saw more violence. Before he or they figured out how to hide it. How to lock it down. If it was going on all our lives—and why wouldn't it be—it makes sense you got the brunt of it. It makes sense, especially when you were a kid, that your brain was not capable of rationalizing that trauma. So it forgot it, blocked it out."

Cal shook his head. He didn't want to think of it as all their lives. It was too awful. Because… "Why would she…" He couldn't finish the question. Couldn't put that even on his mother's memory.

"We'll never know. When you're feeling sorry for yourself, piling all that blame inside, just remember. He took that knowing from us too. *Him.* When he killed her."

Cal wished he could find some of Nate's bitterness toward his father. Some *vehemence*. It was there, bubbling somewhere underneath all this numb guilty exhaustion. "Maybe that's easy for you to say."

"Nothing's easy, Cal. Not a damn thing."

Chapter Twenty-Seven

The Bennet Ranch

ALY WASN'T SURE how she made it through the next few days. She was an anxious wreck. For a wide variety of reasons. It felt like they were in the worst holding pattern ever. Pretending like everything hadn't changed.

If it wasn't for Landon spending nights with her, she might have come completely unglued. But in the safety of his arms, she did manage to sleep. He stayed by her side during the day as they did chores together, and maybe it wasn't *necessary*, maybe she should have been able to handle everything on her own. Hadn't she been on her own for years and years?

Except Landon was always there. Always. He was her rock, and if that was a little codependent, she figured she could deal with that once this was all over.

Every time she had to deal with Ben, which was few and far between, she was a nervous wreck. He'd been in a habit of avoiding interaction as much as possible since Sandy had died, and now she only had to do a few things to make sure she only rarely saw him.

But rare wasn't *never*. Trying to smile and act normal had her nerves stretched tight. That and knowing he was drunk almost every time she did happen to have to deal with him.

It still upset her that he was back to drinking heavily when he'd made that proclamation to her that he'd stop, then she'd get mad at herself for being angry with him for something so pointless when he was a *murderer*.

She'd ended up telling Jill the whole story, after a few days of back and forth. But once she'd gone up for her usual weekly visit, Aly couldn't hold it in any longer. Jill barely left the mountain, so there wasn't really anyone for her to tell. And this way, she and Glenda were forewarned if something should … happen.

Jill had been appropriately shocked, outraged, concerned in her responses. She'd let Aly lay it all out, and something about speaking all this awfulness out loud to someone who wasn't involved eased a *little* of the tension Aly had been carrying around.

"Well, I better get back," Aly said when she'd eked out every last minute that could be spared, being off the ranch, being away from all that tension.

"I don't like you driving back there alone," Jill said as they both got to their feet and moved toward the door.

Aly forced herself to smile. "It's just a short drive. Don't start sounding like Landon."

Jill's mouth curved a little, but Aly knew her gaze was considering. Careful. "So that's going well?" Jill asked, trying to sound casual.

Well. Aly wanted to laugh. It was so easy and comfortable to just slide into being more than the friends they'd always been. Because as of right now, all they'd really added to the mix was sex.

"I guess it's complicated until we're done with this."

"And the police didn't give you any idea when that would be?"

Aly shook her head. "No. I think they're being careful. Even with Landon and me cooperating, we're too close to Ben. They know that's a liability. But I think it's clear, even with Cal's testimony, they need more."

"It's like my grandma, kind of," Jill said thoughtfully. "No doctors have given any physical reason she can't speak. The one psychologist she saw couldn't give a reason, since she wouldn't communicate with him, but his theory was it was trauma based. Part of her brain shut down because of something that happened. Just like part of Cal's did."

Aly nodded. "Yeah, I suppose it is similar." Which Aly had to admit, made her feel some teeny bit better. That maybe this was more common, more believable than she'd given it credit for.

"Would you hate me if I used dissociative amnesia in a book?" Jill asked. "Would Cal?"

Aly laughed in spite of herself. "Please. Maybe something good can come of this nightmare. You writing a runaway bestseller."

Jill snorted. "Maybe *you* should be the fiction writer." Then she pulled Aly into a hug. "Please be careful."

Aly nodded, though her throat closed tight. "I am."

She drove back to the ranch. Tension crept into her with every minute. She was so tired of feeling like she was walking some horrible tightrope. Because the end of this wasn't some happy thing. Even when this was all over, there'd be devastation.

She pulled up to the ranch to find Landon was sitting on the front porch swing. It was almost never used, so Aly was surprised it still held weight. She wasn't sure she'd ever seen Landon sit there as an adult. He was always busy. Always moving. Or he was going to bed. There was no contemplative sitting.

But he'd been waiting for her. Probably worried about her, even though he didn't need to be.

She got out of the truck, and he walked toward her as she walked toward him.

So it's going well? Jill had asked, with some concern. No, it wasn't going *well* because everything was a mess.

But it was somehow still right.

Before they made it to each other, she heard the sound of tires on gravel, turned just as Landon reached her. They stood hip to hip as a police cruiser rolled up.

Aly felt as if the blood simply rushed out of her, leaving her cold and frozen. The police were here. Did that mean…

Landon's hand gripped hers as two deputies got out. One was Brian Mathews. The other Aly wasn't sure she knew.

Brian approached Landon with a grim expression on his face. "Is Benjamin Bennet here?"

"I'll go get him," Landon said, dropping Aly's hand.

"If it's all the same to you, we'd like to come get him ourselves. If you'd show us the way."

Landon inhaled carefully and nodded. "Stay here, Al," he murmured.

Then he led the two deputies inside. Aly didn't know what to do. Go to her side of the house? Hide? Go do some chores? In the end, she just stood here next to her truck and waited.

She heard something like a shout from inside. She took a few steps toward the house, then remembered that both deputies had *guns* and no doubt knew what they were doing.

When they reappeared, Benjamin Bennet—the man who'd acted like a father, sort of, to her for the past near twenty years of her life—was being taken away in handcuffs.

Because he was a murderer.

He was screaming, fighting the officers, struggling against them and trying to get away. They held firm as he shouted and writhed.

"I didn't kill Sandy. I didn't! I loved her. She made me feel alive. I didn't kill her. I needed her." He was outright sobbing now. "Landon! Aly! Tell them!"

Landon came to stand beside her. When Ben looked over at them, Landon put his arm around her waist, turned her around so she didn't watch. He began to move her toward the house, even as Ben howled and yelled.

"They're arresting him for the murder of Mom *and* Sandy. They told him that in no uncertain terms," Landon said, his voice rough. Pained.

Aly looked over her shoulder. They'd finally gotten Ben in the police cruiser, and she couldn't hear him yelling anymore. "So why is he only yelling about not killing Sandy?"

"My question exactly."

Chapter Twenty-Eight

Rental Cabins at Reynolds Ranch

NATE KNEW IT was a strange thing to almost be used to sharing a cabin with his brother at this point. But Cal had continued to take the extra bed in the cabin, and neither one of them discussed how permanent that would be.

Not that Nate knew how permanent *he* was. Everything felt like it was in a strange, awkward holding pattern of waiting for the police to arrest their father. He couldn't go back to Tennessee until that happened.

And every time he thought of that, he was aware how little interest he had in returning to his isolated cabin in the Smokies.

Yeah, he'd needed the alone time. He really had. Isolation had its purposes. But being back here, seeing his brothers, working with Sam, moving through a community he'd once been a part of ... Nate realized that he might not *want* all this, but he needed it. It was better for him, mentally and emotionally, to be amongst the living.

He heard Cal's cell ring from behind the door that was still closed, then low voices as Cal had a conversation. Nate made coffee, and like he did every morning, he tried to figure out what the hell he was supposed to do with himself.

Mostly, it was trying to come up with excuses to head over to Honor's Edge. Poke deeper into this case, maybe try to help the police along in their search for evidence. Action in *some* way.

But Sam had been scarce. She didn't return his calls, just texted excuses. So, he'd stopped trying.

He wasn't sure what about her being right about his father had made things weird between them, but it had.

And still, he missed the weird little reality he'd created in being back in Marietta. He'd *enjoyed* puzzling things out with Sam, and not having that the past few days had made him realize … how little he'd been doing with his life the past year. Injury or no.

It had led him to think about his future. About what came next. He had a few ideas, but he wasn't sure about any of them.

The door to Cal's bedroom slammed open and he walked out, fully dressed in what Nate could only call *lawyer clothes*. A pressed suit that looked far too fancy for this rental cabin on a dusty ranch.

"Dad's been arrested," Cal announced with no preamble.

Nate felt it like a blow, even though he'd known it. All these years, he'd known it was possible. He'd *seen* that in Benjamin Bennet. And still it landed with a force he hadn't expected.

Dad had *killed* their mother. He was being arrested for it. He would pay for what he'd done.

"I'm going to head down to the police station," Cal said, moving through the cabinets to find a travel mug. "Make sure I get all the information. Landon and Aly are staying up at the ranch, and I think you should stay here too. Let me handle this on a professional level before we confuse the matter. I'll keep you all up-to-date and go from there."

Nate nodded slowly, feeling a bit like he was moving through quicksand. It was happening. It was real.

Cal filled the travel mug with coffee. Nate surveyed him. Cal hadn't been quite so quiet and despondent as he'd been in the direct aftermath of remembering and going to the police, but he'd definitely been … subdued the past few days. A bit like a ghost going through the motions.

This was the first time since then Nate had seen him more like the Cal he'd known when they'd been growing up and seen a few times since coming back.

"You seem more yourself."

Cal snorted. "What the hell is myself anymore? But at least work I know how to handle. I'll be back later." And with that, he grabbed his keys and left.

Dad was arrested. Would that mean they'd let Sam's dad go, or would the parole stuff take longer to sort? Did she know? Or was this still new news? He considered, then figured a friend would let the other friend know. He could call her, or…

This was finally a reason to stop by Honor's Edge.

He got himself ready for the day, grabbed his own keys and wallet, then was outside locking the door to the cabin in the light of late morning. It felt like spring. The promise of summer was even there in the air, in the warm sunlight.

He turned to see a car he recognized. Sam's car. He lifted his hand in a wave, but quickly realized she hadn't turned onto the little lane that would have led her to his cabin. She was still on the main drag.

Was she here to see her aunt? Maybe give her the news? But she must have seen him, because she slowed her car. And even though he couldn't fully see her through the window, he could practically *feel* her indecision. Wave and keep going? Stop and have a conversation?

She pulled over to the edge of the drive and stopped, so he walked over the little patch of land that separated the lane and the main drag of the ranch. He walked over to the driver's side as she rolled down the window. "Hey," she greeted.

"Hey. I was just heading over to Honor's Edge. We got news my father was arrested."

"Yeah. My dad's lawyer already got a hearing with the judge to see about getting him released immediately. I have to get Dad a suit though." She gestured in front of her. "That's why I'm here. He lived in a cabin here."

"Oh." Nate squinted out at the land with the little rentals dotted all across it. He should let her go, but… "You mind if I tag along for a minute? There's something I want to talk to you about."

Sam didn't answer right away, and he was about to back away, suggest they talk about it later when she wasn't busy, when she shrugged.

"Sure. Hop in."

Nate did, though he wasn't sure how he was going to broach the subject at hand.

"You're not headed down to the police station?" she asked, driving down the lane, past all the rental cabins and to one at the end of the line, set a little apart.

"Cal thought he should be the one, and only one, to do it. Keep it professional, I guess. I figure he's right. If he needs any of us, he'll call us down."

"Probably smart," Sam said, putting her truck into park. "All that lawyer expertise." She opened her door, glanced at Nate. "You can follow me inside if you want to talk. I just have to grab a few things."

"Okay."

They got out and he followed her up the path to the door. She shoved a key into the lock, pushed inside. It was a little stuffy, a lot dark with the shades drawn, but that made sense since Gene had been in jail for over a month now.

"Come on in," she muttered, striding into the dark cabin.

She flipped lights on as she went. He followed Sam through the main areas, into a neat bedroom.

She went straight to a closet, and Nate hung in the doorway. "So, what did you want to talk about?" she asked, reaching into the closet and pulling out a hanger with a suit on it.

"I figure I should probably stick around, until we know how a trial will shake down. They'll need me to testify, I imagine."

"I will too, obviously, though my motives would probably be questioned. But if the prosecutor can use me, I'll be there. With bells on." She tossed the suit on the bed, grabbed a pair of shoes that she also tossed onto the bed.

"I suppose even if not everyone believes you, they'll want as many people to create the real version of Ben that he hides from the public."

"All that drinking hasn't helped his case lately. Even *I've* heard people whisper about him. Not that they think he killed anyone. Just that he isn't quite the paragon they thought." She pulled a tie out of the dark closet, then frowned. "Why is this heavy?" she muttered, running her hands over it.

Then frowned deeper as she pulled something out of the little fold in the fabric. It was a watch. Gold and old looking. But … familiar. Nate had seen that watch before. He'd *touched* that watch before. Hadn't he? He frowned at is as Sam turned it over in her hands.

"Why was this in a tie?" she wondered aloud.

But the memory was just within his reach. Where he'd seen that watch. Whose watch it was. "Sam, I know that watch."

"Know it?" she replied.

Nate swallowed. "Turn it over. Behind the watch face. Look at the inscription."

Her eyebrows drawn together in confusion, she did as he said. Then her whole body went rigid. Her eyes flew to his. "It's the Bennet Ranch brand."

"That was my grandfather's watch. The watch…" He couldn't seem to push out the words.

Because he didn't know what it meant.

But he knew it wasn't good.

He watched as the truth dawned on her.

And something about that allowed him to say it. "The watch Landon said last night that Sandy liked to wear to piss off my dad."

Chapter Twenty-Nine

Crawford County Jail

SAM WAS NUMB. So numb she hadn't argued when Nate had insisted on driving her to the jail. So numb she hadn't protested when he'd gathered the suit items himself, put the watch in a plastic baggie, and then dragged her along to her car.

He'd taken the keys from her and driven her from the ranch all the way to the jail.

He hadn't said what it meant out loud. Maybe it didn't mean anything. She kept trying to convince herself it didn't mean anything.

A watch Sandy used to like to wear hidden in her father's tie. If it mattered, the cops would have found it in their search of the cabin last month.

Hidden in a tie? A man's watch? Would they have even taken a second look at that?

But no matter how many questions that rattled around, she kept moving forward. Out of her car. Into the jail, her father's suit over her arm, the watch in her purse. She went through the familiar rigamarole, except this time she was led to one of the conference rooms where Dad sat, cuffed and chained, with his lawyer.

Mr. Simpson stood. "Thanks for bringing that along, Samantha."

"I need a moment alone with my father," Sam managed to say.

"Sam—"

"Now." The word was sharp, harsh, and not fair to Mr. Simpson.

But he seemed to sense something was wrong. "All right." He moved to the door of the conference room.

He didn't step out of the room, but he stood far enough away from the table, talking to the deputy, that Sam felt she could have a private conversation with her father. She put the suit across one of the empty chairs, then slid into a chair across from her father. He was smiling at her.

It was different. This time, it had been different. She'd chalked it up to the fact Dad had gone through this before. But shouldn't that have made him angrier? More antsy? Knowing he was close to having to do time for something he didn't do all over again?

Was it something else entirely? Something so terrible she didn't want to deal.

But she had to.

She pulled the bag out of her purse. She slid it across the table. "What is this?"

Dad looked at it. His expression was completely blank. No confusion. No guilt. No questions. Just blank. "Looks like a watch."

"It is indeed a watch. With the Bennet Ranch brand engraved on the back. Hidden in a tie in your closet."

Dad slid his gaze from the bag to her. Then Mr. Simpson and the deputy, who weren't paying them much mind.

"Where did you get it?" Sam demanded quietly, so as not to draw attention. "Why did you hide it?"

He leaned back in the chair, gave a little shrug. "Hell, I don't know, Sammy."

She realized this was what had been dogging her since Cal had said what he remembered, maybe even before all her forever-held truths had been proven true.

Maybe this was why she hadn't been happy to be right.

Because no matter how it *looked* like the murders connected, she'd known, deep down, they hadn't.

At least not by the murderer.

Emotion would win if she didn't get this out.

She forced herself to lean forward, meet her father's gaze, and speak very quietly but very clearly. "You do know. My God, Dad. Tell me you didn't kill her."

"I have told you all these years—"

"Not Marie Bennet. Sandy McCoy. Tell me you didn't kill Sandy McCoy."

Dad shook his head. "Sammy. This is… What are you even talking about?" His gaze dipped to the watch. To his lawyer. "Put that away, Sammy. We'll talk about it once they let me out. Simpson thinks it could be this afternoon. The parole violation was so small. They know it was about the case, and Benjamin Bennet was *arrested*."

His smile was smug.

It made Sam sick. "Look me in the eye and tell me you didn't do this." The emotion was trying to take over, but she couldn't let it.

She needed the truth. All these years she'd fought for the

truth. Not that many days ago, she'd looked Landon Bennet in the eye and told him she wasn't afraid of the truth.

Now here was her own truth she didn't want. She wanted it to be a lie. To be a mistake. She needed it to be.

But Dad leaned forward, the smug smile fading into a scowl, his eyes ablaze with an unleashed anger she'd seen flashes of over the past fifteen years. But then he'd always hide it.

"He deserved it," he whispered. "Now *he* can do time for something *he* didn't do."

Sam felt like maybe she'd been shot. A pain blooming deep inside her chest, while the rest of her felt so numb she couldn't do anything but feel that pain. And struggle to breathe. Even as Dad leaned closer.

"Sammy. No one knows, right? You can't *tell* anyone. It was fair."

"Fair?" She looked at the man she'd been defending for fifteen years.

Who she'd given up just about everything for. To prove he was innocent. To prove he was right and good.

And he'd *killed* someone. With no remorse. None here, even when he was caught. Just Ben deserved it. Ben, who was still alive, even if he too was going to jail.

"A woman is *dead*." Two women were *dead*.

Dad shook his head. "A woman no one cared about," he whispered emphatically. "Except the man who's going to rot in prison for her murder."

Sam shook her head. The tears threatened, she could barely speak. "They found the real killer. They finally have enough evidence. To clear your name. To put Ben in jail for

Marie's murder."

"A little too late for all that, isn't it?"

"Maybe." A tear tripped over onto her cheek, and she quickly brushed it away. "But we'll never really know. What could have been. What you might have done with the rest of your freedom. Because it's gone now."

Dad sucked in a breath. "Sammy, I did my time."

"You killed this poor woman. You ended her *life*. Nothing, not even your fifteen years of suffering, changes that."

"It doesn't have to be that way." He jerked his chin at the watch. "Throw it away, Sam. Throw it in the creek for all I care. This is justice. We're finally getting justice."

She wanted to agree. To accept. To believe. So badly, she wished she could be a different person in this moment. One who didn't believe in right. One who couldn't picture the victims of this all too easily.

But she was her, and she couldn't forget. "Where's Sandy McCoy's justice?"

"Who the hell cares? I am your father. You care more about some stranger than *me*? Is that who you are, Samantha? I raised you. I trusted you. I *believed* in you, and now you're going to betray me?" His face twisted into something unrecognizable.

And it broke whatever shattered pieces of her heart were left. "What are you going to do, Dad?" she asked, pushing to a standing position so hard her chair toppled over. The lawyer and deputy startled, the deputy moving toward Dad, but Sam kept her gaze, her anger on him. "Kill me?"

But Dad wasn't moving. He was glaring at her, but not moving.

"Mr. Simpson, why don't you take Sam on out of here?" the deputy suggested.

But Sam didn't need any help. She was already walking toward the door, even as her dad started screaming her name. She closed the door behind her, even as she heard her father and the deputy scuffle with each other.

It didn't matter. She looked at the lawyer she'd paid so much money to over the years. All for … a murderer.

"We need to talk to Detective Hayes," she managed to say. "Can we get him here?"

"Sam, the hearing is in an hour."

"It doesn't matter, Mr. Simpson. It's really not going to matter once we talk to the detective."

The lawyer clearly didn't like that answer, but he gave a sharp nod and pulled out his phone.

It took a while. Sam moved through it like a ghost. Like she wasn't even there. Even as she handed the watch over to the detective, explained the circumstances, answered questions. It was almost like someone else was doing it, and she was watching from above.

"Sam," Mr. Simpson began as he walked with her out of the jail. But he never finished his sentence.

"I'm sure he'll need a lawyer for the trial, Mr. Simpson," Sam heard herself say in some far-off vague sort of way. "He's paid a price for a crime he didn't commit. That should hold *some* weight. I'm sure you'll be able to handle it. Get a fair sentencing."

He made a kind of noise, but she walked away from him. How had she even gotten here? She moved toward the parking lot without really having any clue.

Until she saw Nate.

Nate was still here. It had been *hours*, and Nate was still there. He was sitting on a bench in front of the parking lot, messing around on his phone, but when he saw her, he stood.

Sam was shaking, but she was keeping the tears in check. She was holding it together. What else was there to do? Nothing really changed. Dad would stay in jail, just like the past fifteen years. She'd have to break it to Aunt Lisa, and that would be hard, but…

But…

Everything had changed. *Everything* she'd built her life on, lost friends over, given up … everything for. Her father's innocence.

And in some warped way he *had* been innocent. But then…

When she reached Nate, stood in front of him, she said what they hadn't said the whole drive over.

"He killed her, Nate. He killed Sandy."

"Shit, Sam. I'm sorry."

"I have to—" She had to suck in a desperate breath. "I have to…" She couldn't breathe. She had to tell Aunt Lisa. She had to … fix this somehow. She couldn't just accept it. She had to … fight. She'd been fighting for fifteen years.

But she couldn't move, because Nate's strong arms were around her, holding her still.

His voice in her ear. "Breathe, Sam. Take a minute. You don't have to do anything."

The first sob escaped, painful and ugly, but against his chest. Maybe, at least for this moment, she wasn't totally alone.

"Just let it out," Nate murmured, rubbing his hand up and down her back.

So she did.

Chapter Thirty

The Bennet Ranch

ALY DID HER afternoon chores. It was the only thing she knew how to do with this anxious energy. Once she was done with this, she'd go into the house and cook enough food for an army. And when she was done with that, she'd give the kitchen a deep, deep clean.

Whatever it took to keep herself busy. Because if she didn't move, she thought she might relive Ben's arrest over and over again for the rest of her life. The horrible, unfixable change of the last few days. From hero to villain.

It hurt, in so many different ways. Not just her own hurt. Not even Landon's hurt. But the whole Bennet family, who had been hers.

And if she let her mind linger, she started to think about what Mrs. Bennet must have suffered. Such a bleak thought, she had to close her eyes and give herself a quick internal shake.

It didn't change anything to think that way.

She finished inventorying the antibiotics, then marched herself toward the house. She was just making spaghetti for dinner, but she'd forgo the shortcuts. Take her time with each step, make a lot of sides. Cook and cook and cook until her brain shut up.

Landon had rounded up the hands to give them the news and squash any exaggerated rumors, so he wasn't back at the house yet. She washed up in the mud room, then headed for the kitchen. She'd gotten most of her supplies together when Landon walked in.

"How did it go?" she asked right away.

Landon sighed. "Hard to say. A lot of surprise, a lot of questions, but … everyone seems content to stay put. For the time being anyway."

"You've been running the show for a long time, Landon. Not much will change on their end. They'll stay."

He didn't say anything to that, just came over to her and wrapped his arms around her from behind, resting his chin on her head.

For a moment, Aly soaked that in. Something as simple as this. Something she'd wanted for so long, but they'd both been wrapped up in … in the Benjamin Bennet of it all.

Now they had to find a new way forward, just them. What did that look like?

He held up his hands in front of her. "Put me to work."

She smiled at him in spite of her dark thoughts. "Always a good worker. But before you help, you should call Cal and Nate and have them come to dinner. The three of you should … sit down and have a meal together."

"The four of us, Al," Landon said, turning her around to face him. His gaze was direct, stubborn. "You've always been part of this family, one way or another."

"Okay, the four of us." But it brought up the other thought she'd been trying to avoid.

Until after. Until things were settled. But she couldn't brush past this moment, it turned out.

She could only push away so much. "Does this change?"

"What?"

"This," she said, gesturing between them. "Us."

"Do you want it to?" he asked, in that careful, obnoxious way of his when he didn't want to take a stand, or was being too noble, or *something* frustrating.

She shook her head. Today wasn't the day. Now wasn't the time. She had no right to be angry, but… "You don't get to do that with me. Not anymore. I asked *you* a question, Landon. Does this change?"

He stared at her for a long time, his dark eyes taking in so many things she didn't understand. He was a man who took in small details, filed them away, made up his own decisions and choices and rarely acted until he was sure of them.

But he reached out, tucked a strand of hair behind her ear. "I don't want it to," he said.

And sure, it wasn't romantic confessions, but this was Landon, so the serious way he said it was romantic enough.

"Good," she said, turning away from him, feeling a little too teary-eyed to keep her pride. "I don't want it to either." She gave a little sniff, got herself together. "Call your brothers. We'll start this whole weird new world with a family dinner."

And she supposed if she could reach out for any good here in all this awful, it was that maybe the Bennet brothers could rebuild the family they'd been missing since Mrs. Bennet had died.

THE NEWS SPREAD fast. Cal received a call about Gene Price when he was still having a conversation with Dad's lawyer. He'd debated whether to call Landon or go to the ranch and tell him in person. Would it risk the news getting to him sooner?

Still, it wasn't the kind of news he wanted to give over the phone. So he drove up to the ranch, a little before the agreed dinner time.

What would change with this information? Everything?

Except when he stepped inside, forgoing knocking on the door though maybe that was a tactical failure, Aly was in the kitchen. In the old days, in the before, this was usually where he found her when he came. Putting together a family dinner since he was coming home.

Back then, he'd considered it … sad. He'd thought Aly should have wanted more for herself than making a dinner for the forever feuding Bennet boys.

But tonight, Landon was at her side, chopping something. They moved in the same, easy rhythm they always did. The way they were partners wasn't anything new. For all the ways they might have resisted anything romantic, they'd always been a unit.

But there was something different here, and Cal couldn't describe it. Except maybe a weight had lifted, even if that didn't fully make sense. Because their father having murdered their mother was a weight. It was a weight that would never go away.

But he supposed that hidden truth, that deep-seated

memory he'd traumatically blacked out, now being free, out in the open. It eased *something*.

And now they could deal with it. So maybe that was what it was. Purpose. And not one born of the bitterness and division Dad had always spread around.

Aly turned to greet him first. "Dinner will be ready in a little bit," she said. "Nate should be here soon. I guess he's got more news."

"Yeah, I think I might know his news. I heard it when I was down at the police station." Cal blew out a breath. He didn't even know how to frame it. How to put it into words. The up and down of this whole bizarre few days.

Might as well just be straightforward about it, he supposed. "Gene Price essentially confessed to killing Sandy McCoy."

Neither Landon nor Aly moved. Cal wasn't sure they breathed.

"But … Mom…"

"Dad killed Mom. I know he did, and to that point, they found trace amounts of Dad and Mom's DNA on the shovel blade. Dad's not confessing, but he's not insisting he didn't do it either, like he's been doing with Sandy. They'll pair the evidence with our testimony and go from there, but the shovel and my memory should be pretty damning."

"There's just … two murderers?" Aly asked, like she couldn't fathom it.

"It seems, according to what I could coax out of people at the station, Gene's motive was to frame Dad. Since he served time for all those years, and he didn't kill Mom. Revenge, I guess."

Aly eased herself into a chair at the kitchen table. She was shaking her head. "What a terrible thing. What a terrible…" She never finished whatever she'd been meaning to say.

She just kept shaking her head, even as Landon stood behind her and put his hand on her shoulder.

"It is terrible," Cal agreed. "But it should be fairly cut and dried. In a few months, this should all be well and truly over."

They all stood and sat there in silence for a long time, before Aly finally got back to her feet. "I need to get to work."

"Let me help," Cal offered.

Aly shook her head. "I could use a few minutes alone. Why don't you two go have a drink out on the porch or something?"

Cal exchanged a look with Landon, who nodded. He went over to the fridge and pulled out two beers. Then led Cal back out through the house and to the front porch.

"She okay?" Cal asked once Aly was out of earshot.

"She'll handle it by cooking a feast, working herself to the bone, then once she's tired enough, we'll talk it over." He handed Cal a beer, then opened his own.

They stood on the porch, drinking in silence as the evening pulsed around them full of insect noises and bird song, the occasional cow mooing in the distance. All sounds of his childhood that made it seem bright and happy, instead of a traumatic mess.

Well, he supposed, things could be both.

"I want to tell you something, Cal, and I'm not sure I'm any good at the words for it, but here goes. We're glad you were here," Landon said. "And I don't just mean because you remembered. I mean because we needed the help. Someone who knew what they were doing. So, thanks for coming."

Cal had never once heard that uttered from a male member of his family. *Glad you were here.* No, not *once*.

He cleared his throat. "Well, I plan on being here more than I have been in the past."

"Good," Landon said.

And even sounded like he meant it.

NATE DROVE THROUGH the gate of the ranch that was his childhood home, not at all sure why he'd agreed to this.

He'd dropped Sam off with her aunt. He'd offered to tell Lisa himself, but Sam had refused his help. She'd needed to do this.

He figured she had a bit too much on her shoulders, but it was none of his business. His business was here. At the Bennet Ranch.

As the house came into view, Nate saw both his brothers stood on the porch, beer cans in their hands.

His first gut instinct was to turn the car around, but he ignored it, because life was different now. Or it was about to be.

He parked, got out and walked up to the porch. There was a pit of something in his stomach, not fully dread but not fully something else either.

"Hey."

"Hey," Landon and Cal replied.

"You want this? It's shit," Cal said, handing him the beer can.

Nate didn't really want it, but he took it anyway. "Thanks."

"Come on in. Food should be just about ready," Landon offered, then turned and led them inside.

Nate hesitated for a second, but Cal clapped him on the back. "I heard about Gene Price, already told Landon and Aly."

"Oh. Good," was all Nate could think to come up with as Cal gave him a little nudge inside. Inside a house he hadn't been inside in fifteen years.

The house was different. And somehow exactly the same. Nate felt an itch between his shoulder blades. The phantom fears of a child. It wasn't pleasant but, when they walked into the kitchen, Aly turned and her smile was bright, welcoming. Like Mom's had been once upon a time.

"You came," she said, and she sounded delighted about it. "Dinner is almost ready. Go on and sit down." She waved them toward the dining room table through an archway.

Nate did as he was told, not sure what else to do. But when faced with the dining room of his youth, he didn't know where to sit.

"Let's mix it up," Cal said, charging ahead. He sat himself in Dad's seat, smirking at Landon like he was daring him to argue.

Since Cal was in Dad's, and Landon was scowling his way into his usual seat still, Nate figured he'd take Cal's.

Aly fluttered around, bringing out bowls and bowls of food, getting drinks, until Landon finally took her by the hand and nudged her into the seat between him and Cal.

"If we need anything else, we all got two feet," he said to her.

She nodded. Nervous energy pumped off of her, but as she looked out over the table, her eyes got a little shiny.

She swallowed. "I just know your mom would be so happy. The three of you here. Even with all this ugliness. It's right."

Nate didn't know what to say to that. It didn't *feel* right, but it didn't feel particularly wrong either.

And that was the real reason he was here. The past few days, even before Dad had been arrested, he'd been thinking a lot about what came next. How to step forward into a life that now involved his brothers knowing he was alive.

"And because it is," Landon said. "Aly and I will keep the ranch running just like we have been. Cal told us he'll visit more, but I want you both to know you're welcome here. Not just to visit. To work here. Live here. Whatever it is you're wanting. We're a family, even if we haven't acted much like one yet."

Nate hadn't planned on telling anyone his plans. Certainly not before he actually got to talk to Sam about them, but … it just seemed right.

"I'm thinking about staying." He studied his glass, not sure how to meet his brothers' gazes.

There was no way to explain just how alone he'd been. How even with all the terrible shit around all of this, there had been something … settling about being back where he grew up. Where people knew him. Where his past was seeped into the dirt—even if it was seeped with blood.

It was connection. It was life. And he'd been avoiding *life* for a very long time.

He shrugged, irritated that he had to clear his throat to speak clearly. "It was … I liked it. Trying to piece together a case. I've been looking into what it would take to get my private investigator license."

"Going to give Sam a run for her money?" Cal asked.

He shook his head. "Nah, I was thinking about seeing if she'd hire me."

A little silence followed that, and Aly began to pass around the food, but then Cal spoke.

"I've got work to get back to in Austin. But I'll visit. And I'll … think about more than a visit." Cal looked around the dining room. "Maybe it'd be good, really good, for all three of us to be here. At least for a while."

"You know, I was talking to Jill today. She was wondering if you'd consider letting her talk to you about a book she's working on," Aly said to Cal. "Needs some help with the lawyer details."

Cal shrugged. "Sure, I can do that."

"I'll give her your number then."

So they ate, and they talked. There were some stilted silences. Topics that hurt too much—Mom, murder, violence—that they tripped over then backed away from. When it was time to clear the table, Nate offered to help Aly while Cal took a work call and Landon had to go deal with a ranch problem.

He brought the dishes from the table to the sink, and she began the process of rinsing them off and filling up the dishwasher.

It was absolutely none of his business, but he couldn't help but think about Sam. All she had now was her aunt. All she'd had, all this time, was that one woman and a goal.

Now the goal was dead.

"She could use a friend, Aly."

Aly didn't even pretend to be confused. She looked at him coolly. "Seems like she has you."

"She does. But she's been on her own, fighting her fight for fifteen years. And she was right. Even if her dad turned out to be a piece of shit too, she was right. All those years when everyone turned their back on her. I don't say that to guilt trip you. I say it so you remember."

"I remember," Aly said on a sad sigh. "I think we've all got a lot of … fixing to do."

"Mom was always the fixer around here."

"Yeah, she was, but guess what, Nate? You're an adult now. You can be a fixer too."

Which he supposed was true.

By the time he finished helping Aly, Landon and Cal were back, and trailed after him as he walked to his car.

"You know, the one thing I can't figure is that pocketknife in the creek." Nate mulled it over.

The shovel connected, the watch, but what about the pocketknife?

"Maybe it was just a coincidence," Landon offered, more hope than belief in his tone.

"Maybe it connects to some other mystery," Cal offered, so very unhelpfully.

The grin on his face told Nate he knew it. And since he didn't want to think about any more mysteries that involved his family or that creek, he turned his attention to the one they'd solved. He couldn't *fix* anything there, but maybe he could close the door on something.

"I'm going to go see Dad tomorrow," Nate said. "I want to hear him say it. You think they'll let me talk to him?" he asked Cal.

"If I come along, I can make sure of it."

Landon sighed. "Well, if you two are going, count me in. Can we do it around lunch, so I don't miss chores?"

Cal rolled his eyes. "This fucking place," he muttered, but with some humor, like he might have years ago. Then he sobered. "He might deny everything."

"He might," Nate agreed. "But maybe we all get the closure we need. Once and for all."

Chapter Thirty-One

Crawford County Jail

CAL HAD TO do some fancy talking, offer just the right compliments, and invoke just the most careful of threats to arrange the visitation. It required the involvement of Dad's lawyer, and Dad's agreement.

Cal wasn't sure they'd get it, but eventually, they were led to a visiting room. It was empty to start, but eventually a deputy led Dad in.

Dad surveyed all three of them. Dark eyes, that all his sons shared, assessed his three boys. There was a bitterness there, and it wasn't new, was it?

It had always been there. Carefully used.

"You all think you're pretty slick," he muttered as the deputy sat him down. Dad shook his head, with an impressive mix of disdain and hurt. His gaze focused in on Landon. "I never thought you'd betray me like this, Landon."

Landon held the gaze, even though there was still a phantom visceral response to his father's disappointment and blame. Some tiny part of him, perhaps the small child, wanted to apologize.

But Landon was a man now, and he understood all too well the way he'd been manipulated. He held his father's gaze. "Same goes, I guess."

Dad looked away. "I don't know what you're talking about."

"You killed our mother," Landon said clearly. Because the more he said it, the more it became a truth he could deal with instead of hide from.

"My lawyer is going to clear me," Dad said, jerking a chin toward the lawyer in the corner. "Gene Price killed both women. Clearly." Dad smirked.

But he looked *old*. His hands shook, probably jonesing for a drink.

"It's actually not at all clear. What with the DNA evidence," Cal returned. He had some concerns about the trial, just because he knew from experience that the little things could undermine a case like this. Could let his father go free.

But that DNA was important and damning. He'd hold onto believing it was the key.

"Your mother and I shared a lot of DNA," Dad replied. "The three of you case in point."

"You almost killed *me*," Nate said, in that quiet, military way of his.

"I don't remember that," Dad said, so dismissively that Nate's insides twisted with rage. "Your word against mine I guess," Dad offered then, with just enough of a hint of self-satisfied for Nate to know Dad remembered.

Nate didn't let the rage show. *That* was a lesson he'd learned out there and learned well. "And Sam Price's word against yours."

Dad snorted. "Yeah, I'm shaking in my boots. The little girl that hates me is really going to convince a jury."

"You hit Mom," Landon said, holding his body still because he was afraid the words might shatter him. "You beat her too."

The way he delivered those words, held Dad's gaze, had Cal and Nate both realizing that by staying, maybe Landon was the strongest of the three of them.

But now all three of them would work together to be the strongest unit. One way or another.

"There's a lot you don't know about your mother. And never will."

"A smart mouth has to be shut, right?" Cal offered, because he heard it in his father's voice in his head suddenly, and as much as he wanted those odd things to be dreams, not reality, he understood now more often than not, they were memories.

Dad's gaze snapped to Cal's.

"I know my own mind did a hell of a number on me, but so did you," Cal said, holding that blazing gaze that had his insides turning to ice. Cal didn't let it show. "You made sure I didn't understand what I saw. What I *saw*."

"Your generation just *loves* blaming the older one."

"Yeah, that's the problem. My *generation*. Not years of you making sure to twist what I saw, and Mom covering for you."

"Did it ever occur she wasn't *covering* anything, because if everything you're pretending was actually true, why would your mother have stayed with me all those years?"

None of the brothers had quick answers for that, but Cal remembered what Nate had told him the other night. That lack of answer wasn't their mother's fault.

It was on the man who'd killed her.

"I don't know why you three are here, having this immature little tea party. I don't have to admit to anything, and I never will." He stood, spoke to the guard. "I'm done here."

The deputy nodded and began to lead him away, but Dad stopped, looked at them over his shoulder. "But a woman should know her place. And she never did when it came to you three." With that, he was escorted out of the room.

Leaving three reeling brothers, and no real closure. Because they'd come into this sure he did it. They came into this *knowing*. So whatever he'd said, none of it was particularly groundbreaking.

And even if he'd admitted it, tearfully apologized, would it really offer closure? No. Actually, Nate realized, nothing could give them closure on this. Except themselves.

But what Dad said in his parting shot did give Nate a *glimpse* into what might have been on his mother's mind if she had indeed *chosen* to stay. "She was protecting us. She didn't leave, because she was protecting us. And who knows, he played all of us, maybe he played her too."

Cal nodded slowly. "Yeah, I think so."

Landon didn't say anything as they left the room, checked out of the jail, stepped into a gray afternoon that suited their moods.

They'd all go their separate ways, but Nate had a feeling Aly would gather them all for dinner again.

And that … it would be a good thing to come out of all this bleak. But there was still some bleak he wanted to deal with. "I'm going to the cemetery."

Landon and Cal turned to him, questions in their expressions.

"I ran into Dad there when I first got here. He left her flowers. I want them gone. Nothing he touched should touch her."

Landon agreed. He was ready to scrub Dad from everything he'd ever known. Because the Bennet name was tainted, the world Benjamin Bennet had held control over was all lies.

But that didn't mean it had to be abandoned.

It just had to be scrubbed clean.

"I'll have Aly meet us there with some flowers from her garden," Landon said. "Most of the flowers are from Mom's seeds and plants, so it's right. We'll all go."

Nate and Landon turned to Cal, who sighed, then nodded. "Yeah, we'll all go."

Because from here on out, they were an *all*, instead of three separate men hiding from the violent, awful truths of their childhood.

Now they were a unit, and they would scrub this new world clean.

Chapter Thirty-Two

Honor's Edge Investigations

SAM THOUGHT SHE was starting to feel more like herself. It was strange. The days passed in the way they had for years. Dad was in jail. Aunt Lisa helped at Honor's Edge and Sam helped out at the cabins when she could. She had a few minor boring cases to investigate.

But all the drive, all that had been fueling her for fifteen years was gone. So, no matter how stable she started to feel, sometimes it hit her, out of the blue.

All that she'd worked for.

And how she now had ... nothing.

Less than she'd had, because her father wasn't the man she'd thought, she'd loved, she'd believed in and fought for. He was a *murderer*. And she had nothing.

Except Honor's Edge, she supposed. Cases for other people. It was *something* anyway.

She tried to remind herself of that this morning when her current case was investigating the mystery of the dug-up roses.

Not a mystery. A loose dog, no doubt. But which loose dog? Mrs. Cather simply *had* to know and was willing to pay.

Yippee.

The bell on the door to the main office rang so Sam got up and stepped out of her office, only to pause.

It was Nate. He was dressed as he usually was, jeans, T-shirt, boots. His hair was getting a little longer and looked windswept. But there *was* something different about him. She'd been a student of people enough in her job to be able to recognize the physical changes in someone when the psychological weights they carried lifted, even if only partially.

She was glad to see it, even if she didn't know what to say to him. How to be around him now. She hadn't seen him since he'd dropped her off at Aunt Lisa's after Dad's … confession. And yes, that had been on purpose. She'd avoided him and his occasional text.

In some ways, she figured she needed to figure herself out before she figured out how to deal with anyone else. With fifteen years of … *everything*.

In other ways, she was just a coward.

Hesitantly, she stepped forward, noted he was holding something behind his back. "Hey. What's up? On your way out of town?"

Because he had to be leaving soon. He'd had a life somewhere else, and he might visit now, come back to testify against his father, but he'd be going back to where she dragged him away from.

That loner cabin in the middle of nowhere. Sounded pretty nice right about now.

"Not exactly," Nate said.

He pulled flowers from behind his back. A scraggly little

clutch of wildflowers, but flowers nonetheless. Her heart did something foreign in her chest, clattering around like nerves.

"Flowers," she said, dumbly.

"Sure. We took some up to my mom's grave the other day, and it reminded me of funerals and such. It's a kind of condolences."

"It's not a funeral," Sam said flatly.

Because her father wasn't dead. He just wasn't the man she'd believed in.

"Maybe not literally," Nate agreed, maybe understanding too well that *literal* didn't matter when you were dealing in the murky waters of upending everything you'd trusted. Part of her wanted nothing to do with someone who understood.

Part of her wanted to reach out and hold on for dear life.

"Besides, you said no one's ever brought you flowers, and it's not exactly a fun time. So, regardless, condolences."

"For wasting my life?"

He shook his head, his eyes somber and direct. "It wasn't a waste, Sam. He was innocent."

She looked away from him, because she didn't want his pity even if it was soft, and damn if she couldn't use some soft. "Yeah, *was* being a pretty operative word."

"It's also a thank-you," he said, stepping closer, still holding out the flowers.

"For what?"

"You brought me home, Sam."

He didn't have to explain that it was more than just coming back to Marietta and the Bennet Ranch. It was facing what home had been. And now maybe … building something with his brothers off that. She hoped he would.

"Are you going to take them?" he asked.

She didn't want to. Mostly because she wanted to too much. But if she didn't, that would be weird, so she took the little bouquet. Looked around for something to put them in. Found a mug.

"I'm thinking about sticking around."

Her heart did a strange lurch to go along with the clattering. She kept her gaze on the flowers. "That a fact?"

"Yeah, I'm going to need some gainful employment though."

"Lots of jobs around here. I bet Landon could have you ranching in no time."

Nate nodded thoughtfully, his gaze moving around the room. "I might help out at the ranch now and again, but I had something else in mind. Something more along the lines of … this."

"This?"

"It'll take some time to get a PI license, but not too long. I can answer phones or whatever in the meantime. Be a kind of intern."

Sam blinked at him, trying to work through this … surprise. She'd expected him to leave. Sure, visit more often. Not leave his brothers without knowing his location, but stay? Become a PI? Like her? *With* her?

"So, to be clear," she said, choosing her worlds carefully because everything inside of her suddenly felt precarious instead of heavy and unwieldy. "You're staying in Marietta, and you want a job here. At Honor's Edge. A PI job, once you're licensed."

"We make a good team. Solved two murders in a few

weeks."

"Put both our dads in jail. Some team."

"Well, they *are* murderers."

It wasn't funny. But sometimes if you didn't have a bit of dark humor, the dark ate you whole. She realized Nate understood that, better than most.

"Probably need to fill out an application, submit a resume, go through an interview process and a background check."

"If you want to waste everyone's time," he replied evenly, calling her bluff. "Sure."

This time she did laugh, and it felt *nice* to lift one of the heavy weights on her heart a little bit. To think about what might come next, rather than everything she'd lost.

Expanding Honor's Edge, adding another PI, it was all in her plans for a murky future *after*. But the after was here. Her father was going to be in jail for a long time, and deservedly so. There was nothing to change, nothing to fix.

Except other people's problems, mysteries, and secrets.

And Nate was right, they made a hell of a team.

So, she held out a hand. "Well, in that case, you're hired, Nate."

He took her hand in his much larger one, gave it a squeeze and a shake. "Can't wait to start."

The End

More books by Nicole Helm

Bad Boys of Last Stand series

Book 1: *Homecoming for the Cowboy*
Book 2: *Christmas for the Deputy*

Big Sky Brides series

Book 2: *Bride for Keeps*

Firefighters of Montana series

Book 3: *Ignite*

The 77th Copper Mountain Rodeo series

Book 3: *Keep Me, Cowboy*

Montana Born Brides series

Book 3: *Bride by Mistake*

Available now at your favorite online retailer!

About the Author

Nicole Helm writes down-to-earth contemporary romance—from farmers to cowboys, midwest to *the* west, she writes stories about people finding themselves and finding love in the process. She lives in Missouri with her husband and two sons, surrounded by light sabers, video games, and a shared dream of someday owning a farm.

Thank you for reading

Double-Edged Reckoning

If you enjoyed this book, you can find more from all our great authors at TulePublishing.com, or from your favorite online retailer.

Made in United States
North Haven, CT
16 June 2025

69795011R00185